Readers Love GREYSON MCCOY

Bridging Hope
"I truly enjoyed this short, poignant story of overcoming what life has thrown at you and rising above to succeed and live."
—Love Bytes Reviews

"Pierce and Dalton experiment, take risks, and learn that when you have kids, love alone isn't enough – the kids are the most important thing."
—Rainbow Book Reviews

Bridging Lives
"This was a sweet, gentle story…the book was easy to read and I liked the quiet feelings of coming home it gave me."
—OMG Reads

Mending Bridges
"Both men realize that they must do better so that they don't wind up losing out on something they both want…this was a very sweet story of two men who don't want to lose what they have."
—Paranormal Romance Guild

By GREYSON MCCOY

BRIDGING HEARTS
Bridging Hope
Bridging Lives
Mending Bridges
Bridging the Divide
Water Under the Bridge

Published by DREAMSPINNER PRESS
www.dreamspinnerpress.com

Published by
DREAMSPINNER PRESS

8219 Woodville Hwy #1245
Woodville, FL 32362 USA
www.dreamspinnerpress.com

Water Under the Bridge
© 2025 Greyson Mccoy

Cover Art
© 2025 Reece Notley
reece@vitaenoir.com
Cover content is for illustrative purposes only and any person depicted on the cover is a model.

Trade Paperback ISBN: 9781641088527
Digital ISBN: 9781641088510
Trade Paperback published September 2025
v. 1.0

Acknowledgments

*With special thanks to Jo Bird and Renee Mizar,
who helped whip this book into shape!*

Prologue

Landon Carter

"HEY, LANDON, you wanna hang out?" I turned around, surprised to see the familiar trio of Marisa, Owen, and her cousin Jason in my garage.

"Oh, hey, guys. Sorry, I was zoned out."

"Whatcha doin'?" Marisa asked.

I looked over at the junk my dad had asked me to sort. "Dad chores," I said.

"Ugh, sorry," Owen said, and I laughed at his pained expression. "Why don't you skip out and join us? We're going down to the river."

I glanced at the crap I still needed to go through. "I don't know. My dad will throw a fit if I don't finish."

"We can wait outside," Marisa said, pushing the boys toward the door. "You look like you're almost done."

I shrugged, and now that I actually had some motivation, I quickly finished sorting the piles. Most of it was not worth keeping, but that was beside the point. It'd pissed Dad off when I told him I wasn't going on the family vacation this summer, and this was his way of paying me back.

I tossed a pair of old roller skates on the Donate pile and popped outside to find the three friends leaning up against the garage waiting for me. They were a familiar sight. They'd all been best friends since they were little, to the point I thought of them as a unit.

They didn't usually spend time with me, but it was pretty cool when they did. Out of the blue they'd show up, we'd hang out, have some laughs, and then they'd ignore me like I didn't exist until they wanted to hang out again. Not that I minded. They were the cool kids, and I was the oddball nerd who spent all his time with his nose in a book.

"Okay, I'm done," I said. "Ready?"

"Sure, come on," Marisa said as she grabbed my hand and pulled me down the road while Jason and Owen followed.

We trudged along the empty road for a few minutes, then ducked between some trees and onto the path that led behind old Mr. Weston's property and then below a bridge and down to the riverbank.

"So, you graduate this year?" Marisa asked.

"Yep, in a few more weeks. So does Jason."

She smiled. "Yeah, you two are the same age. I always wondered why you didn't hang out with us more."

I laughed. "Really? You three are thick as thieves. I'm the odd man out. Always have been."

"Not on purpose," Owen said as he came up behind Marisa and me. "It always seems like you're too busy for us."

I looked at them, dumbfounded for a moment. "I mean, no, not really. We hang out, then you all seem to lose interest in me. I mean, it's not a problem. I like hanging when you want me around."

Marisa sighed. "We didn't mean to ignore you."

"Wait, why are y'all concerned about this all of a sudden?" I asked, confused.

"Well, 'cause we were talking about how few people we know in this town. Like, in school and out. When Jason mentioned your name, I realized how little we hang out with each other. It sorta feels personal."

I laughed, thinking she was joking, then looked at the three friends whose faces remained stoic. "Wait, you're serious? Dude, you three are practically glued to each other. It's not like you've opened your clique up to anyone else. But it never bothered me, and I've enjoyed when you let me hang from time to time. Besides, in a few months, I'll be going to college in Eugene."

"Cool," Marisa said, but Jason frowned.

When we reached the river, I plopped down on the riverbank and leaned back against one of the old posts that held the bridge above us. Marisa and Owen joined me, but none of us really said much.

After a while, Jason, who'd been throwing rocks into the river, came up and said, "We can hang out together for a few more months. We've still got the whole summer ahead of us."

I shrugged. "Yeah, if you want to. I have a lot going on, but as long as, you know, you don't mind working around me." I thought for a bit, then smiled. "Hey, we can make a schedule. I know what nights I work. We can…."

Jason snickered. "You always overthink things, don't you?"

I tried to play it cool but couldn't hold back a pout. "No, I mean, I'm really busy with school and, you know, work and stuff. Aren't you?"

Jason just shrugged. "Nah, I'm not into all the clubs and stuff you are."

I shook off what felt like an insult. Yes, I was busy with clubs and stuff. I served on the student council and had honors club to manage, being its freaking president. But it had all paid off, since I got into college on a nice scholarship. Never mind it also gave me some semblance of a friendship circle outside of this hot-and-cold trio.

When Jason snorted, I looked back up at him. "You're thinking about what I just said, aren't you? Always overthinking."

"Fuck off, Jason," I said and got up to leave.

Jason's eyebrows did that thing where he cocked one side. It had always been one of the hottest things I'd ever seen. I spent a lot of nights thinking about Jason Murrin looking at me that way.

Blushing, I dashed away from the group. I heard Marisa say something about Jason being a dick, but I didn't care. I didn't like being teased. Hated it, actually. The thing was, Marisa, Owen, and Jason had never done it before. *Oh well*, I thought, as I rushed back to the house and up to my room. It wasn't like I had that much more time here anyway.

I was going to finish high school, go to college, and then leave Oregon behind for good. That's the only thing that made sense for a closeted gay boy like me.

Jason Murrin

"Ouch, Marisa, stop hitting me."

"Did you not just tell us you wanted to get to know Landon better?" She whacked my arm again.

"Damn, stop. And yes, but he *is* an overthinker. That's why we're not closer to him. First he overthought our asking him to hang out, then he overthought our being friends."

"And you think he's cute, and haven't made a move 'cause you overthought that."

I sighed. "I should've never told you guys."

"You didn't. Your first cousin there forced it out of you," Owen said, pointing to Marisa and laughing.

"Listen, I'm eighteen, have a car, and am on Grindr. I can name at least six guys I could call when I have that need. What I don't need is a relationship. That's something y'all want."

Owen looked at Marisa and sighed. "So, you know Marisa and I…."

I rolled my eyes. "No duh, Owen, I already know. You two have been making goo-goo eyes at each other for the past year. But you know that doesn't mean I need to shackle myself to someone too, right?"

"You need to do more than fuck a bunch of men who are honestly too old for you anyway. You know, all six of those guys could go to jail for screwing around with you."

"Save your breath, Marisa. I didn't even sign up for Grindr until I turned eighteen. Besides, they're all my age or a year older. You make it sound so weird."

"It is weird. Why do you want to randomly fuck men who mean nothing to you?"

I looked at Owen, who was stifling a grin. "I'm so not going to try to explain to you why guys like random hookups. Just think of it as a difference in our natures," I said as I walked in the direction Landon had gone.

"Wait. For real, Jason, you've got a good heart. Don't become one of those nasty men who, you know, fucks anything that moves."

Owen snorted—the asshat—and I flipped both of them off but didn't stop. I was a typical young guy with a healthy sex drive, but I didn't fuck anything that moved. Just hot, available men who showed mutual interest.

Marisa and Owen had begun asking me a week ago who in Northport I'd consider getting serious with, and the only person I could think of was Landon.

I thought about Landon a lot. He was so bookish and nerdy, but he had a tight body too. We had swimming classes together last year, and I'd lusted after that body of his more than a few times. Not that I ever told him. Outside of my two best friends, no one at school knew I was gay.

I could sorta tell he was too, but I had already convinced myself I'd never pursue anything until after we graduated. Being out in a rural high school would've been pretty awful, not to mention dealing with my dad. If someone mentioned me being gay to him…. Shit no, that would not be happening. Even now, living with Marisa and my aunt, he would still be a pill if people knew.

As I reached Landon's house, my resolve began to crumble. What if I never saw him after this summer? *Fuck it.* I knocked on the front door.

Landon's mom answered and immediately invited me inside.

"Honey, your friend is here," she called up the stairs, then disappeared into the kitchen.

Landon came to the railing looking confused. His eyebrows shot to his hairline when he saw me.

"Hey," I said, rubbing the back of my neck. "I wanted to say sorry."

Landon stood watching me, then sighed. "Come on up," he said. Then he turned around and went back into his bedroom.

I took the steps two at a time and watched as he plopped down in front of an old TV and began gaming. "Join me," he said. "I just started, so you can play too."

"Landon," his mom called up the stairs. "I'm going to take this over to Mrs. Hughes. I won't be back until late. Your dad's bringing home fried chicken for supper."

"Okay," Landon hollered after pausing his game.

"Oh, and Jason, tell your aunt I'll call her about the community picnic."

"Yes, ma'am," I yelled back. Unlike my sexuality, it felt good that most people knew I was living with Marisa and her mom, my aunt Kathy, now. No more awkward excuses about why I wasn't going home. Besides, with my grandparents gone, Aunt Kathy and Marisa were the only real family I had left. It felt right to live with them.

I heard the front door open and close and looked over at Landon, who had his bottom lip caught between his teeth as he resumed playing.

He blushed when he glanced toward me, the cute way he did when he was feeling self-conscious. "I like you," I said, and his blush deepened.

"Yeah, Marisa said. I still think—"

Before he could go on, I leaned over and kissed his lips gently, in a way he could easily pull back from if he didn't want to take it that far.

When I pulled back and searched his face, feeling a little unsure if I'd made the right move, he put his fingers to his lips. "Wow."

Then it was my turn to be shocked when he slid his hands around the back of my head and pulled me in for a real kiss. Tongue and all.

I didn't even register he'd maneuvered me to the floor and straddled me until I felt his crotch grinding into mine. "God, you're so hot," I managed to say. That must've shocked him back to reality because he froze mid-thrust.

"Oh shit, wait. I mean, we shouldn't be doing…."

He moved to get off me, but I put my hands to his hips. "Wait, just a second ago, you were into this. What changed?"

"You and I have known each other for years, and the three of you want to be friends with me now, and my mom and your aunt are doing the community picnic together, and—"

My laugh cut him off, and I released my grip. "All of that was true before you stuck your tongue down my throat," I said as he rolled to the floor and I turned onto my side to face him. "Geez, you really *do* overthink everything."

I could see that last comment irritated him, so I leaned over and kissed him again. When Landon whimpered, I took that as my cue to drape a leg over his hip and pick up where he'd left off. "Mmm, no fair," he said between kisses.

I licked the shell of his ear, then sucked on his earlobe. "Stop thinking. Just enjoy," I said as I began to pull his shirt off.

I wanted Landon Carter, and had for a long time. Now we had a house to ourselves and he was showing me he wanted me every bit as much as I did him. I'd be damned if I was going to stop. He was perfectly capable of stopping if he wanted.

As he lay naked under me, I let my fingers explore his sexy, lean swimmer's build before I retraced every inch with my tongue. Landon squirmed under the attention, which sent a thrill through me.

I was affecting Landon as much as he was me, and I relished the feeling. If I hadn't been so wrapped up in him and this moment, I might've been the one to overthink what all that meant.

Landon

JASON LAY half on top of me, and the pressure of his solid, warm body on mine felt glorious. "That was—"

"Shh, don't analyze. Don't think. Just, you know, be."

"Okay, maybe you're right. I do overthink things a bit, huh?" Jason chuckled but didn't move. "You know, that was my first time ever." He didn't respond. "You seemed pretty experienced," I pressed, wanting to know more about him in this way.

Jason remained silent. I forced myself to lay still as I stared at the ceiling and tried to simply enjoy everything that'd just happened.

After a few moments, Jason rose and looked down at me with that sexy cocked eyebrow. "I can feel you overthinking."

"Shut up," I said and went to get up.

"No, I'm determined to turn that brain of yours off." His hand wandered down my body, waking me back up the farther it traveled.

When he kissed me again, the only thing I could think of was how much I wanted to do everything we'd just done all over again. Jason was every bit as hot as I'd always let myself imagine, and now he was all mine.

FOR THE following week Jason occupied all my thoughts. I'd never planned to return to Northport after I graduated college, but I let my mind wander to moving back here, buying a house, and living in marital bliss with him. Did that make me weird? Yeah, I knew it, but Jason Murrin, the sexiest man at Northport High School, made love with me, not once, but twice. I couldn't get him or my new vision of our shared future out of my head.

Grandma came into the store looking harried, which tore me out of my romantic daydreams. "What's wrong?" I asked.

"We're running out of supplies. I swear Clayton didn't order one damn thing before he left. Honey, I have to stay here to get the paperwork done. Can you run to the Restaurant Supply and pick up stuff for me? I'll call ahead and have them get it ready."

She smiled, kissed my cheek like she always did, and then swatted my behind—also something she always did.

If I was quick, I'd miss the evening rush-hour traffic. I'd made good time when I pulled into the parking lot and dashed through the front door. When the woman who worked the customer service desk recognized me, she smiled.

"Your grandmother already called. They'll bring your order right up, but it'll be a minute. Why don't you leave your keys with me and I'll have JJ load everything. You can go on back and grab a hot dog or something."

I smiled at her, handed over my keys, and headed for the concession stand. I'd just sat down with my hot dog at the table near the employee entrance when movement caught my eye. A man poked his head out the door, gestured toward someone, and then disappeared back through it. I froze. The man was Jason.

A few seconds later, a guy I'd never seen before looked up the aisle, spotted me, then looked toward the door. He must've figured I was a clueless customer because he proceeded through.

I put my uneaten hot dog down and walked toward the employee entrance. When I reached the door, I pushed it open and stepped inside.

It didn't take long to find them. I heard rustling coming from what I guessed was a supply closet. My hand shook as I turned the knob and found Jason kneeling in front of the stranger, looking up at him as he reached for his zipper. I gasped.

Jason must've heard me because he looked over and we locked eyes. "Oh shit, Landon!" He jumped up and made a dash for me.

"No!" I put my hand up and shook my head. "No," I said, this time more of a whisper, before I turned and forced myself to walk calmly out.

"Landon, wait," Jason said behind me. "I can explain."

I nodded. "So can I. You don't owe me anything, Jason. I've got to go," I managed to say, even though I wanted to cry.

I reached the front of the store just as JJ returned with my keys. I took them and signed the paperwork without looking over the inventory. My grandmother would've had a fit if she'd been there, but I didn't care. I just needed to get the hell away before I broke down and embarrassed myself.

Jason followed me out of the building. "I can explain, Landon. I mean, it's not like we're a thing, but I know you."

I didn't respond. Instead, I climbed into the truck and drove away. I lasted until I got onto the interstate before the tears fell. I'd always been gullible.

It'd been silly to expect Jason to be exclusive. After what we'd shared, I thought we were a couple—boyfriends—but I'd been wrong. After the tears subsided, it struck me that Jason had been at the Restaurant Supply in Eugene. It was a members-only store, where you had to run a food-related business to get in, and located in a city nowhere near where we lived.

Did he or the stranger work there? Had Jason known I'd be picking up supplies? That could only mean he wanted me to see him, catch him in the act. He'd somehow set all this up, and for what? To hurt me?

Now that I thought about it, Marisa and Owen must've been involved as well. The last time we met I was wary. At least in light of this, it felt suspicious. Take the geeky virgin kid on a head trip and fuck his mind up. The more I thought about it, the angrier I got. Overthinker, my ass. I'd been played.

"Well, fuck all three of you," I said as I drove back to Carter Store. I could get through the next few months and not have anything to do with those losers. Thank God this happened at the end of my senior year. I'd be off to college soon and never have to see those three again as long as I lived.

Eleven Years Later

Landon

"Grandma, stop already," I said, laughing. "I told you I'm happy to come help. Besides, with the sale of Traguilla Industries, I've got no job to go to anyway."

"I'm so happy you did well with that," she said and patted my hand. My grandmother, even at seventy-three years old, was still a tough businesswoman, and she'd been proud of my position with Traguilla.

I'd worked my way up in the Chicago-based grocery supplier. Mr. Traguilla himself had taken a liking to me and moved me up to work alongside him.

They paid for my master's degree, promoted me as high as I could go without being family, and then when I helped broker the sale, they paid me a broker fee. With that generosity, I was set for the lifestyle I wanted to live. I'd never be ridiculously rich, but I could live on the interest and do just fine for the rest of my life.

I wasn't thrilled to be back in my hometown, but when Grandma was in the hospital, I didn't hesitate to pack my bags. Now she was chomping at the bit to get back to work. "So, tell me again, you need me to check on the managers and do what?" I asked.

She shook her head. "You can go with me and see what I do. There's no reason for me to stay at home like I'm an invalid or something."

I looked down to hide my grin. Short of lying in a hospital bed, my dad's mother wouldn't tolerate anyone butting into her business. Dad might've been able to take over, but he wasn't really management material. Mom was better at it. She'd been a manager at the original Carter Store, which is how my parents met. Now she was retired.

Dad's skill was growing the chain—getting the new stores built on time, on budget, and without the headaches I knew many other companies like ours had to deal with. But managing people—at least those who didn't cuss like sailors—wasn't his thing.

"Okay," I agreed, "but if you get tired, we come home without argument. You have to promise me."

Grandma squared me with a look. I recognized her intimidating expression but had long ago become immune to it. And she'd shown that when push came to shove, she would give in… at least for me.

"I will *not* get tired, and like I've said at least fifteen times, I had a little TIA. It wasn't a full-out stroke, and they said I didn't have any blockages, so stop fussing over me like I'm sick when I'm not."

I chuckled, and before she could resist, wrapped my grandma in my arms. "You are as stubborn as an old mule. Okay, we're in agreement. But a transient ischemic attack is still an attack. You've only been out of the hospital for a week, so you need to take it easy, and I'm here to be your grunt worker so you can."

After I let go, she slapped me on the behind and laughed. "Who are you calling old, kid? You've always been so cocky. I swear, I have no idea where you got that."

The lady behind the register, pretending not to listen to the conversation, cocked an eyebrow, and I snorted. If I was stubborn, the entire world knew the only place it'd come from was my grandmother, Gloria Carter.

I dropped Grandma off at her apartment in the new fifty-five-or-older community a few miles out of town and drove back to her house just outside Northport. She had it up for sale, but probably because it was the most bizarre home ever built, with weird angles and strange doorways, it hadn't found the right buyer. I loved the crazy building that reflected its owner so well that I looked forward to staying here until Grandma was back on her feet.

I never knew my grandpa. He died when I was little. My grandparents owned the first Carter Store, still in operation near the intersection of two major highways. Back then, Grandpa ran the store and Grandma ran the register and cooked the food they sold to customers who came in for gas.

As my dad tells it, Grandma went a little off the rails after Grandpa died. She revamped the old store, upgraded everything, and began cooking amazing fried chicken. She put Carter Stores on the map.

When she began to buy up other old country stores in the area, it didn't take long for them all to start doing as well as the original. I found it both admirable and sad how Grandma channeled her grief into running the business. It made Grandma a formidable businesswoman, if a lonely one. But I'm sure it would have made my grandpa proud.

I unlocked the front door, turned off the alarm, and went to the bedroom I'd always considered mine—the one I stayed in when I came to visit when I was young.

I opened my computer and stared at the dozen or so emails from my latest bad choice, Orion Kurt. I'd already told him it was over. I had no idea why he couldn't get that through his head. No, I didn't want an open relationship. No, I didn't want to have a three-way with a random stranger.

He hadn't cheated on me—at least I had no evidence—but when he said he couldn't be monogamous, I finally threw my hands up and ended things for good.

I should've done it sooner. Being buried at work with the sale of Traguilla put my personal life on the back burner. But I'd put the brakes on our relationship even before that.

I quickly looked through the emails to ensure I didn't need to do anything about the apartment or our other shared responsibilities. No, they were all just him begging me not to quit on us.

I took a deep breath, let it out slowly, and clicked to compose a new email.

Orion,

I know you're hurt and I'm sorry about that, but as I've told you before, we're over. That isn't just your fault, of course. I'm at fault as well.

The apartment complex has agreed to remove my name from the lease, so you're welcome to remain there as long as you like. I've already taken the stuff I want. You can do what you want with the rest.

I care about you, Orion, but you know my reasons for why we broke up. I'd recommend that, in the future, if you know you need an open relationship, let the other person know that before you become lovers.

I wish you well and hope you find what you're looking for, but it's not me.

Sincerely,
Landon

I hit Send, then answered a few other emails, checked social media, shot a message to the Traguilla family to check on them, and then closed my computer and crashed on the bed.

I pondered my latest breakup. It seemed that no matter what I did or who I was with, I ended up in the same damned situation. I was old-fashioned and tried hard to make sure the men I dated knew that before we got serious.

I had a healthy libido, but I had no desire to sleep around. I wanted the house, the picket fence, the happy little family. But no matter how many times I said it, wrote it in my dating profiles, or reiterated it to guys on dates and even to boyfriends, they almost always wanted to open things up, take a break, invite a third….

I guess most men want those things. Every guy I'd ever gone with, from Jason Murrin to Orion Kurt, was all the same. Then there was me, always the oddball, needing something different. I wanted a guy who wanted only me, who thought I was enough.

"And that's why you're going to be single for the rest of your life," I said to myself. I got up, brushed my teeth, and changed into pajamas. I needed sleep in order to meet Grandma tomorrow at six. Being late would be a really bad idea.

I climbed into bed, closed my eyes, and pictured that idyllic house with its picket fence and the happy husband and two adorable kids waiting for me inside. Then I watched in my mind's eye as an old school eraser laid waste to it. Time to focus on reality.

I was back in Oregon, back in my small hometown, and back in a world where it was unlikely I'd ever meet a man who wanted the same things I did. If I couldn't find him in a huge city like Chicago, I sure as hell wouldn't find him in the sticks.

I need to be okay with that, I thought, and fell asleep.

"Morning, Grandma," I said as I walked into the store.

"Morning, yourself. You're late," she said.

I looked at my watch and saw I was ten minutes early, though I didn't dare call her on it. "So, you ready to go?"

"Yes, but we've got a change of plans," she said. "I forgot about an appointment with my attorney in Wilcox. We're having some problems with one of the acquisitions. So you can take me to meet him."

I glanced at my watch again. "What attorney meets clients at six in the morning?"

"One who likes to manage my accounts," she said with a wink.

I followed her to my rental car, then held the passenger door open for her. "I want you to spend some time with this attorney in case you need to deal with him. He's good," Grandma said, and I smiled over at her.

"Okay, and why would I need to deal with him?"

"We both know you're here to learn how to take over the business. To do that, you need a good attorney. I swear people wanna sue about everything these days."

"Grandma, I'm not here to take your place."

She put her hand on my arm. "Grandson, it's you or no one. Now you've come home, the least you can do is consider it. Who knows, you might love the work as much as I do."

I had thought about it. Of course I had. "Listen, Grandma, in a few years, when you're ready to retire, maybe I'll consider it, but for now, I'm enjoying not having a job. You know, letting myself be free from responsibilities for a change."

Grandma laughed out loud. "Son, you're too much like me. We both know if you don't have responsibilities, it'll drive you insane. Trust me."

She wasn't wrong. I'd always been like her, and the thought of endless downtime *did* make my head swim a bit. But I was determined to turn over a new leaf. I needed to learn how not to overthink everything. Of course, that made me think of Jason Murrin. How was it that eleven years had passed since I'd seen him, yet he still occupied my thoughts? He'd been right, though; I did overthink things.

When we pulled up to the curb, Grandma waited for me to come around and open her door. She was old-fashioned to her core, but I didn't mind. She was also my rock.

I followed her to the old wooden door that led into one of the nineteenth-century buildings in Wilcox's historic downtown. If I'd been paying more attention, I might've noticed whose name was on that door as we entered, and I wouldn't have been blindsided. I thought I must be hallucinating.

My vision narrowed, almost like I was about to pass out from shock. I had visions of me lying on the floor like some diva in an old Hollywood movie while my grandmother used smelling salts to revive me. Along with being an overthinker, I clearly had an overactive imagination.

"Thank you for meeting us so early," Grandma said. "Jason, you remember my grandson, Landon."

Of all people, Jason Murrin was my grandmother's attorney. How in the hell was I only now learning this? I met his gaze, and he smiled, then held out his hand for a shake. "I do. Landon, it's a pleasure to see you."

The desire to glare at him was overwhelming, but I didn't want to give him the satisfaction. Despite wanting to flip him off and walk out the door, I smiled, which probably looked like a grimace. This was not what I signed up for, but we were here on Grandma's business.

"Jason," I said curtly as I shook his hand, ignoring the tingly feeling that shot through me as our hands touched. God, I hated that, even now, a single touch from him could send me into a tizzy. I sighed inwardly and resolved to act like a mature adult.

I followed Grandma into Jason's office and sat back as the two discussed some snafu around the acquisition of a new store.

I focused on looking at his office décor rather than at him and listened warily as he explained that the old store was in a trust and one of its trustees wasn't interested in selling.

"So, this will kill the deal, then?" Grandma asked, and I could see her disappointment.

"Wait, who's the unwilling trustee?" I asked, finally switching into full business mode.

Jason smiled at me again, though it didn't quite reach his eyes. "It's a family business, and there's some estrangement between family members at play."

"Have you spoken with the reluctant family member personally? Explained what we're offering?" I asked.

"I have, and she won't budge."

I let that settle in as I listened to them conclude the meeting. Jason might be my grandmother's attorney, and she might trust him, but I doubted I ever would again. Not wanting to ask too many questions in front of the man, I decided to bide my time and then speak to Grandma in private.

When we stood to leave, Jason shook my hand. "It's nice to see you again, Landon," he said.

I looked down at our clasped hands and stifled a sigh. No one, least of all Jason, needed to know his touch lit up every nerve in my body. Even after all these years, even after the hurt and embarrassment he'd put me through.

I released his hand too quickly and was met with the quirk of an eyebrow. I swear the bastard knew what that sexy trademark move of his did to me. It felt like a thousand butterflies took flight in my stomach, and holy hell, I needed to get the fuck out of there.

"Thanks, Jason," I replied and quickly escorted my grandma out the door.

Dickhead, dickhead, dickhead, I repeated in my head as we made our way to the car, though I wasn't sure if I was referring to Jason or myself. I trusted my own judgment, and for the last decade, I'd known to the core of my being that Jason Murrin was a selfish asshole. The sooner my traitorous body remembered that, the better.

Jason

"You're never going to guess who just walked into my office," I said, probably sounding too eager.

My cousin let out a long-suffering sigh. "What's so important that you'd call and wake up Reena at seven in the freaking morning? My baby girl needs sleep, and so do I."

"I happen to know my goddaughter wakes up at six every day like clockwork, so don't pull that crap on me, Marisa," I countered. "Turn on speakerphone. Your husband will wanna hear this too."

I heard Owen chuckle and couldn't help but smile. Sometimes I still marveled at how close my two best friends and I had remained our whole lives, even after they became high school sweethearts, then got married, and most recently became parents.

"Whatever," Marisa said. "We can both hear you now, so spill. Who came to your office?"

"Landon Carter," I said excitedly, though I kept my hopeful thoughts to myself. I didn't think I'd ever see Landon again, but he never really left my thoughts. Now I was wondering… could I have another chance with him? Would he even consider it?

There was silence on the line. Even Owen's constant chuckle had stopped.

"Hello?" I looked at my phone to see if the call had dropped. "Are you guys still there?"

"We're here," Marisa said, sounding hesitant. "It's just, last time he was around…."

I sighed. "I know, I fucked… sorry, *screwed* that up," I said. I'd been working on not cussing so much now the baby had arrived, with limited success so far.

"What did Landon want?" Owen asked.

"He was with his grandmother. I don't think he knew I'm her attorney. He seemed a bit caught off guard but hid it well."

"Jason, you shouldn't get your hopes up," Marisa said, reading me like an open book, as always. "You know how things ended."

I did know, and it still gut-punched me when I thought about it. I'd been so wild back then, screwing anyone or anything halfway decent-looking and willing to fool around. I'd been screwing Opie James for over a year. His uncle owned the Restaurant Supply in Eugene, and messing around in a public place always gave me a thrill. Much more than Opie did, though he was cute enough.

"You know he's probably forgotten all that. It was a long time ago," I said hopefully.

Silence lingered for a bit, and then I heard muffled voices before Marisa came back on the line. "Meet us at the donut shop downtown in thirty minutes. Reena will be in a good mood, and I could use some out-of-the-house time before Owen has to go to work."

"Wait, we don't...."

"Yes, we do," Owen said. "Don't argue, just come."

Like I could argue with two against one. Besides, Owen had become the man of reason in our little tribe. If he agreed this necessitated a meeting, fine by me. I'd teased him more than once about being the perfect dad.

"Okay, but I have an appointment at ten, so I can't linger."

"And so do I," Marisa chastised. "Do you think Reena would tolerate us being out that late? Nope, nap time is ten o'clock, or there'll be hell to pay."

I laughed as I hung up. My goddaughter loved routine. Of course she wrapped me around her little finger the moment I held her for the first time. So if Reena wanted to be in bed by ten, we'd make that happen.

I'd already grabbed a dozen of our favorite donuts and ordered coffee when Owen, Marisa, and Reena came into the shop. Marisa had decided to forgo caffeine since she was breastfeeding, so I'd had to ask them to brew a pot of decaf, which meant it wouldn't be coming for a few minutes. But Marisa dug into the donuts as soon as she sat down.

After the pregnancy, she'd lost a ton of weight and said it was because Reena was voracious. I watched as she piled two huge donuts onto her napkin and forced myself not to be jealous. Even though I was only nearing thirty, if I ate two of those sinfully delicious things, I'd have to run to Northport and back to work them off.

Thank goodness I didn't mind exercise, otherwise I'd have to steer clear of the donut shop altogether. If I overindulged, I'd end up bigger than my extremely unhealthy great-uncle Harris. I shuddered at the thought as I savored every bite of my one donut.

"So, let's talk about your morning encounter," Owen said.

For thirty miserable minutes, I listened as Marisa reminded me what an ass I'd been when Landon and I had fooled around. What I'd never told either of my friends was that Landon had been a virgin and I'd initiated getting intimate. Deep down, I think I knew even then that Landon hadn't just been getting his rocks off. What we did had been special to him, had meant something. He was just that kind of guy, and I'd gone and pissed all over it.

Marisa and Owen never judged me for anything, but I couldn't stand the thought of how they'd react if they knew the whole story. Teenage me had royally screwed up. I knew it the second Landon saw me on my knees in the Restaurant Supply.

Marisa put her hand over mine and sighed. "Jason, you've turned over a new leaf and you're different now, but Landon doesn't know this mature version of you." She glanced over at Owen with a pained expression. "You know he refused to even look the two of us in the eye after everything went down. He acted like Owen and I didn't exist. That tells me his hurt ran deep and likely still does."

I shrugged. "I know, and you're probably right. I guess time doesn't heal all wounds, huh?"

Marisa nodded, then pinned me with a look. "Just be friendly and don't make a move on him."

I opened my mouth to argue when I noticed Owen was giving me the same *don't even try it* look. "Jeez, you guys, I'm not a horny teenager any longer."

"Were you thinking about making a move?" Marisa asked.

I was about to deny it, then took a breath and let it out slowly. "I hadn't decided yet. I mean, this might be my only chance to make amends. If he forgives me and still finds me attractive, which I think he does, maybe he'd be open to seeing where it leads."

Marisa practically groaned. "Okay, we'll decide for you. No moves on that poor man. You already stomped on his heart once. Try just being his damned friend." She looked at her daughter. "*Darn* friend," she corrected, and we all laughed.

"We need a cussing jar," I said. "At this rate, it might fully fund Reena's college education."

Marisa gave me a wry smile. "Mom already lectured me about my potty mouth, saying if I didn't cut it out, we were in for a lot of 'heck' when Reena starts school."

I smiled in agreement. "Okay, you've convinced me—no moves on Landon Carter. I'll be my smooth, easygoing self and see if that doesn't earn me some forgiveness."

My best friends eyed me suspiciously, but when Reena began fussing, they focused on her. I winked at my goddaughter and inwardly thanked her for taking the heat off me, at least for the moment.

Landon

ONCE WE left Jason's office, it took me a few minutes to regain my composure. I hadn't told my grandmother about all that'd happened between him and me. I hadn't told anyone. I'd been very firmly stuck in the closet at eighteen years old.

Not that I needed to be. My conservative-acting family had absolutely no issue with me being gay. Despite all the drama inside my head at the moment, I couldn't help but smile as I thought about my coming out. I'd built it up to be some huge, dramatic event, but when I announced it at a family dinner, I basically received nods and knowing smiles. Even my construction-manager father just blinked twice and said, "I have a couple of guys your age who work for me that're single. I could introduce you." I almost laughed out of surprise as I declined his offer, but I'd never felt more loved and accepted as I had in that moment.

I felt my frown return as I thought of Jason the Jackass. Regardless of my family's open-mindedness, I'd kept Jason and me a secret and suffered in silence—something else I was determined to change in my life. Keeping secrets was eating me up inside. When work got tough in Chicago, I almost had a breakdown. The panic attack I *did* have put me in therapy.

"I just hate that," Grandma said as we got into the car, pulling me from my thoughts.

"Hate what?" I asked. She hadn't sensed the awkward tension between Jason and me, had she?

"That store has been on my radar for decades. It's literally just down the road, and I've always wanted it as part of the Carter chain."

I smiled over at my grandma and said, "So this is a challenge for you?"

She shrugged. "No, not really. That place holds good memories for me." She stared out the front window, a sweet smile on her face. "When I was out of school, sometimes I'd go with Dad to the old store and buy us peanuts and bottles of soda. My dad loved salty peanuts in his Coke."

She chuckled at the memory. "We'd sit over in the picnic area off to the side of the store, prepare our drinks, and sip them while watching the traffic go by."

I nudged her with my elbow. "It sounds like a good memory."

She smiled sadly. "You know, it doesn't matter how old you get, you still miss your parents. Landon, you should know your great-grandparents were good people. They loved me and my sisters with all their hearts and did everything they could to give us good lives."

We sat in silence for a while before I started the car. "Do you know who owns the store?" I asked, getting a nod.

"Same family who has always owned it. The son runs it now, and the rumor is they want to sell it and move south."

"Then what's the problem?" I asked, confused.

"Oh, family feud. I don't know all the gossip, as I disapprove of that sort of thing, but from what I've been told, two siblings split the inheritance and weren't happy with the terms. Come to think of it, Jason's dad is one of the siblings. I would've asked him for details, but I steer clear of meddling in other people's family drama."

"Wait, your attorney is on the wrong side of the family feud? Grandma, that's probably why they said no. I'm kind of surprised Jason is representing you in this. Seems like it's a conflict of interest."

"I have full confidence in him handling this like a professional," she said. "Jason is an honest man and won't do me wrong."

How ironic, I thought, but I kept my mouth shut as we pulled onto the street. I couldn't let go of my grandmother's disappointment as easily, though. "You know, I'm pretty good with negotiations. Want me to see if I can persuade them to sell?"

Grandma was already smiling when she looked over. "Please do," she said and patted my hand. If I didn't know better, I'd think that's why she'd invited me along.

FIRST THINGS first, I had to talk to Jason to get the full story. My grandmother might not be a meddler, but *I* had no qualms about sticking my nose in when it impacted our family's business. Grandma had given me her blessing and even contacted Jason to schedule another meeting with him.

Unfortunately, the day of our appointment, Grandma came down with a serious fever. Having just had a TIA, my parents and I demanded she stay home to rest. Luckily, instead of it being me in the line of fire this time, my mom got the lecture about how Grandma was a grown woman and didn't need people telling her how to live her life.

Of course, Mom, being the diplomat she was, talked Grandma down with a promise to bake her one of her famous blackberry pies. There weren't many things more delicious than my mom's pie, and because they were so much work, she didn't make them very often. I couldn't blame Grandma for being sweet-talked by the offer.

I arrived fifteen minutes early to the appointment, thinking Grandma would approve. Despite my reservations about seeing Jason again, I put on my professional game face and strode into his office feeling confident and laser-focused.

When I saw his smile and his outstretched hand, I was gripped with an intense desire to rip into him. I would forever fantasize about all the things I could've said to wipe that shit-eating grin off his stupidly handsome face, but I was a consummate professional. That, and I wouldn't give him the satisfaction of knowing how much he still riled me up.

"Hello, Jason. My grandmother isn't feeling well, so it's just you and me, I'm afraid."

Jason's grin seemed to grow, making me want to throttle him that much more. "So, to what do I owe the honor?" he asked.

I sat down across from him and, leaning forward, asked, "How about we start with you telling me exactly why one of the owners of the store we're pursuing doesn't want to sell."

His smile faltered a bit then, but he didn't lose his composure. "Well, the property is held in trust between two siblings. The one who operates the business wants to retire and sell. The other wants to keep it in the family."

"Let's not beat around the bush here," I said. "This is *your* family we are discussing, correct?"

I inwardly patted myself on the back as Jason's irritating smile completely disappeared. He nodded. "Yes, my father is one of the owners. My aunt Kathy is the other."

"Why didn't you disclose this to my grandmother?" I asked in an intentionally accusatory tone.

"Because your grandmother already knows. Everyone from here to Northport knows," he said, sounding tired and annoyed. "My family has been gossip-mill fodder for years."

I shook my head. "My grandmother doesn't partake of town gossip. Yes, she knows your family owns the store, but not the particulars. I'm guessing your aunt not agreeing to the sale is as much about you negotiating the deal as it is about her not wanting to sell."

Jason's infuriating smile returned. "No, my aunt adores me. She has never held her issues with my parents against me."

"Then why won't she sell?"

He shrugged. "Pride? A way to punch back at my father? I don't know, Landon. Even Marisa tried to help, but her mom wouldn't budge."

I sat back in the chair. "Do you think she'll meet with me?"

Jason just laughed. "That'd be a hell no. Once Aunt Kathy makes up her mind about something, there's little chance of convincing her otherwise. Kind of like someone else I know."

He gave me a pointed look, and I nearly leaped across his desk. Instead, I stared daggers. "Well, we're not done with this. What's to prevent your father from boarding the place up and retiring? Could your aunt take it over, or is selling now in everyone's best interest?" I asked. "Once a mom-and-pop shop like that closes and people develop new routines of going somewhere else, it's almost impossible to get them back. Could you ask your aunt to at least meet with me? Surely she'd see no harm in simply talking."

Jason thought for a moment. "Maybe, but you'd be better off talking to Marisa and approaching it that way. If my aunt thinks I'm trying to force a sale for my dad, that'll end this before it ever begins."

I hadn't talked to Marisa since the incident my senior year of high school, and the betrayal I'd felt from her and Owen back then once again hit me in the solar plexus. Suddenly I felt my stomach twist at the awful memory. I shook the thoughts off as best I could and stood to leave. "Please set up a meeting with Marisa," I said and was already heading for the door.

"Landon, before you go…."

I stopped but didn't turn around. There were so many things I wanted to say. Hell, to be honest, I'd absolutely never wanted to kick someone's ass as much as I had Jason's, and that feeling hadn't changed in all these years. But instead of indulging my fantasy, I kept my clenched fists in my pants pockets. "If this is about the past, I don't want to rehash it. I'm here on my family's behalf, that's all," I said flatly. "Please let my grandmother know when you've arranged things with Marisa."

Then I left without waiting for a reply. I was a dedicated and hardworking businessman. I wouldn't let shit that went down when I was still a kid get in the way of work, no matter how much the betrayal still stung.

As I drove through Wilcox, I resolved to make the deal happen no matter what it took. Grandma's career was coming to an end, and this store mattered to her.

If she could have one more opportunity to apply her magic touch, it should be on a business that held such good memories for her. I decided to drive out to the old store to get a look at it for myself.

The place sat near the river and at a busy crossroads between Northport and Wilcox. Three old gas pumps sat out front, and most of the front of the building was glass, while the rest was cinder blocks. I stared at it from the empty parking lot of the elementary school across the way, hoping to go unnoticed. I needed to keep this very official and not play favorites, and couldn't risk Jason's parents recognizing me—not that they would after all these years. We never met when I was growing up.

I smiled sadly as I looked next to the building at an overgrown area where you could barely make out a few ancient-looking concrete picnic tables. I could imagine my grandma as a little girl sitting next to her dad, drinking a soda with peanuts in it—something she'd done with me when I was a kid.

It made sense now why Grandma insisted all Carter Stores have an outdoor seating area. I'd always thought it a savvy business decision that'd become a sort of trademark, but now I recognized it as well-placed sentimentality. Restoring those old picnic tables would be a top priority when—not if—we purchased this place.

Jason

As soon as Landon left my office, I texted Marisa.

Me: *The man was just here. You've got ten minutes to call me or I'm calling you.*

I'd decided to text her first as fair warning. But my cousin was notorious for not calling back, so it only worked if she looked at her damned phone. Dammit. I mean, *dang it. Darn* phone. Jeez, I'd never learn not to cuss.

To my surprise, my phone rang. "Hey, you called. I think you set a new speed record too."

"Well, of course I called. Why wouldn't I call?"

I decided not to answer that since I could tell by her tone she was in a bad mood. My playfully arguing with her would just make it worse.

"Landon is assisting his grandmother on their business endeavors. He wants to meet with your mom about selling the store property to them."

Marisa groaned. "Jason, I told you…."

"I know, and I told him what you said, but he seems determined. Gloria Carter is my client, so I'm obligated to reach out again about the sale, but you know what'll happen if I go to Aunt Kathy with this."

"Oh yeah, don't do that. Da…. Dang," she corrected, and I knew she must be holding the baby. "Let me think about it."

"While you're thinking, I told him he should probably talk to you first."

"That's the right answer. Okay, yeah, let's do that. Why don't you ask him to meet me at Wilcox Café? It's neutral ground, and if I plan it right, Mom might accidentally show up while we're chatting."

"Oh, nice plan. That way, you can play innocent."

"Bingo," she said, and I could almost see her touching a finger to her nose.

"Cool, okay, then we have our plan."

"Sounds good," Marisa said. "So, um, how upset did he seem about, you know, what happened?"

I shrugged even though she couldn't see me. "Marisa, he shut me down before I could even bring it up."

"Well, okay. That gives me some direction. Best to steer clear of the topic. Anyway, Mom usually goes to the café for pie with her girlfriends on Wednesday mornings. They usually arrive around eleven to beat the lunch rush. So, assuming Owen can stay with Reena, you should try to set it up for ten. That way, we'll finish up just as Mom comes in."

"You are devious, cousin," I said with a smile.

"You'd be wise never to forget that," she said. Then as Reena began to fuss, she said she had to go. "I'll text you what Owen says."

I leaned back in my chair and thought about Marisa and Owen. It hadn't surprised me when my two best friends became high school sweethearts, just as it hadn't when they finally got married. They'd found their life partner early on, but I knew they actively worked at maintaining a strong relationship. I hungered for what they'd created together.

I stared out of my office window, thinking about all the years since high school. I'd been just as boy crazy in college, but law school was different. I liked to think I matured a lot during that time, but whatever the reason, I stopped wanting empty hookups.

I tried having meaningful relationships after that. Unfortunately, the longest was just over a year, but I was the one who kept it going. When we finally parted ways, I had to accept that we weren't a good fit. Looking back now, we should've called it quits within a couple of months of getting together.

Since then, I resolved to let relationships run their course naturally. If they were meant to be, they'd be. If not, nothing I did single-handedly would make them work out. Besides, even living my entire life as a bachelor didn't mean I wouldn't have fulfilling relationships. I already did and counted myself fortunate for it.

My best friends and now their amazing little girl were the most important people in my life. Those three plus Aunt Kathy were my family, and I loved them unconditionally. Some days, I was determined that would be enough for me. On others, like today after Landon left my office, I secretly longed for a partner to share my life.

Landon

MARISA SAW me enter the café and stood as I approached her table.

"Hi, nice to see you again," I said, lying through my teeth. Call it a honed skill, but I knew how to remain outwardly cordial amid inner turmoil, at least around anyone but Jason. For a moment it looked like she was going to hug me, but instead, she gestured to the seat across from her.

"It's good to see you again too. Have you been here before?" she asked.

I shook my head. "No, we didn't come into Wilcox much," I admitted.

"Well," she said as she leaned in so only I could hear, "the food is awful, legendary in being the worst within miles. But the pie is amazing. I recommend you go for that."

She was right. I ordered a slice of peach pie that was beyond yummy. I considered adding vanilla ice cream to it, but figured the sizable slice was indulgence enough.

Marisa clearly didn't have the same inhibitions, because she had two slices of pie on her plate and a huge scoop of ice cream piled on top. When she followed my surprised gaze, she laughed. "I'm breastfeeding, and my baby is, well, let's just say she has quite the appetite. I have to put away a lot of calories to keep up with her."

I sat with a smile pasted on my face as she caught me up on the local gossip, then talked about Wilcox and how much she and Owen loved living here. All the while, I packed down painful emotions that threatened to surface. The visceral memory of how Marisa and her now-husband had pretended to be my friends, then played a part in Jason's twisted games, nearly made me lose my lunch.

"Anyway, Owen's office is just across the street, but he's not there now or I'd pull you over to see him. He gets to take time off to spend with the baby, to give me a break." Marisa pushed her plate away just in time for a server walking by to whisk it away along with mine. "So, you wanna talk about my family's store?"

I nodded, feeling a bit overwhelmed at how the woman managed so many topics in one sitting.

"You need to know, there's a lot of bad blood between my mother and uncle. I'll catch you up so you're prepared for the 'no' my mom is bound to give you."

She waited until I nodded in understanding, then went through myriad details about her family history. Marisa recounted how, for all the years her grandparents owned their store, it truly was a family venture and source of pride. All that changed when they died and their assets were divided between the two children. The house, which was worth considerably less than the business, was given to her mom. The store was more complicated.

"Between you and me, my grandparents thought they'd come up with a good solution. They put the store in trust, with my mom and uncle named co-trustees. The terms were that my mom would receive a monthly stipend until the store closed or transferred ownership, and my uncle would run it. He has full control over day-to-day operations."

"So, your mom feels cheated?" I asked, hoping to get to the crux of the issue.

Marisa nodded. "She always felt cheated. I think mostly because my uncle told her he didn't need her to work there any longer. It'd been the only job she'd ever had at that point. Hell, up until the age of ten, I spent copious amounts of time stocking shelves there myself." She shook her head. "It was just a bad way for my uncle to handle it."

I considered Marisa's story and how it stood in contrast to how I'd seen other family-run businesses, namely Carter Stores and Traguilla Industries, successfully navigate change. "It sounds to me like the whole thing has been a sore spot for nearly twenty years. I guess I don't understand why your mother refuses to sell now."

Marisa shook her head. "Well, that has to do with a couple of things. If my uncle no longer wants to run the store, my mom has the right to take it over from him. So when Jason approached her about selling, she again felt betrayed. He unknowingly put himself directly in her line of fire. Of course, he was just telling her that your grandmother had asked to buy the store. Being estranged for so long, Mom hadn't heard about her brother's plans to retire, let alone his desire to sell the business. It all blindsided her."

"Is she still mad at Jason?"

Marisa nodded. "A little, but mostly I think she's just hurt. Regular visits from her baby granddaughter have eased some of the sting, though."

I chuckled. "Grandbabies seem to have that effect on people," I said, thinking of how insanely attached my former boss was to his grandchildren. In fact, he decided to sell so he could spend more time with them.

"I have to ask, why would your mom want to take the store over? I mean, with what we're offering, she could use the money to supplement her income and spend more time with your daughter."

Marisa put her finger to her nose. "And that, my friend, is what we've been working on helping her understand." I'd been so caught up in Marisa's story that I'd set aside my dislike of her until she said friend. I did my best not to cringe. Fortunately, she didn't notice and continued on. "Mom retired at the same time as her boss, Tim Bradford. She worked as the administrative assistant at his law firm for years. In fact, for a while, she even worked for Jason. Anyway, I think once she gets past the hurt all this has dredged up, she'll see retirement is worth a lot more than that old store."

Just then, Marisa waved at a group of women near the entrance, one of whom I vaguely remembered from my childhood. She approached our table while the ladies she'd come in with found seating elsewhere in the café. I put two and two together and realized this woman was Marisa's mom.

"Marisa, how on earth are you here without that baby of yours?"

Marisa huffed. "That baby of *mine* is just fine and you know it. Besides, it's more than fair that her father shares some of the parental duties. Mother, do you remember Landon Carter?" she asked, clearly attempting to divert her mother's attention.

The woman looked at me in surprise and smiled. "I do. Landon, It's been a month of Sundays since you've been around these parts. What brings you back home?"

"Well, ma'am, that'd be a grandma who had a health scare and was told to slow down a bit."

"Oh, I did hear about that," she said. "You tell your grandmother I said hello."

"Maybe you could do so yourself," I said quickly, thinking if anyone could talk sense into Marisa's mom, it'd be my grandma.

She smiled and winked at me. "Good try, but I'm guessing I'm being set up, since I know you haven't spoken to my daughter since high school, and your grandmother has made an offer on my parents' old store. I'm sorry, Landon, but we aren't interested in selling right now," she said and patted my shoulder like I was a puppy. Then she leaned over and kissed the top of Marisa's head. "You really should get back home to my grandbaby."

She disappeared around the corner of the restaurant to join her group without looking back.

I gaped after her, and when I turned back toward Marisa, she burst into laughter. "Oh, that woman," she said. "Well, it was worth a try."

I shrugged. "I guess that's that."

Marisa nodded, then looked thoughtful. "Why did you stop talking to me in high school?" she asked, catching me off guard.

"We've had a nice time. Let's not drag up old grievances."

"Let's do," she said.

I eyed her warily and saw the same resolve in her expression that I'd just seen in her mother's. That was my cue to go. But Marisa put her hand on mine to stop me before I had the chance to excuse myself.

"Landon Carter, I left my four-month-old baby at home to come meet with you, knowing my mother was going to nail my ass for running around town. All so you could *accidentally* run into her here at the café to hear for yourself that she doesn't wanna sell. The least you can do for me is answer my simple question. Why did you dump me as your friend all those years ago?"

Simple, right. Nothing about my past with Jason and his friends was simple. All the emotions I'd been working so hard to stamp down now bubbled over. "How can you ask that?" I practically hissed, keeping my voice low.

"I didn't do anything to cause you to give me the cold shoulder. I thought we were going to hang out more, become better friends, and then it's like you flipped a switch. Wouldn't give the three of us the time of day."

The incredulity in Marisa's voice only pissed me off. "Better friends? I was never your friend, Marisa. You all made that very clear with everything that happened."

"You mean with Jason? I know that you two hooked up. What did that have to do with me, or Owen for that matter?"

"Did Jason tell you that after we hooked up, I caught him in the Restaurant Supply days later with a different guy?"

She nodded. "He did, but—"

"No buts, Marisa. There's no sugarcoating what Jason did. He fucked the starry-eyed virgin, then fucked me over by deliberately setting me up to see him blowing some random guy. You can't tell me that was an accident. Never mind the assholery of the situation, but it was at one of the only places my grandmother did business." I stood up to go. "It also only makes sense that the two friends he was stuck like glue to all the damn time helped him hatch that plan. What I'll never understand is why he didn't have the dignity to just dump my ass like a man. Oh, wait, I do know. Because he's an asshole."

I shook my head, embarrassed now because despite trying to talk quietly, I'd drawn some attention. So much for remaining professional. "Thanks, Marisa, for trying to help with your mom. I'll let my grandmother know things aren't going to work out."

She stared at me, her mouth agape, but I didn't stick around for her response. Instead I left the café and wandered around town on foot, trying to get my head on straight. Finally I sat down on a bench that faced a pretty, newly painted covered bridge that led across the river and into what appeared to be a sweet little neighborhood.

How, after all these years, could these feelings still be so raw? I felt on edge and fileted open, all from one so-called *simple* question. This was why I'd avoided coming back home for so long.

I put my head in my hands and let myself process what had just happened. A few moments later, I heard someone sit down next to me. My body language didn't exactly scream friendly, so I figured it must be Marisa.

She didn't speak for a while, and I didn't look up, hoping she'd just go away. I didn't know if I had the emotional wherewithal to hash this out, especially in public. But apparently Marisa did.

"First, you need to know neither Owen nor I had anything to do with what happened between you and Jason." The firmness in her tone told me she was struggling with her own emotions. "Second, had I known, I'd have tarred and feathered my cousin myself."

I looked up then, surprised. Marisa held my gaze. "That day, the three of us had talked and decided we needed to do better at being friends with other people. You in particular. If Jason's motives all along had been to toy with you, please know that Owen and I knew nothing about it."

I was leery about her sincerity. But I also knew I had trust issues and always had. I wanted to give her the benefit of my doubts. "How are you so sure about Owen?"

She laughed. "Trust me, Landon, my husband is a good man, through and through. There are seldom any thoughts that go through his head that he doesn't share with me, then and now."

She reached over and grasped my hand. "I didn't know the details about all that happened between you and Jason. According to him, you two fooled around a bit, and then you saw him fooling around with someone else and lost it. His statement, not mine," she said.

"That sounds like him," I said, and despite my best efforts, the self-protective fortress around my heart began to crack.

Marisa smiled ruefully. "He was a total ass when it came to guys back then. Even he'd admit that. But if I'd known he was going to make the moves on you while fooling around elsewhere, I'd have told him not to. I have to believe it was never his intent to hurt you, though. My cousin may have been a boy-crazy teenager, but he's always had a good heart."

She sighed and leaned back on the bench. "I usually wouldn't put his business out there, but you have some rights here since he screwed up so badly. Jason's dad, my uncle, was and is a jackass. He did take advantage of Mom, and she's not wrong to be upset. He would've taken that store away from her entirely if my grandparents hadn't created the trust before they died, so even they knew he was a jackass. The problem is, when my uncle found out Jason was gay, he lost his shit." She hesitated, and I could tell she was holding back. "He did some bad things to Jason before he was able to get away from him. Jason even lived with me and Mom for a while." She sighed and shook her head. "Anyway, I'm not making excuses for him, but for a long time, my cousin was lost. I always thought he was using sex as a way to heal his wounds. Not that it makes what he did to you okay, but it dos explain it, maybe."

We sat quietly for a while, staring at the historic bridge in front of us. Finally Marisa said, "I was very disappointed when you iced us out. Hurt, really. I guess I understand now, but I've been mad at you for a long time. I suppose I should apologize for that. Especially since I now understand why you did it."

I sighed. As uncomfortable as this conversation was, I needed to finally say my piece. Keeping this shit bottled up for another decade would only tear me apart inside. "I was so angry with you and Owen, almost more than I was at Jason. Hell, even now I'm struggling not to be mad. I kept thinking of the three of you laughing at my awkward ass, and it would send me into a dark place. Took me years to get past it, and hell, I'm still not past it. I want to be, I really do, but I'm still struggling with all this," I admitted.

She squeezed my hand, still held in hers. "I tell you what, you come to dinner one night and meet our daughter. It's what friends do."

For a few moments I studied her. "That sounds nice. Thanks."

"So, we good?" she asked.

"We're better. Now when do I get to meet your little one?"

We laughed as she filled me in on the antics of her daughter. I'd left the café without paying, but when I tried to pay Marisa back, she said she and Owen owed me this one, but next time, it'd be on me.

Despite all the raw emotions still swirling around inside me, I truly did hope there would be a next time.

Jason

"YOU ARE an asshole, a total *stinky* asshole," Marisa said as she stormed into my office.

"What are you talking about?" I asked.

She paced in front of my desk. "You fucked him, then threw him away like a piece of snotty tissue."

"What? Marisa…."

"Don't you *Marisa* me," she said, pointing a finger in my face. "You told us you fooled around with Landon, but you didn't tell us the whole story, did you?"

Realization dawned, and I leaned back in my chair and sighed. "I didn't tell you all the details because they were private. Frankly, they still are."

"Bullshit," she said and began pacing again. "You didn't tell us because you knew how we'd react. We'd just started trying to build a friendship with him, and you treated him like another piece of meat to fuck! How could you do that to someone?"

I nodded. "I made a mistake," I said, then waited until my pissed-off cousin finally sat down. "But I'm not that same stupid teenager, Marisa. I've done a lot of growing up since then, and I cringe at some of the awful shit I pulled. How I treated Landon ranks at the top of the list."

"I know you're a good man, Jason. You wouldn't be my baby's godfather otherwise, but you were so fucking selfish back then."

"I was," I agreed sadly. "And I didn't realize how selfish until I hurt Landon. That was when I first began to wake up to it. I liked him a lot. Still do."

"Why haven't you done anything to clean all that shit up? Did you know he thought Owen and I were in cahoots with you? He thought we were trying to make him look bad or humiliate him or something. Like a bunch of fucking bullies."

"I figured."

"Yet you said nothing."

"Yet I said nothing."

"God, sometimes I want to pop you upside the head, Jason. Quit being so damn agreeable when I'm raking you over the coals. Anyway, I'm inviting Landon over for dinner, and Owen and I are gonna try our darndest to salvage a friendship out of this. The one we should've all had for the past decade. And no, you're not invited."

"Understandable."

"Damn right it's understandable. Just answer me something and then I'll go," Marisa said, leaning toward me with her hands on my desk. "Why did you do it? Did teenage you really need to get his rocks off that badly, or was it something else?"

"Yes and no. I wish I had a better answer, but it's not like I fully thought my actions through in those days." I shrugged. "I'd been fooling around with that guy from the Restaurant Supply for several months. His dad owned the place. There was the whole thrill of doing it in a public place, but I had no idea Landon would be there."

"So you were just cheating on him, not setting him up to catch you in the act?"

"Of course I didn't set him up. I might've been an inconsiderate asshat, but I was never vicious. Damn, Marisa, give me some credit. And I didn't cheat on him. We never talked about being exclusive."

She held up her hand. "Okay, so you weren't a bully who tried to make him feel worthless. But if you seduced him, took his virginity, and weren't clear about considering it just screwing around, then you're a liar by default." She let out a frustrated sigh. "I know your teen years sucked. I know how Uncle Lee treated you, but that's no excuse for how you treated Landon."

"I know," I said as my voice hitched. "I… I just…." I trailed off, unable to find the words.

Marisa got up to leave, but before she disappeared out of my office, she turned back and looked me in the eye. "I'm disappointed in you, Jason. Surely you don't need a law degree to know time doesn't heal all wounds. The boy whose heart you stomped on may be a man now, but he's still hurting. I know you are too, for not setting things right."

Left alone with my thoughts, I sat staring out the big window looking onto our small main street. I'd set up my law practice in Wilcox when my buddy Dalton's aunt became mayor and her attorney husband began talking about retiring. It felt like a homecoming of sorts, but I never anticipated my past and present would collide like they had today.

Landon Carter was the one man from my past who still haunted me. I guess it shouldn't have surprised me that in some respects I haunted him too. But hearing confirmation of that from Marisa offered cold comfort and didn't get me any closer to a resolution. Regardless of the time that had passed, I needed to fix this. I needed to talk to Landon.

Landon

Little Reena was placed in my arms the moment dinner ended, and her parents bounced around clearing the table. She cooed a few minutes and then fell asleep.

"She captivates you, doesn't she?" Owen asked with a lopsided smile. "Hard not to be smitten with her."

I could've sworn both parents sighed simultaneously, but I tried not to notice. It was great seeing two old friends, people I'd hardly gotten to know, who'd fallen in love and created a happy family.

It also helped convince me Owen and Marisa weren't the mean-assed bullies I'd believed them to be.

"I hope you don't mind," Owen said when his phone pinged. "I need to sign some paperwork for the city, and the mayor and her husband are going to run it by."

"No problem for me," I said and leaned back in the rocker while the baby continued snoozing against my chest.

We chatted for about half an hour, and then the doorbell rang, waking Reena. "I'll go change her while you meet the mayor," Marisa said as she scooped the baby out of my arms. "I think you'll like her and her husband."

Owen led the couple into the room. They kissed Marisa on the cheek and played with Reena before Marisa whisked her away.

"Polly, Tim," Owen said, "meet our high school buddy, Landon Carter. Landon, this is our mayor, Polly, and one of Wilcox's most esteemed attorneys, Tim Bradford."

I shook both their hands as Polly looked me over. "You wouldn't happen to be related to Gloria Carter, would you?"

I grinned. "Yep, that'd be my grandma."

"Oh, that's nice. We both adore your grandmother," Tim said.

"Well, I'm pretty partial to her myself." I smiled.

"So, you've been gone for a while, at least that's the word around town," Polly said. Things never changed in small towns. Folks didn't hesitate to dive nose-first into your business.

"Yes, I lived in Chicago until recently. I'm back helping my grandmother with her business as she recovers from an illness she had a few weeks ago."

"We heard about that," Tim replied. "We were concerned. I heard it was only a TIA, but still, can't be too careful about those things."

Polly shook her head. "So, now that we've demonstrated we're typical small-town folks that know too much about each other, tell us what you were doing in Chicago. Your grandmother, last I saw her, mentioned you were running a big grocery-store chain."

I nodded and smiled again. In short order, I'd already begun to like the couple. "I helped with acquisitions more than running the business, but I did about anything they needed me to do. The family sold it not long before I moved back here."

When our conversation lulled, I decided to ask the mayor about her city. "I don't remember much about Wilcox growing up. It seems my memories are mostly of a town that was dying. Now it seems to be quite the happening place."

Polly grinned wide. "Yes, we've worked hard at that, haven't we, Tim?" She nudged her husband. "We've been rebuilding our downtown, getting business to come back that'll keep the area historical and quaint. But we're also hoping to attract larger companies to bring in a few more amenities. Which is why we were talking to your grandmother. She was considering a plot of land five miles out of town, but unfortunately, it wasn't quite the right fit."

"Did you speak to her about developing closer to the town center?"

All three cringed. "We're trying to maintain a certain aesthetic in the downtown core, one that's less modern. We're hoping to build up our outskirts, though."

"Well, I did my master's thesis on incorporating modern commercial amenities into historical areas. Why couldn't we bring a Carter Store into downtown and give its exterior a vintage look?"

"Well, son," Polly said and looked over at Tim, "we sorta offered that solution to your granny, but she was pretty dead set in her belief that all her stores should look the same."

"My grandmother's strong opinions about branding have served our business well," I said. "But if the right property became available, especially in a town as up-and-coming as Wilcox seems to be, I'd be willing to create a proposal for her to consider."

Polly, Tim, and Owen all smiled at me, then at each other. "Why don't you come by my office tomorrow morning?" Polly asked. "I've got a property that would be perfect, as long as the store design meets our strict requirements."

I couldn't help but be excited. Maybe this could be something my grandmother and I did together, something that'd take the sting out of her losing the other store. Of course, I would have to convince her that embracing a style that befits the town's historical elements instead of our bright red, white, and blue trademark design was in our best interest.

I waved at Polly and Tim as they left, buoyed by the knowledge that I had a secret weapon. My grandmother wanted me to take over the business. I wasn't keen on doing so—not yet—but that didn't mean I wouldn't use her desires to my advantage. As more and more downtowns preserved their heritage, Carter Stores lost more and more opportunities. Grandma didn't take kindly to losing out on a good business deal, which is exactly how I needed to present this to her.

THE NEXT morning I sidestepped my grandmother by telling her I needed to tend to some personal business. Then I went to the town hall in Wilcox to hear what the mayor had in mind.

Polly met me at her office door when I arrived. "This is an impressive old building," I said as I shook her hand.

"Hard to imagine, but this place was on the verge of being condemned when I was elected mayor. Our friend Xander did the renovations, and one hell of a job he did too," Polly said, sounding proud. "So, the property I'm thinking about for you was an old service station in the twenties or thirties. It closed sometime in the sixties and has sat vacant ever since."

"No offense, but those tend to be too small for modern businesses. Unlike those days, gas is a loss leader. We make our money from the stuff we sell inside the store."

The woman smiled indulgently and nodded. "True enough, but there's a bit more to it than that." She gestured toward a map displayed on her desk, and as we both peered at it, she pointed at a rectangle on the edge of Main Street, not far from the café. "The property encompasses a little more than five acres right in town. That old station is a blight that's been creating trouble for years. And before you ask, all the chemical pollutants were cleaned up long ago. It's just a vacant piece of property looking to be upgraded."

"Why hasn't someone bought this and built on it?" I asked.

"We're at the beginning of our renaissance. Xander is our biggest investor at this point, and he has his hands full with upgrading the buildings downtown, and finding people to come occupy them when he's done. We just haven't built enough interest for that part of town yet."

I smiled and all but jumped up and down to see what stats she could show me. As I suspected, traffic in and out of Wilcox was significant. The mayor's data revealed an almost equal distribution of traffic along the four roads that went in different directions out of town. It meant the downtown area was consistently busy, and the outlying areas less so. The fact that Wilcox wasn't very far from the interstate would help us too.

Making the case to my grandmother for a downtown location suddenly seemed relatively easy, if she could look past the branding issue.

"So, talk to me about your vision for keeping the place historically accurate," I said, and Polly launched into her ideas for the property.

"For the most part, we'd need to maintain the building's vintage look. It sits in a highly visible location and is a historical landmark. Compromising its historical integrity would defeat the purpose of our downtown revitalization efforts. If the original design could be incorporated into your overall plan, it'd go a long way to convincing the town aldermen to green light your petition."

"My dad is going to struggle with the historical aspect of it," I said out loud, although I meant it as an inward thought. "We'll need an architect who specializes in that sort of thing. Do you know anyone locally who might be up for the job?"

The mayor laughed more than I thought the question warranted. "Xander and his new husband Rhys are both property developers. As I said, Xander revived this ol' building, and he'd love the opportunity to work on the service station. As for local architects, Rhys's stepfather Johney is the only one in town. That doesn't diminish his abilities. He helped design the historical restoration of the homes up by the covered bridge on the other side of town. I'd recommend you talk with him first."

That sounded easy enough, though I'd have to do my due diligence. My grandmother would give me the side-eye if I pitched a bad plan to her.

"I'm going to walk over and take a look. Who owns the property?" I asked. Polly's smile grew.

"It's actually in probate. The owner died almost a decade ago without any known heirs, and the estate languished for years until I began to push the state for information. Finally, a judge got ahold of it and gave it to one of our local attorneys. Let me get you his card."

I closed my eyes and said a quick prayer that said attorney would be anyone but Jason Murrin. I opened them just as the mayor turned back around and handed me the business card.

Jason's name sat staring at me in raised black font on crisp white cardstock. "You should be able to speak to him about where it is in the process. His office is just down the way from here," Polly said.

My heart dropped. Clearly, I'd pissed off some ancient god who wanted me to face all my demons at once. Unwilling to give away how much I dreaded dealing with Jason, I simply smiled and nodded. "Thanks for your help in this. I'm going to head over to the property and poke around a bit. If I decide to create a proposal, I'll need the town's assistance. I can promise you my grandmother will be an absolute no if we run into a lot of red tape."

The mayor nodded. "As long as you create something accentuating our downtown, you won't have much trouble. I can't promise you won't have *some* pushback, but no more than you'd expect in any small town."

We were on the same page, or at least it felt like we were, so I shook Polly's hand and walked over to where the derelict service station stood behind years of overgrowth. I only surveyed the perimeter, afraid of chiggers and no telling what else would greet me if I tried to venture farther.

I couldn't tell what the hell I was looking at, even though I was on the property, so I decided I'd be much better off using satellite views to formulate my plan.

Now comes the fun part, I thought sarcastically as I walked back toward the downtown core. *A visit with Jason Murrin. How fucking wonderful for me.*

Jason

I HAD JUST gotten a call from my friend Adam, who was all worked up over a mutual client who'd spent the night in a Portland hotel and woken up to find the place trashed. Apparently, he'd gotten so drunk he passed out, but his entourage of mostly groupies quite literally ripped the suite to shreds. Or so he claimed.

"The hotel is threatening to sue, even though we've offered them a fair price to repair the damages," Adam said.

"And I'm guessing they're threatening to go to the press," I replied.

"Bingo," Adam said.

"Okay, send me their information and I'll send the cease and desist. We'll go the blackmail route since they threatened to go public. But Adam, the guy needs to spend some time in rehab, 'cause you know it's not the first time we've had to clean up his mess."

"I know, I know," he replied. "I've already given him my ultimatum. Shape up or find someone to replace me."

I smiled. Adam was one of the best PR reps in the film industry and always in high demand. Even the most famous stars practically had to beg him to represent them. The threat of losing Adam was probably more of an intervention for our client than anything else.

I wasn't opposed to assisting in legal disputes, celebrity or not, but I preferred real estate law. Fortunately for me, with all the property development in and around Wilcox in recent years, business remained steady.

I was just about to finish up with Adam when I heard my front doorbell jingle. I still loved the old-fashioned sound of it. I'd deliberately kept it when Tim retired as city attorney and I'd bought the building and moved into the apartment on the second floor. It just felt important to keep that little piece of history intact, and I smiled every time I heard the bell.

I peered out of my office into the entry and almost swallowed my tongue when I saw Landon. Damn, he looked good. My eyes drank in every inch of him before my brain came back online. Why did he have that effect on me? Thank God he'd been looking the other direction so he didn't catch me ogling his body. "Hey, Jason, arc you still there?" Adam asked, and I realized I'd gone silent.

"Yeah, sorry, I-I've got to let you go. A client just came by. I'll let you know when I've sent the letter."

I hung up and walked out of my office feeling both excited and nervous. For a split second, seeing as Landon had come alone, I entertained the wild notion he was here on anything but business. "Hey, it's good to see you," I said with a smile.

"Yeah, we both know it's not. Anyway, do you have a moment? We need to have a chat."

I nodded and tried to maintain my poker face. I was having a hard time keeping my heart from beating outside of my chest, and I couldn't tell if it was because I was still so attracted to Landon or if it was because I knew it was time to face the music.

I gestured toward the sofa in my waiting room. "Have a seat. I don't have any more client meetings scheduled today, so we shouldn't get interrupted out here."

Landon sat, back ramrod straight, on the edge of the sofa. His body language screamed discomfort, which told me I was in for it.

He made eye contact with me as I sat down. "So, you and I have a lot of water under a bridge I thought long ago destroyed. But apparently, since you work for my grandmother *and* Wilcox, it appears I'm forced to deal with you."

That last part sounded like he was talking through his teeth. Not surprising, seeing how his jaw was clenched so tight, it had to hurt.

I nodded but didn't say anything. Truthfully, I wanted to fall on my knees and beg Landon to forgive me—tell him I'd been a stupid teenager who didn't understand how relationships worked. But now wasn't the right time.

He glanced over my shoulder at a painting I purchased when I took over Tim's law practice. It depicted one of our area's covered bridges. "Wow, that's gorgeous," Landon said, and I couldn't keep the smile off my face.

"Local guy. He and his wife used to operate a gallery downtown."

"You did good," Landon said, then returned his attention to me and sighed. "Listen, Jason, let's face facts here. You hurt me. There's no getting around that. Yeah, I know it was a long time ago when we were both basically kids, and I know I should be able to let it all go, but…."

"But when someone hurts you like I did, it leaves a scar."

Landon stared at me for a long moment. "Why? Why did you do it? I have never been able to figure out what was in it for you. I never took you for someone so cruel."

Damn, his words stung. For all these years he'd viewed me as a heartless bastard, and right now I felt like one. "To be honest, nothing was in it for me. I used you and all the other men back then to forget my problems. For a fleeting sense of peace. It's not an excuse, but I used sex to escape my shitty life."

"So I was just a quick fuck for you?"

I hated to admit the truth of that. It bared my soul and all the ugly parts of me I'd worked damned hard to bury the past several years. But Landon deserved my honesty, however brutal. "I think if circumstances had been different… if my dad hadn't…." I cleared my throat, surprised by the lump in it when I swallowed, and started over. "I was a lost kid, Landon. Had I been a normal kid with normal crushes, it's possible you'd have been my first too. That what we shared would have meant as much to me as it did to you. It wasn't entirely meaningless, though, even if I couldn't process it at the time. Yes, I hooked up with a ton of guys back then, but you weren't just another notch on my bedpost. I hope you can believe that."

Landon maintained eye contact for several seconds before he let out a deep breath he'd clearly been holding. "I don't want to forgive you, Jason. I don't trust you. I honestly don't even want to have to deal with you at all, but life has other ideas."

He stood up, indicating that he wanted me to stand as well. "Let's agree to put aside the past for our mutual benefit. No lies, no pretenses, just working together for the betterment of my grandmother's business, which you have a fiduciary relationship with, correct?"

"I do, and I agree." I put my hand out for a shake. Just from that minimal contact, all the attraction I'd felt for him as a confused and stupid teenager came rushing back. I had to force my thoughts away and remember that I had just agreed to remain professional.

Landon held my hand a bit too long for what would be considered a typical handshake, but I might have been seeing my own deep desire to have more with him. Or perhaps his hesitation was about not wanting to work with me.

I was even less sure when the moment ended and he smiled at me for the first time in over a decade   a genuine smile, not the courtesy one he pasted on his face the first time he visited my office. The sight sent electrical currents through me… currents I was now forced to ignore.

"So, now's as good a time as any to talk business," Landon said and sat back down. "Tell me everything you can about the old Wilcox Filling Station."

Landon

STUPID, DUMB-ASS heat. And I don't mean the weather. After all that'd happened, all I'd just said about staying professional, and all the years of anger and hurt, one touch of the fool's hand sent scorching heat up my arm and about melted my damn brain.

No. I won't even consider it. Jason Murrin's a tool. Okay, maybe he *was* a tool, but "once burned, twice shy," or something like that. Maybe it's "fool me once…." Regardless, I refused to allow myself to feel anything for Jason besides professional courtesy.

And yeah, I'd heard Lee Murrin was an ass. I remembered seeing Jason looking like someone had beaten him down when we were in our junior year of high school. There'd been rumors that his dad was abusive, although no one really knew, and I tried, even back then, to avoid the gossip mill. Being a gay kid in Northport, I could only imagine there were plenty of rumors about me.

My mind wandered as Jason showed me all the information he had on the defunct filling station, including some pretty good photographs of it from back in the day. "If you want more pictures, go see our town historian, who works at the library. He received some pictures from the probate attorney when this case started. 'Bout the only thing that worthless attorney sent me."

I almost missed that last part because Jason said it under his breath. Of course, if the property had been languishing in probate for over a decade, his frustration was justified.

"I gave those to the library to store in the archives since they also included some old pictures of other buildings in town as far back as the early nineteen twenties."

"Cool, yeah. I'll go over when we're done here. So, tell me about what we should expect to pay for the property. If Carter Stores decides to pursue it, is there any reason to think the acquisition wouldn't be straightforward?"

"There shouldn't be any legal hoops to jump through. There are no living heirs, which is why it's languished for so long. Any proceeds from the sale will go back to the state to pay off back taxes. There was a little cash left in the estate, but the other attorney sucked all that dry. Two years of taxes are owed, which will have to be paid by whoever purchases the property."

"Okay, so you'll send me the file that shows the resolved brownfield? The mayor said any pollutants were mitigated years ago."

I'd already given Jason my business card, so he smiled and nodded. "I'll get that to you as soon as possible. Your grandmother will be so excited."

"I doubt it. Speaking of my grandmother, I need you to keep this between us until I can confirm if it's even viable. I'll run numbers and should know in a few days if it is or not."

"I can hold off, but only because I'm the probate officer. If this becomes particularly business-related for Carter Stores, I'm obligated to inform your grandmother. As you said, my fiduciary relationship is with her, after all."

I bit back a groan as I thought about the hot water I could get into with this. "Okay, but give me the week at least. I'm proposing something completely different from our normal business model. If it works out, it could even be more lucrative, but I need a little time to figure that out."

"Okay, deal. You've got one week, but if she asks, I'll have to tell her about it."

"If she asks, you should, but she won't. She knows the deal on the other store has fallen through, and from what I can tell, you aren't working on the out-of-state projects, so it's unlikely she'll call, correct?"

"Correct." Jason about blinded me with a bright smile—the same one that used to stop my heart. It threatened to do the same now.

"Okay, off to the library, then," I said quickly as I dashed out of the office. As soon as I was outside, I mentally patted myself on the back for having not humiliated myself in front of Jason. Hopefully meeting with him would get easier going forward. One down, likely several more to go.

Jason

I COULDN'T WIPE the smile off my face for the rest of the day. Granted, it wasn't like Landon forgave me or even wanted to see me. In fact, he made it clear he didn't, but it felt good to… to what? I wasn't even sure. Does it feel like he hates me a little less? Do I feel not quite as guilty now?

I still had some shit to work through. Regardless, it felt good to be on speaking terms with him again. Meanwhile, I was now behind with a whole bunch of work, but I looked at my phone and had to resist the urge to call Marisa.

I already knew she'd kick my ass if she knew how insanely attracted I felt to Landon. Not that I could control that, but still. Marisa told me just yesterday to behave. "And I will," I said to myself out loud. "I will behave, but I can also enjoy being around a sexy man."

"Well, nothing wrong with that," Adam said as he strolled into my office. "Thanks for the compliment."

"Damn, Adam, you just about gave me a heart attack. How did you get in without ringing the bell?"

"Practice. I hate that thing. Why don't you get rid of it and hire an assistant?"

I shook my head because this was an ongoing friendly argument between us.

"'Cause I don't need an assistant, and not all of us have money flowing out of our ears," I said, not even looking at him. Instead, I began shuffling my papers. I wouldn't be getting any work done now that he was here.

"You are a proper law firm, and you need an assistant."

I rolled my eyes. My friend was like a freaking dog with a bone. "Adam, to what do I owe the honor?" I asked.

"Oh, I popped into town hall a while ago, and the mayor said there might be some interest in that eyesore on my side of town. She said you were meeting with the potential buyer, and I wanted to get the gossip."

"Damn, news travels fast in this town. Before we get into that, what's going on with our hotel-room-trashing client?"

Adam shrugged. "He'll be spending a few nights in rehab. Actually, that's another reason I came by. Did you get the cease and desist letter out yet?"

"No, I've been a bit preoccupied since we talked." I looked at my watch. "Three hours ago."

"That's good, actually. Hold off on it. I'm going to give the hotel manager a call, and I think I have a way to motivate them that doesn't require attorney intervention." I cocked my eyebrow at him, and he laughed. "Don't give me the look. It's nothing that'll cause legal issues. Another client of mine, Layla, who is a big social media influencer, needs a place for her baby shower, and it'll be a big deal for whichever venue hosts it, since it's bound to generate massive publicity. I'll see to that personally. I'm thinking about offering it to the hotel. I was already considering that before all this went down. Now it just provides extra incentive."

"But didn't they threaten to expose our guy?"

"Yes, but they've been known for discretion for years. I doubt they'd jeopardize that, even if they are pissed about the destroyed hotel room. Regardless, I'm going to head up to Portland tomorrow and exert some charm on them. I've already gotten the okay from Layla." Adam chuckled. "Not that you need all the details. Anyway, what's the scoop on the filling station?"

I sighed, not wanting to give too much away, even if Landon wasn't technically my client. I didn't want to tell Adam that I felt an odd protectiveness when it came to Landon, a revelation that I hadn't even examined for myself yet. "Polly totally sent you over here because she didn't want to get in trouble for spilling the beans, but she knows I can't disclose anything either. Attorney-client privilege and all that."

"So the interested buyer is a client? Anyone I know?" Adam asked, but I just shrugged. He knew better than to even ask. "Okay, what *can* you tell me?"

"If this works out, it'll fill a big void while getting rid of a blight on the town. It'll be a boon for Wilcox."

"And?" he asked.

"And that's it. If the buyer wants to move forward, then and only then will I give you more details," I said, then added under my breath, "not that you won't find out anyway."

"Hey!" Adam said. "I'm not that nosy."

"Says the guy who's quizzing me like I'm on the witness stand."

"Okay, touché, but you know I was considering buying that myself. It'd be a great location for a boutique hotel or maybe even a pocket park."

"And you might still have that opportunity, but if this deal works out, I think what it brings would be more in line with what our little town needs."

My friend's eyes lit up. "A café that can serve more edible food than pie? Maybe blink twice if I hit it on the nose. That way, no one could accuse you of squealing."

"You're the worst." I stood to escort him out.

"Come on. You can at least tell me what kind of business."

"Bye, Adam," I said as I gently pushed him out my front door. I deliberately jingled the bell twice before I closed it on him, and chuckled all the way back to my office.

Adam and I attended law school together and had become friends, though I never expected he'd put down roots in Wilcox, of all places. But when a famous actress bought property in town, he followed her up from Los Angeles and fell in love with the area. Recently, he bought a sweet home that Xander and Rhys, who'd become his friends as much as mine, had built.

Adam hadn't wasted any time getting involved in local business, to the point that now he acted like he owned the town. And Wilcox was all the better for it. He'd been helping spearhead revitalization efforts, and if that's what ended up keeping Landon around for a while, I'd be secretly indebted to my friend.

Landon

I STRODE INTO the library, intending to conduct my business and get out of there as quickly as possible. My grandmother would be calling any minute. In fact, I was surprised she hadn't called already.

"Excuse me," I said to the man at the front desk who had his back to me.

"Hi," the man said as he turned around, smiling. "What can I help you with?"

"I just came from Jason Murrin's office, and he mentioned the town historian works here and that pictures of the old filling station are on file. May I take a look?" I was a little concerned this guy might let the cat out of the bag, but I wasn't sure if asking to keep this confidential might make things worse.

"Certainly you can. Our archive is open to the public," he said. "I'm Corey, the historian that Jason mentioned. By day, local historian, and by… well, still day, I guess, Wilcox's one and only librarian." He gave me an adorable lopsided grin then, and if things weren't so up in the air with my grandmother, it'd be worth my time to find out if he was gay.

I followed Corey around the corner and into a room that he unlocked. "I keep all our historical information back here to keep it safe, but our patrons have free access. I've been slowly working my way through our archive to properly document everything. The photographs you're interested in are still on my to-do list, but I did manage to get them placed in archival photo sleeves for easy viewing." He reached on top of a tall file cabinet, pulled down an archival box, and placed it on the table. "Here it is. These photos are fragile, so please handle them with care. But you're welcome to take pictures of the pictures, if you like. When you're done, just leave everything out on the table. I'll put it all away."

I nodded. The pictures were exactly what I'd hoped to see. They showed a typical nineteen-thirties-style service station with two antique-looking gas pumps in front. Photographs couldn't tell me if the building remained salvageable, but they confirmed the place oozed small-town charm in its heyday. My mind drifted to how we might go about recapturing that with a Carter Store.

I flipped through the other photos, thrilled to see images of people smiling—mostly kids with a soda or a lollipop in their hands. I realized how important that station must have been to the townsfolk. So many family memories happened in stores like that one and in the ones my grandmother had created with Carter Stores.

I snapped out of my reverie and took a few photos with my phone. If I could convince my grandmother to take this project on, I'd come back and ask if reprints could be made to incorporate into the artwork for our building.

I was just about to get up to leave when my phone buzzed. "Hi, Grandma," I said without looking at the caller ID.

"Hello, Grandson. Are you done gallivanting around Wilcox, or are you needing more loafing time?"

I snorted. "I'm not gallivanting or loafing, thank you very much."

"Then why did Lorine say she'd seen you walking into the library?" she asked.

I shook my head. "Well, first, whoever Lorine is, she needs to mind her own business, and second, I'm not prepared to tell you yet. It's a surprise. But I will be coming your way in a few minutes. I just finished up here."

"Good. I need you to run me over to Edward's Crossing."

"Okay, give me about thirty minutes and I'll be there. Oh, can you have one of the cooks put together a fresh chicken sandwich for me? I'm starving, but I don't want something that's been sitting out all day."

"I'll have you know our sandwiches never sit out all day. We…."

I laughed. "Grandma, I know, but you know they taste better when they first come out of the fryer. If I'm going to have to run an extra mile tonight to get rid of the fat from that sandwich, at least it should taste its best."

"Fine, just get here soon," she said, and I could hear her muttering under her breath about young people wanting everything to be their way or the highway. I was still smiling when I approached Corey at the front desk.

"Did you find what you needed?" he asked.

I nodded, then almost asked if he had plans tonight. Luckily I noticed he sported a wedding band. "I'm done with the photos, but I'm considering taking on a project involving the old filling station property. If I do, could I get high-quality reprints made?"

"Not sure why not. The photographs officially belong to the estate. Jason has loaned them to the library until the new owner takes over. If that's you, then they'll officially be yours anyway. If you decide to donate them to the library, we can digitally scan them and make you copies."

"Perfect, thanks. I'll be in touch. I'm Landon Carter, by the way. Nice to meet you."

I walked back to my car wondering what had gotten into me. Had it not been for the wedding band, I'd totally have flirted with the man. Something I usually didn't do.

My mind immediately returned to Jason, and I realized I'd gotten caught up in my attraction to him and had projected that onto Corey— not that the town librarian wasn't damn cute in his own right. Good thing I noticed that wedding ring when I did.

Jason

"Hello, Madam Mayor," I said as Polly came in and sat comfortably across from me. "To what do I owe the honor?"

"Weeeell." Polly stretched the word out like folks do when they're about to ask for something they shouldn't. "I heard through the grapevine that Landon Carter came by yesterday to see you." I nodded but didn't comment. "I know that he's considering buying the old filling station property."

She held my gaze but stayed silent, another small-town tactic when fishing for information. I'd learned all the tricks early on, considering an attorney had to know when to keep his mouth shut.

Finally Polly just chuckled. "Well, okay. I see you're gonna keep those cards close to your chest. So let me just share my two cents. Old Miller Haskin wants that land to put in a water park for the kids. It's absolute nonsense, but until the Carter boy came nosing around, I seriously considered it 'cause you know that's a mighty big eyesore in the midst of our town."

I nodded, already aware of Mr. Haskin's interest. I also knew he didn't really want it but was tired of the blight in an otherwise up-and-coming area.

"Anyway, I want to let you know, if that boy can do what he's considering *and* keep the historical elements in place like we discussed, I'd be very interested in that. A damn sight more than a water park. Do you catch my drift?" she asked.

I chuckled. "Polly, we all want that property developed, and yeah, I understand what you're saying. I don't have any power, though. I work for his grandmother, not him."

"Well, no matter. Oh, that reminds me, Adam wanted me to talk to you about expanding your practice and bringing in a few more attorneys."

I groaned. "Adam wants to nose his way into everyone's businesses here in Wilcox. I'm not looking to expand 'cause I don't want the headache. Not only that, but Henry Erickson officially works for this firm, and so does your technically retired husband when he wants to dabble. They may not be here around the clock like I am, but that's still more attorneys than we need here in Wilcox."

She cocked her eyebrow at me, and I laughed. "Listen, Tim had the right idea all those years. He worked alone. If I wanted all the crazy that comes with managing attorneys, I could've remained at the law firm I started with in Portland. I'm here 'cause I want simple and easygoing."

"I can respect that." Polly smiled. "I also already told Adam as much, but you know how persistent he is when he gets hold of a thought."

I shook my head. "Well, keep telling him to back off. Maybe when we're all retired, he'll get the point."

At that, Polly stood and moved toward the door. "You know, with all these business plans, I'd guess that Carter boy is planning to move back here permanently." She winked at me. "He seems like a fine young man. Easy on the eyes too."

"Oh Lord, you're worse than Adam. I'm not shopping for a husband right now, even if everyone in this town is obsessed with playing matchmaker."

Polly's smile never left her face. "Oh, I've heard all that before, but trust me, a good man makes life worth living. You'll see."

With that, she was out the door. I liked Landon, but even if we didn't have a past, I wasn't sure any man would want to settle down in a small town with a guy making a modest living. My law firm turned a profit, but I was never going to be rich. If I couldn't find a husband while living in a metropolis like Portland, I doubted I'd find one here.

Although I'd given up hope of finding a lasting relationship, I wasn't exactly living like a monk. Hookups were rare these days, but I couldn't deny taking a quick trip to the big city when the urge hit. Thankfully, I could still rely on Grindr to take care of my physical needs.

I shook my head as I tried not to think about that too much. I hated wanting two things that opposed one another. I'd chosen Wilcox, no turning back now, even if that meant a life without the companionship I secretly craved.

Landon

I ROLLED MY head from side to side to relieve the tension in my neck. Glancing over at the clock, I saw it was past one in the morning. I needed to shut down my spreadsheet and head to bed. Grandma had no idea what I was doing, so she'd expect to see me at the crack of dawn.

I closed my laptop and slipped into bed, then got up. Mayor Polly had recommended a small-town architect, and I decided to stop the treadmill in my mind and send the guy an email.

Too many people were learning about my project, and I hoped it didn't bite me in the ass. I needed to come clean with Grandma before she heard through gossip that I was making business plans behind her back.

The next morning, I met her at one of her first business purchases—a store she says "runs like a top." She wanted me to observe the manager there so I could "see how it's supposed to be done."

Unfortunately, even though I arrived ten minutes early, she recognized my sleep-deprived state the moment I walked in the place. She immediately pulled me into the back office and demanded I spill.

I flopped down on the chair next to her and shook my head. "Grandma, I'm chasing a lead, a project that I think would be good for Carter Stores. But before you get all uptight about it, it's something I studied in college."

"The old Wilcox Filling Station?" she asked, and despite my exhaustion, I couldn't help but laugh.

"Yeah, didn't take long for you to figure that out."

"Well, son, you know I'm friends with most folks around there, considering I've lived in the area my whole life. Polly approached me about reviving that station over a year ago. But they want it to be a small, old-timey thing from the nineteen thirties or something. That's not what we do."

"But it's five acres in a prime location, and I think we could build a regular-size store that looks historical. There's a compromise to be found there. That's what I've been researching."

"You're gonna have a committee of people over there watching over your shoulder too. That town is full of busybodies."

I nodded. "Yeah, I figured that. But if our plans are clear from the beginning…."

"Then they'll still walk right over them." She sat for a moment, looking down at the paperwork on the desk. "Listen, I'm not going to say no, because I want you to test your sea legs out a bit, but trust me, I've walked out of more than one deal when a town tried to micromanage me. Wilcox is designed to be one of those towns."

I released the breath I was holding. "I know you're probably right, but I'd like to pursue this. Just let me chase down the leads and see if I can make it make sense financially. Then, if you and Dad approve, I'll take it to the city council and see what they say. If they give us a lot of grief, well, we can drop the whole thing. And since you aren't paying me anyway…."

Grandma chuckled. "Okay, you've got me there. But no on involving your dad. He's got more on his plate than he can handle right now. If you really want to put this together, you'll have to find someone else to build it."

I couldn't hold back my excitement at getting her blessing. I stood up and pulled her into a hug. "Thanks, Grandma. I'll make you proud. Even if it doesn't work out, I think it's good for us to keep our minds open to other ideas."

She just shook her head and sat back in the chair. "Well, you know I disagree. Find what works and stick with it, that's my philosophy. But I'd be a hypocrite to discourage you from following your gut instincts. Besides, if you take over, you'll do things your way, and I'd prefer you fall on your face while I'm still around to help you get back up."

"Yes, ma'am," I said, and she nodded her approval.

"Okay, get on out of here. You look like you're about to fall asleep on your feet anyway. Lord knows I've seen you get hold of things before, so I know you won't let it go until it's done. But son, don't stick on this too long. I've got a lot to show you, and I'm not gettin' any younger."

A twinge of guilt struck me. I hadn't decided to take over for her. But then, I hadn't decided *what* I wanted to do. Maybe I *would* like to run Carter Stores. Maybe, if I could focus on stuff that inspired me—like this potential Wilcox project—that might make it all the more desirable.

Those were questions for another day, as was whether I would even want to live in the area long-term. As a teenager, I couldn't wait to leave small-town Oregon behind. But the more I saw of Wilcox and its people, the more I liked it. Even a certain local attorney was causing me to reconsider things.

Landon

WHAT THE fuck was I doing here? My leg bounced, and I gripped the steering wheel hard—all too obvious signs of how nervous I felt. Apprehension and excitement warred within me as I sat in the café parking lot and mentally prepared myself to go inside.

I'd spent the day and night before working, poring over spreadsheets, and sometime in the early morning I'd fallen asleep at my computer. When my buzzing phone woke me an hour ago, my eyes went from bleary to the size of saucers as I read who texted.

Jason wanted to meet me at Wilcox Café. Was I ready for that? Fuck no. I felt too vulnerable, and tired on top of it. I was likely to bite his head off or drop to my knees, neither of which was a good idea.

I let myself have the internal argument for a few minutes. *He's gonna mess with your head again. He's being a player, don't fall for it. Forget how hot he still is... he'll stab you in the heart like last time.*

However, if he had information about the old filling station project, I'd be stupid not to go. So I'd texted him back.

Me: *What time do you want to meet at the café?*

Jason: *I can get away by five. Does that work?*

My brain hesitated, but my traitorous fingers flew across the screen.

Me: *Sure, see you then.*

This was such a bad idea. I decided to take a long shower to hopefully soothe some of the kinks out of my shoulders before I restressed them by meeting Jason. For a moment I missed Chicago and the ability to schedule a massage at the drop of a hat. Small-town Oregon didn't have a lot of those places.

Maybe a trip to Portland this weekend would be in order. I needed a deep tissue massage if I was going to complete this business proposal.

By the time I finished my shower, I barely had enough time to get dressed, brush my teeth, and get to Wilcox Café on time.

After my internal debate in the parking lot, I walked into the café five minutes before our agreed meeting time and had to force my grandmother's voice out of my head about that being late. Jason was sitting at the far corner table, looking over a bunch of paperwork. I smiled at the lady at the front, let her know I was going to seat myself, then walked toward Jason's table.

"Hey," I said as he looked up.

The smile he gave me lit his entire face. Once again I was forced to deal with the tummy butterflies that went ballistic at that expression.

"Hey, sorry. I was focused on… well, you probably don't care about all that." He stuffed the papers back into a folder and shoved it to the side. "I didn't want to get any food until you got here, so why don't we order before I show you what I've found."

I nodded and sat across from him, sighing as I looked at the menu. I'd been here enough to know the only edible food was the breakfast, and even that was questionable, so I decided to order from their breakfast menu.

When our food came, I dove in. Only when I looked up did I notice Jason staring at me intensely, and I immediately blushed. "How's your waffles?" I asked.

Jason shook his head. "Sorry, yeah, it's good. Well, as good as it gets here. I normally don't eat at the café, but it's not like we have many options in Wilcox."

The comment brought me back to my senses enough that I could eat my oatmeal and not worry about the *I want to rip your clothes off* look he'd just given me.

I noticed then that Jason's cheeks had taken on a faint pink, and he nervously forked his food around his plate. Was he sweating? Oh my God, was he actually sweating?

I didn't know how to react, and we ate in silence for a while before he broke the tension.

"So, I've been looking at tax credits and other options to help make the deal more enticing, but so far no luck."

I smiled, genuinely this time, because it was sweet that he was trying to think outside the box. "I know a fair bit about incentives. I was training to be a community planner before I gave that up for the business route," I admitted.

Jason nodded. "I was going to be a partner in a highfalutin Portland law firm. Spent a year there and hated it beyond what I can tell you. So yeah, now I'm a broke small-town attorney and couldn't be happier with that decision."

For some reason, it pleased me that Jason had found himself at home in Wilcox. I couldn't picture him spending his life in a big city like Portland. Not that he couldn't be successful anywhere, but he had always struck me as someone who'd be most content as a big fish in a small pond. I wondered if I might be that sort of person too.

My breath caught as I watched Jason lick syrup off his fingers. I remembered sucking on those fingers myself, and the heat of that moment filled me with longing. What would it feel like to have those fingers working me? To revel in every sensation, not as an inexperienced teenager but as a man—a man who could now return the pleasure he'd given me?

My mouth went dry. *Holy hell, this can't be happening. I still want this guy. Fuck me sideways.* I couldn't hold back a chuckle at that last thought because *yes, please.* Then I realized Jason hadn't missed how hot and bothered I'd been moments ago.

His gaze bored into me, and his cheeks were even pinker now, but he was quickly working to manage it. Good, he deserved to be as flustered as I felt. He only looked away when two men I didn't recognize approached our table.

"Hey, Jason, who's your friend?" one of the men asked.

Jason cleared his throat. "Hey, guys. Adam, Joey, this is a high school friend, Landon. Landon, Adam is our resident busybody, and Joey is his long-suffering husband, who should be given an award for dealing with his nosy self."

Adam gave Jason a dry look, then smiled at me. "Ignore my wannabe comedian friend. I'm a respectable member of the Wilcox community. Do you mind if we join you?" he asked, and I saw his husband roll his eyes at Jason.

Of course, I now wanted to know what these two were all about.

Joey and Adam pulled up a couple of chairs. "Nice to meet you, Landon," Joey said as soon as he was seated. "My husband is a bit of a busybody, but he's got a good heart."

Adam gave Joey a warm smile and didn't try to contradict him. "So, high school buddy of Jason's, what brings you back to this part of the world?" Adam asked.

"I'm helping my grandmother while she's recovering from an illness," I said, not wanting to put all my family business on the table.

"That's nice of you," Adam said. "Your grandmother must live around here, then?"

"Yes, not far from Wilcox," I replied, realizing Jason's introduction of his friend as the town busybody had been a warning. "And you, what do you do, Adam?"

Adam talked for several minutes about his PR business. He didn't name-drop any clients, but I gathered that he ran a very successful company. "And Joey, do you work in Wilcox?" I asked.

The man, considerably shyer than his husband, nodded. "Yes, I'm a musician. I compose music for movies."

"That's cool," I said with a smile as we then chatted about our respective careers. When our conversation slowed, and having finished my meal, I pulled out my wallet to pay and go.

"No dessert?" Adam asked.

"No, I need to hit a gym before I start eating food with too many carbs," I admitted.

Joey grinned. "I'm from New York, and trust me, you'll come to accept there's going to be a little more thickness around your middle living here. Despite its reputation, Wilcox Café is the center of our town's social life, and none of us can resist their pies."

I sighed. "I shouldn't, but the company is certainly good. Why not?"

"They've got homemade ice cream too," Jason said. "You'll want to top it with that."

Although I knew better, I had to make good with the locals, so I decided to give in to sweet temptation.

Once dessert was served, the three men began chatting about local politics as we dug in. "Freaking mother of God," I blurted after swallowing my first bite. "How do they make it that good?"

Everyone chuckled. "Peggy is an expert. None of us can get her to tell us her secret," Adam said.

"I think it's witchcraft," Joey added, to laughter all around us, not just our table.

"You don't listen to these three," a hard-looking older woman said as she walked toward us. "That's not magic at all, just a lot of experience." She winked at me, then asked, "How's your grandmother doing? I heard she had a stroke. Also heard she was back at it in less than a week."

I laughed. This was only my second time in the café, but this woman, who I'd never met, knew who I was. Wilcox really was a small town. "My grandma's fine, ma'am. And no, you can't hold her down for long. The woman is made of steel."

"Oh, son, that's a great description of Gloria Carter. I'm Peggy, by the way. If you need anything else, you holler, okay?" she asked, then quickly moved around the tables to chat with other customers.

"Your grandmother is Gloria Carter?" Adam asked. "As in, the owner of Carter Stores?"

I nodded.

"So you're the secret Jason and Polly won't tell me," he said in a whisper, then squared me with a look. "Are you considering putting a store on the old filling station lot?"

Knowing to keep the cards close to my chest, I just smiled. "Oh, don't believe everything you hear. Now, back to this homemade pie and ice cream, do they make it to go?"

Joey gave me a bemused look but helped divert his husband's attention before Adam could ask any more questions. Okay, points for Joey. A moment later, I couldn't resist the yawn that escaped me. "Sorry," I said, a bit embarrassed. "Been burning the candle at both ends."

I fished out my wallet, placed some cash on the table to cover my bill, and rose. Then I shook Joey's hand, then Adam's, waved at Jason, and left the café. Everyone I'd met in Wilcox so far had been welcoming and inviting. There really was something special about this little town. Even in the short amount of time I'd been here, I was beginning to feel it.

Jason

Hanging out with Adam, Joey, and Landon had felt right—like we were all old friends. Landon kept the discussions fairly formal, but the way he and Joey practically tag-teamed to maneuver around Adam's nosiness was impressive. Adam being Adam, I wouldn't doubt if he respected Landon all the more for it.

I had to admit my feelings for Landon, which had never gone away, were getting stronger the more time I spent with him. I needed to go sit down with Marisa and Owen so they could talk some sense into me. I'd never been one to hold back when I liked a man, and this was the first time I hadn't made a move on someone when I wanted. And boy, did I *want*, but this was Landon. I couldn't risk fucking things up with him. Not again.

The way he looked at me today—with enough heat to spark a damn fire—made me think he was as attracted to me as I to him. But mutual attraction was never a problem between us. *I* had been the fucking problem.

I could've kicked my teenage ass about now. "So you're going to keep this a secret for real," I heard Adam say next to me, pulling me from my thoughts.

"You can't be in the middle of everything, as much as you try to be," I told him. "As I said, and as you damn well know, I'll tell you only when it's something I can share publicly with Landon's blessing."

"And that's all you can do." Joey quickly reached across the table to take his husband's hand.

Adam sighed. "It's just, this town means a lot to me, and you know I've put a lot of energy and money into it. And now that I've invested in Rhys and Xander's company, I'm about to invest even more."

"And you've made a lot of improvements, there's no disputing that. But not even Polly knows everything that's happening in town, and she's the mayor."

Just then, Polly turned around. I hadn't even noticed her come into the café and sit at the next table. "What is it that I don't know?" she asked. Polly and Tim sat across from Xander and his mom, Ellen McLeroy, the county commissioner. I could see the humor on all of their faces.

"I give up." I gathered up my file folders on the table and stood to go. "This town? Nosiest place in the Pacific Northwest."

Everyone around me laughed because it was the dang truth. "I'll see y'all later, and Polly, come see me when you have a chance. I want to talk about, well, you know what."

She gave me a little salute in acknowledgment, and I went up front to pay my bill.

It was a nice evening, and I'd normally have enjoyed a stroll around town. Instead I wandered over to the property Landon was considering. Weed trees and blackberry vines had taken over, so the place looked like hell, but it remained a prime piece of real estate.

If Landon decided to pursue the project, he'd have to flush out the mice and other creepy crawlies hiding in there—all easy enough to do. The bigger issue was the filling station itself. The small building was dilapidated, and the whole roof looked like it could fall in at any minute. I wondered if there was any saving it.

Then I walked back to my place, pondering how best to deal with my not-so-new obsession with Landon. Should I make a move? Could I let it be? Either scenario had potentially devastating consequences. That is, unless we somehow salvaged a happily ever after from our disastrous teenaged start. Did I even dare believe that was a possibility, however remote?

I sighed and sat heavily on the bench outside my office while I scanned my hometown. There was so much progress being made here, more than in most little towns these days. Northport was still bustling when I was young, but now it showed signs of struggle. Wilcox felt like a totally different place, and not only economically.

Together, Xander and Rhys had been a leading force in the downtown revitalization effort. Thanks to a generous grant from an anonymous source—aka Adam—the town hall had also been renovated in recent years. Ellen had even managed to carve out enough money to renovate our very dilapidated library, which was now being run by a young gay man who moved here with his husband and two kids.

I felt fortunate to have purchased my building for next to nothing. With Rhys's help, I'd done some minor repairs and renovated my apartment above the first-floor office.

Our town had made great strides, but some major work was still needed. The old dry goods store and the building next to it still sat abandoned, as they had for at least a couple of decades. They butted up against the filling station property, and all of it stood out like a sore thumb.

The two derelict buildings would probably be torn down, which would be a shame. It was obvious both had been impressive structures in their heyday. I wondered if maybe I should speak to Landon about them. I had no idea how he could incorporate either or both into a service station model, but he should be made aware of the opportunity. I went inside, fired up my computer, and sent him an email.

Landon,

I got to thinking. The two buildings next to the filling station are also for sale. The town owns them because they're derelict.

I'm guessing if no one buys them soon, they'll have to be razed. I know one of the buildings has lost part of its roof. Not over the main building, but a lean-to on the back.

Let me know if you want more information.

My fingers hovered over the keyboard, and I was unsure if that's how I wanted to close the email. Should I just keep it professional? *Fuck it*, I thought. No harm in being friendly.

Thanks again for meeting me at the café today. I'm glad you got to meet Adam and Joey. If you ever want more of Peggy's famous pie and ice cream and want company, just say the word.

Jason

Landon

I'D BEEN knee-deep in spreadsheets when my inbox dinged with a new email. It was from Jason, informing me that two properties next to the filling station were available for purchase. He also all but asked me out for another round of pie and ice cream, but I chose to ignore that… for now.

I'd noticed those abandoned buildings during my recent walkabout, but I still looked them up online for a better vantage point… though "better" was a relative term. "How the hell are they still standing?" I asked out loud.

Offhand, neither looked salvageable, but I wondered if it might be worth asking the architect. Still, the old filling station already came with five acres, more than enough for a store, parking, and a little picnic area to the side.

Rather than reply to Jason's email, I texted him.

Me: *Hey, I got your email. Interesting idea. I'll think about it, but I'm not sure I can do much with those buildings.*

He must've been on his phone, because mine pinged with a text a second later.

Jason: *I figured. But they need an owner, if you can think of someone who might be interested.*

I was glad our conversation died after that. I'd be much better off not communicating with him at all. The fact that this realization caused me to want to cry only further confirmed how much I couldn't trust myself where that man was concerned.

So, instead of texting Jason again, I called the architect.

Johney answered after the first ring.

"Hi, Johney, my name's Landon Carter. I was given your name by several people about consulting on a building project here in Wilcox. I have some ideas and wondered if you have time to meet me tomorrow."

When he said he did and we set a time to meet on-site, I decided to bring one of my dad's standard plans for Carter Stores to our meeting.

When I ended the call with Johney, I texted Dad.

Me: *I need a basic Carter Store blueprint by tomorrow morning.*

Dad: *Those are confidential.*

Me: *I've got Grandma's blessing. I promise not to share with anyone not under an NDA.*

He didn't respond, not that I expected him to. I knew he wouldn't refuse if Grandma had given a green light.

My next text was to Jason.

Me: *Can you shoot Johney an NDA regarding the filling station? My dad's request before I share any store blueprints.*

Jason: *On it!*

I leaned back in my chair and smiled. I really liked the nuances of running a business and working out all the little details. I could see myself operating a large chain like Carter Stores. But I would have to move back to Oregon since we were headquartered here.

Had anyone asked me a week ago if I'd be willing to permanently relocate, I'd have flat-out said no. Jason, Marisa, and Owen all lived in the area, and together with the rampant homophobia in our hometown growing up, they were massive turn-offs for me. But Wilcox was clearly crawling with gay folks who were out and apparently fully embraced by the town. Marisa and Owen seemed like decent people too, and as for Jason, the man… well, I still wasn't entirely sure how I felt about him.

The next morning I got up early and headed to my parents' home in Northport. The rolling hills along the drive were mostly wooded with a few pastures in between, and I was surprised by the feeling of nostalgia that flowed through me. I loved this part of the world.

Other than my late teen years, I had excellent memories of the area. I'd spent my entire childhood helping at Carter's, even when it was still a one-pony show, as my grandma called the first store she ran with Grandpa. Those were amazing years.

I smiled as I drove past my grandparents' old farm, which Grandma sold several years after Grandpa passed away. The current owners of the sprawling brick Greek Revival wannabe had painted the old house white, making it look even more regal than it had when Grandma lived there. That place held many good memories too.

But seeing the state of the land made me sad. It was mostly overgrown now, the pastures long ago reverting to woodland. Based on what I'd been told and seen in photographs, it was a spectacular farm when Grandpa was alive. Grandma had sold the house but sectioned it off from most of the acreage beforehand because Dad wanted it. In fact, he still owned it, but I knew he hadn't gone out there in years. All the traveling he did for Carter Stores didn't mesh well with maintaining a sizable property like that, or even visiting it much.

I arrived at my parents' place just as Mom finished making breakfast. "Mmm, Mom, that smells good," I said as I walked into the kitchen.

"Well, you're just in time," she said as she hugged me.

"Is Dad in his office?" I asked.

"Yes, and tell him breakfast is ready."

I found Dad poring over some paperwork. "You're getting an early start." I flopped down in a chair across the desk from him. "Mom said breakfast is ready."

He looked up and smiled when he saw me. That was another typical response. Dad could be tough as nails. His rough, calloused hands, scarred by years of manual labor, and the fact that he didn't take shit from anybody, might speak to having a rough personality. But he was a big softie at heart and always had a grin on his face for me. A wave of emotions washed over me as I took that in.

I'd seen more than a few kids on the streets in Chicago because their parents hadn't accepted their sexuality. Yet I was from a small conservative town in Oregon and my family had only ever embraced me. If not for them, my teenage years could have been as hard as Jason's.

Before I had time to dwell on Jason's upbringing, Dad's voice brought me back to the present. "So you wanted our blueprints. Mind telling me why?" he asked.

I shook my head. "Grandma told me not to. Said you were busy enough without my wild ideas getting in your way."

He laughed. "Sounds like Mom, but I do need to know if this is going to end up with me having to build something."

I sighed. "You tell Grandma you forced it out of me, 'cause she'll wring my neck once she finds out I told you against her wishes. I'm putting together a proposal for a store in downtown Wilcox that has historical elements to go along with it."

"Your grandmother let you get away with that?" he asked.

I nodded. "She wants me to take over, so she's giving me more rein than she normally would."

Dad laughed out loud at that. "Well, you better use that sparingly, 'cause you and I both know she won't let you get away with much. So, tell me about the project."

"He can when you're both seated at the kitchen table," Mom said from the doorway, her face clearly showing her impatience. "I swear, I don't stand in there cooking just to post pictures of it on social media. Now come on, you two."

Dad winked at me as he stood and followed her down the hallway. My parents might argue with each other on occasion, but there was always an undercurrent of love. When I let myself dwell on my nonexistent love life, I wondered if I'd ever have that with a partner—someone who balanced me out and saw the best in me, who knew all my faults and insecurities and loved me anyway, and vice versa. Someone who'd never give up on me, even in the tough times.

We dished our own food and took a seat. Then I told my parents about my project—everything from how I had enjoyed this type of project in college, to my conversations with Polly and Jason, to viewing the historical photos at the library.

"I think it's a good idea for Carter Stores to have a presence in Wilcox," I said. "I mean, how often do you get five full acres in an up-and-coming area for that good a price, let alone with all the brownfield stuff cleaned up already?"

Dad nodded, and I internally fist-pumped. "So, if Mom doesn't want me to be all over it, who do you have in mind?" he asked.

"I'm still figuring that out. I'm meeting with an architect—Johney McMann—later today to put together some preliminary plans. But I'll have to find a local builder."

"Don't you think Mark Healy's company can do that?" Mom asked Dad. "You remember how we worked with them years ago, before you built your crew."

Dad nodded slowly as if thinking it over. "I think his son Rhys took over most of that, but I've heard good things. They've even pilfered a few of my best men who wanted to work locally instead of traveling. Despite that, I'm guessing they're good folks."

"Okay, that bodes well, and he was already recommended to me," I acknowledged. "Do you think they're reasonable cost-wise?"

Dad shrugged. "Been a long time since I used them, and I've heard they're building some pretty fancy houses for the Portland elite, so you can bet they don't come cheap. But in this business, you get what you pay for. You shouldn't be too worried about shelling out a little more if it means getting a project done on budget and done right the first time."

"Okay," I said. "Can you get me Mark's contact details? I'd like to talk to him."

"Well, I don't have his number," Dad said. "But ask Polly next time you're in town. She knows everything happening in Wilcox, and she did long before she ever became mayor."

"That's been my impression of her as well. I first met her when she and her husband dropped off paperwork while I was over at Marisa and Owen's."

Both my parents stopped eating and turned to me. "You went to Marisa and Owen's?" they asked in unison.

"Yeah, why?"

"'Cause they stopped coming around your senior year, and when I asked about it, you told me they could get bent. Honey, I didn't even know what that meant, but I knew it wasn't good," Mom said. "I figured you'd say more if and when you were ready. Later on, Kathy was so upset. She told me that Marisa was completely distraught over whatever happened."

"Yeah, we had a misunderstanding back then. Marisa cleared it up and invited me over."

"Well, that's good," Mom said. "It's never a bad thing to reconnect with old friends."

I didn't want to ruin Mom's nice sentiment by admitting Marisa and Owen had never been my friends. But then, that cut both ways. Maybe now was the time to be the friend to them that I'd always wished they'd been to me.

AFTER BREAKFAST I drove to Wilcox. I had some time to kill before my meeting with Johney, so I decided to check out the homes he'd designed near the newly painted covered bridge.

The houses were impressive from the outside, and when I saw one with an Open House sign in front, I decided to take a peek inside.

The house was stunning. You could tell it was meant to mimic homes from the nineteen twenties and thirties. When I walked in, a woman I assumed was a Realtor greeted me and asked if I was looking to purchase a home.

I shook my head. "No, just curious is all. I'm about to meet the architect who designed all this, and I wanted to get the lay of the land before I hire him."

The woman looked amused, but she smiled. "I'm assuming you're meeting Johney McMann?" she asked, and I nodded. "I'm Linda, his wife, and I'm also the mother of the man who built this house. Here, let me show you some of the design elements."

We toured the house as Linda explained a lot about the visible design nuances as well as things built into the walls and floors that made the home more comfortable and livable.

"Was it Johney's idea to make these homes look like they were from another time?" I asked.

"Oh no, that was all Rhys. He wanted them to have the same feel as his house, which sits right across the street." She pointed at a sweet two-story cottage directly across from us.

The balance of vintage and modern was exactly what I had in mind for the old filling station. When Johney came in and his wife introduced us, I knew instinctively his would be the right company to hire—a family-run business that obviously took pride in their work.

"I saw you come in and thought I'd let Linda give you her speech about the homes before I rescued you," Johney said, clearly teasing her.

She gave him a regal cock of the eyebrow and then said to me, "It was a pleasure, and if you're ever in search of a home, you can find me here."

Johney chuckled. "I work from home, and we can walk to my house from here. Jason sent over your NDA, and I've signed it. Keeping things quiet is smart until you've figured out all the particulars."

I felt relieved Jason had come through with that. Perhaps he really was a man of his word now. In any case, a signed NDA meant I could speak freely with Johney. "Agreed. If too many opinions get expressed, my grandmother will bow out quicker than you can spit."

Johney shook his head and laughed. "Believe me, I've seen that show before. Anyway, let's head to my office and you can show me the blueprints you brought."

As soon as we were in Johney's office, he handed me the signed NDA, and I rolled out the blueprints. "This is a typical Carter Store. My dad wanted to ensure you understood this is confidential, as it's our original design. The closer you can get to recreating this while still honoring the historical elements, the more likely this project will work out."

Johney took his time looking over the blueprints and jotted down a few notes, which I appreciated. This project would take a lot of thought, consideration, and ingenuity on the architect's part, and he was already demonstrating those qualities.

"I don't see why blending historical elements into your basic designs wouldn't work. That said, I doubt the original structure can be salvaged," Johney said. "But the good news is it's still standing, so we can take measurements and gather all the information needed to create a new and improved structure that will look like it's always been there—just like we did with these vintage homes, including the one we're in now."

"Do you think the town aldermen will let us tear it down?" I asked.

Johney shrugged. "They're a very opinionated bunch, but if the building is already dilapidated to the point that I assume it is, they won't be able to salvage it anyway." He stared at the drawing in silence for a bit. "What's your overall vision? Do you want the old building incorporated into the actual store or use it as something that's separate?"

"To be honest, I have no idea. The mayor was pretty adamant about accenting the historical, hiding the modern. I do like that concept, but I don't know how to go about implementing it."

Johney nodded, still not looking up. "So, what if we could use that old structure, or at least a recreated version of it, as a drive-through? Would you be interested in selling coffee and some of your other convenience items through a drive-through window?"

I stared at him, dumbfounded by the idea. "Um, maybe?"

He looked up at me. "Oh, sorry, I'm just brainstorming. If you don't like it…."

"No, no, I like it a lot. All of our stores have food. I don't know any that allow you to buy food from a drive-through window, though. It doesn't really fit with our current business model, but that's for me to figure out. Please work up some blueprints that incorporate a drive-through option."

I shook Johney's hand and could barely keep myself from jumping up and down. It was such a clever design and more than I'd even hoped for. His ingenuity, even just spitballing ideas in the moment, boded success for the whole project, because we needed outside-the-box thinkers to make it work.

Now I just needed to figure out why Jason Murrin's stupidly handsome face popped into my mind when Linda showed me the romantic bedroom suite....

Jason

"MARISA, I HAVEN'T done anything. I'm telling you how I feel so you *keep* me from doing something I probably shouldn't."

As if I were her second child, I'd just endured a lecture from my best friend about having and maintaining boundaries, so I was frustrated and trying to keep my cool.

Marisa stared at me for a long time.

"I ain't your damned mother, Jason. It's not my job to keep you in line. You need to do that yourself, like all of us adults do. After the way you acted when you were a kid, that man feels used by you and has for more than a decade. The best you can do is be a friend, or at least friendly, and prove to Landon you're not that same teenage-jackass version of yourself. If anyone is going to make a move, it needs to be him. Capisce?"

"Yeah, I know. That's why I'm here. It's almost all I can do not to set up ways to see him. I mean, I like him. I've always liked him. I was just stupid back then, immature."

My heart felt like someone had poked it with a stick, so I put my head in my hands and tried to manage my frustration, mostly with myself. I was in this tiny town by choice, but still, all the gay men here were either married or not for me. Then Landon, someone I've always wanted more with, returns out of the blue, like a gift of a second chance. Royally fucking things up with him was the biggest regret of my life. Now I had to sit on the sidelines and watch one of the best chances I'd had at a great relationship—the kind Marisa and Owen had—slip through my fingers again.

I felt Marisa sit down beside me. "Listen, Jason. I think Landon is interested in you too. But like it or not, you can't erase your history with him, and it doesn't favor you. If he likes you as much as we all think he does, he'll make a move. If he doesn't, well, then you know, right?"

"Yeah," I said without looking at her. "You know I'm a patient man, not that same reckless kid. But this not knowing just… it sucks."

I leaned back with my eyes closed. Damn, I felt so tired. It'd been a week since Landon and I met up at Wilcox Café. I wanted to call him and almost had today, but I decided to call Marisa instead. She immediately told me to come over. Luckily—for her, not me—the baby was asleep, so she could lay into me about Landon. I hated it, but it was what I needed to hear.

Probably to give me a chance to get my thoughts aligned after her tongue-lashing, Marisa changed the subject. She was good about that sort of thing. "So, I've decided to start helping out at the town hall. Polly asked me to assist with applying for grants and stuff. I think this whole Landon thing has lit a fire under her."

"I'm sure Aunt Kathy loves that, huh?"

"Do not get me started," she said, rolling her eyes. "That woman has been driving me insane."

"She loves her grandbaby, but I think she also regrets all the time she spent working when you were born."

"Yeah, I've figured that out too. The fact she did, then Uncle Lee screwed her over with the business, just made it worse. But my situation is different than hers was, and I think she forgets that sometimes."

I looked down. I hated how my dad treated his family. First his only sibling, then his only child. I hated that he beat the shit out of me when I came out and now acted like I didn't exist, but none of us could change who he was. *What* he was.

"I wish your mom would just sell the store so Dad could go away for good. I'm sick of seeing him around."

Marisa put her hand on my shoulder. "Has he been giving you shit again?"

"No, not since Aunt Kathy threatened to expose what he'd done to me. He likes his standing in the community." I ran my fingers through my hair and then said under my breath, "More than his family, at least."

"I talked to your mom a few days ago," Marisa said. "She was asking about you."

A bitter laugh escaped me. "She knows where I live and where I work, Marisa. She has my phone number and email address. She doesn't have to go through you as a personal messenger."

Marisa didn't make excuses for my mother, or anyone, to be honest. She believed that people who made their beds deserved to lie in them. My teenage fuckup with Landon was a perfect example. "I'm sorry, Jason. You should've been treated better. I know I've said it before, but had our grandparents been alive when you came out, I'm sure it would've been a better experience for you. They were the only ones who seemed to be able to deal with your dad."

"Oh well. I've got a good life—better than most—and you and your mom are more my family than my parents ever were. But I wouldn't mind at all if they moved anywhere else."

"Give it time. Mom isn't as mean as your dad, but she's definitely as stubborn." We both laughed at the truth of that.

I slipped out of Marisa's house before she went to get Reena. If my goddaughter saw me, she'd demand to be firmly placed in my arms and would have to be pried out, which would only lead to a lot of screaming and tears. I loved her fiercely, but I'd intended my visit with Marisa to be a relatively quick one.

I intentionally drove by the old filling station, mostly to see if I might accidentally run into Landon. I was surprised to see a couple of guys I recognized walking around the property, so I immediately pulled over and got out.

"Hey, Jason," Johney said as I walked up to him. "Do you mind holding this since you're here?" He handed me the end of a measuring tape. "I'm just getting some rough measurements of the building, nothing formal yet."

"Did I see Xander with you?" I asked.

"Yeah, I'm over here," Xander yelled from somewhere behind the building.

"This place looks even worse up close," I said just as Xander leaned out the back window.

"You aren't wrong. Sorry, Johney, the termite damage is the worst I've ever seen. The whole building would've come down long ago had it not been for those two other buildings somewhat protecting it from the elements," he said.

"Yeah, that's what I figured, but can you write that up for me?" Johney asked. "If this project goes ahead, we may need to tell the aldermen in detail why the building isn't salvageable."

"No problem, I'll include it in my initial bid."

"Wait, initial bid?" I asked. "You've already been asked to bid out the design?"

Xander nodded. "Hold on a second. I'm afraid I'm going to fall through the floor. I'll come around back."

A few moments later, he was standing next to us as I held the tape measure for the last measurements of the base. "So yeah. I know you're aware of the buyer, but the build is pretty damned simple. Basically, it's a long box with this thing," Xander said, gesturing toward the filling station, "built onto the front."

"I thought you couldn't salvage it?" I asked, confused.

"The building as it barely stands, no. As we did with the other buildings in town that we've renovated or rebuilt, we'll preserve and reuse anything we can—like recycling the original bricks—and the rest will be new construction built to look old. It's not historic preservation in its truest form, but the powers that be in town should be happy with the end result."

"This is cool," I said after Johney left. Xander was jotting notes in a pocket-sized journal.

"It will be. Customers will be able to come in through the door on that side, keeping it hidden." He pointed toward the building. "But it'll be easy enough to see from the street, so people will still know it's an actual convenience store."

"Not that the big Carter Store logo on the building won't give them that clue."

Xander chuckled and resumed scribbling down notes until I interrupted him with a question that'd been gnawing at me. "What's the likelihood all this will work out? I mean, let's take off the rose-colored glasses and get down to brass tacks. Knowing all you do now, would you bet on this being a successful venture?"

Xander shrugged. "I don't know anything about the convenience-store business. But the few times I've met with Landon, he seems positive. I guess we won't know until he gets all his numbers put together."

I nodded and stared at the building for a while until Xander nudged me. "So, you and him are more than just attorney and client?"

I snorted and nudged him back. "I thought you were above small-town gossip."

Xander sighed. "I did too, but how can you live here and avoid it entirely? Eating at the café is like listening in on a town-sized party line straight out of the nineteen fifties."

I laughed because, for real, the local gossip mill could run rampant. "To answer your question about Landon? No, we've got nothing going on besides a professional relationship."

"But you'd like more?"

"Yeah, maybe, but we grew up together and I sorta fucked it all up. Water under the bridge and all that."

Thankfully Xander didn't press for details. Instead he went back to focusing on his notes, and I turned to go. "Jason, before you leave, Polly asked me to come up with some solutions for the two derelict buildings over there, and I wondered what your thoughts were?"

"Tear them down, probably. I doubt Gloria Carter will be keen on having dilapidated buildings threatening to fall on her fancy new digs. I've already been thinking about it, but I don't have any easy answers so far."

"I was hoping Landon might want to incorporate them into this project, but he assured me the land that comes with the filling station is more than enough."

"He's smart, 'cause if you have to tear down this old thing, the repercussions will likely be bad enough. If the townsfolk think he's responsible for tearing down two other buildings, I honestly don't know what the collective reaction would be."

Xander snorted. "We all know what the response would be, and it isn't good, even if the whole thing is a giant liability waiting to happen. Still, they do sit in a prime location between town and the new station. I'm sure someone will want the land, even if it isn't as big as the lot the station sits on."

"In how long? Ten years?" I asked, and Xander smiled. We were growing, and most of that was because of the work Xander and Rhys had done on our town. That being said, attracting new businesses to our small town was tough. Building something the town council would approve of would require some significant capital. I just hoped the land didn't sit vacant for that long.

I shook Xander's hand and headed back to my office. It had been a good day on both the business and personal fronts. I still felt a jumble of emotions as far as Landon was concerned, but at least he was talking to me, and Marisa had provided some helpful insight therein. Now I just needed to heed her advice about following Landon's lead.

Landon

XANDER'S BID came in exactly one week after I agreed to Johney's preliminary plans. Overall, the store would retain a lot of the filling station's old-timey charm, and I absolutely adored the design.

I especially loved the drive-through window on one side and the walk-up window on the other. I'd been working the past few weeks, letting Grandma take me around to all our stores to show me the ropes, and all the while gleaning as much information about the business as possible.

Despite my excitement, I was bummed that I hadn't seen more of Jason—even though I'd put those boundaries in place to keep him at a distance. I shouldn't want to see him, so why the hell did I always think about him?

How could I want the man who'd squashed me so entirely as a teenager? I sent a quick email to my therapist in Chicago to ask just that. Luckily, she could provide support via telehealth, and I talked to her for over an hour. She basically concluded that, as long as I wasn't trying to hurt myself by dating Jason, it was plausible that I simply liked him.

Plausible maybe, but probable? I struggled with that. I still had so much pain wrapped around that incident that it was difficult to separate the past from the present. I'd never met someone I liked as much as I liked Jason, and that seemed as true now as it had then.

Not that I really knew Jason as an adult. Since I'd been back, I typically met up once a week with Marisa and Owen, sometimes twice if Marisa wanted to take Reena out to meet for coffee at the café.

Developing those friendships felt good, and they rarely mentioned Jason. When they *did* talk about him, it was because I prompted it. "He's different now," Marisa told me just last Friday. "Something clicked while he was in law school, and he stopped fuck… um, I mean, screwing around."

Obviously, both Marisa and Owen still struggled to clean up their potty mouths. Reena hadn't uttered her first word yet, but I could only imagine what it might be. For a baby, she was strangely tolerant of me.

I knew most babies weren't too keen to be held by strangers, especially as they began moving toward independence, but she had no such qualms with me from the get-go.

Reena was just shy of nine months now, and she was going to be a very independent young lady. I loved spending time with them, and I felt like I belonged for the first time in a very long time. Becoming a fixture in Wilcox played a large part in that too.

I sat at my laptop and had just finished inputting numbers into a spreadsheet when my phone rang. "Hello," I answered without looking at who was calling.

"Landon, your grandma's being taken to the hospital in Eugene," Mom said. "I'm following behind the ambulance."

"What?" I bolted up out of my chair. "Mom, what happened?"

"The paramedics aren't sure—maybe another TIA, maybe something more serious. She was at one of her stores when she suddenly felt dizzy. That's all I know. Honey, I'm getting a call from your dad. I'll talk to you when you get to the hospital."

When she hung up, I took several slow, deep breaths to keep the panic attack at bay. "Not now. I need to hold my shit together," I said out loud to myself.

Thank God I was already dressed, so I grabbed my wallet and keys and dashed out the door. Fortunately I didn't get caught in any traffic or stuck behind a slow tractor, so I made good time reaching Eugene from Grandma's house. When I rushed into the emergency room, Lamont Jameson, a kid I knew from school, looked up from the front desk.

His expression showed compassion. "Hi, Landon. Your grandmother is being taken care of. Why don't you have a seat in the waiting room. Can I get you some coffee or something?"

I shook my head, thankful as I could be to be greeted by a friendly face who knew me. "Um, my mom, is she here?"

"She's with your grandmother."

"Thanks, Lamont," I said. "Can you let them know I'm here?"

"Of course I will," he said, and I went to take a seat.

I didn't recognize anyone in the packed waiting room, so I found a quiet corner and began looking at anything and everything on my phone to keep me distracted.

Well over an hour later, my dad rushed into the ER, and I got up to intercept him just as he asked about Grandma.

"She's still going through some tests," I heard the woman who'd taken over front desk duties tell him. "I think someone is already here for her in the waiting room."

"Hey, Dad," I said as I came up behind him. He instantly grabbed me into a bear hug. My dad didn't show emotion that often, so when he did, it was a bit overwhelming. "Hey," I said again. "Come over here and sit with me. We'll wait for Mom to come get us."

He just nodded, a mix of worry and fear still playing across his face. He looked like I felt.

Dad sat beside me and leaned in slightly while he absently thumbed through the magazines in front of us. We sat there for another half hour without saying anything, but we took silent comfort from one another. Finally Mom came out, and it was obvious she'd been crying.

Dad and I both stood, and he wrapped a comforting arm around my shoulders as Mom approached us. "She's okay, she's okay," Mom assured us as she wiped away tears. "They say she's going to be fine, but they think she threw a clot. They're making sure there's no damage to her lungs or heart."

Dad sagged in relief beside me, then hugged Mom. "Is that why she had the TIA?" I asked.

"Honey, I don't know much. They just took her up to the floor for observation. Said we could come up later, once she's settled."

We all three sat down, Dad now leaning against Mom. "Did you eat?" she finally asked him.

"You're always worried about food. Yeah, I ate before you called." He nudged her shoulder in the sweet and playful way they did sometimes, then sighed. "I'm worried about her," he admitted.

"We all are," I said. "She refuses to slow down, but…."

"But she's gonna have to," Dad said on a long exhale.

It took a long time before we were allowed to go to Grandma's room. She was sitting up in the hospital bed when we came in, and I could tell she was annoyed. Leave it to my grandmother to be aggravated at a time like this.

"You okay?" I asked.

"Oh yeah, I passed a clot. Don't think it's anything to worry about, though."

Dad harrumphed, clearly frustrated. "Mom, you don't think a clot is something to worry about? What about Aunt—"

"Your aunt was a stubborn old goat who wouldn't go to the doctor. That's not me," she said, and when all three of us laughed, she sighed. "Okay, maybe stubbornness is a bit hereditary." She sighed. "You all need to grab a chair. You're making me nervous."

As we sat down, she told us what the doctor had said. "I had a pulmonary embolism, which is just a fancy way to say I threw a clot. And before you all go getting any ideas, I looked it up on my phone, and they say sittin' around doing nothing can be the cause of it as much as anything else."

"Well, that's sort of correct, just not in your case," a woman said as she entered Grandma's room. "Hi, everyone. My name's Eloise, and I'm the nurse for Mrs. Carter."

We looked at Grandma, who was giving the middle-aged nurse a very cross look. To the nurse's credit, she didn't seem at all intimidated. "DVT is often the cause of the pulmonary embolism you've experienced," Eloise said to my grandmother while checking the machines. "You were lucky. Had that clot stuck, it could've caused some very serious damage. Now, is there anything I can do to make you more comfortable?" When Grandma just crossed her arms, the nurse smiled. "Okay, then. If you need me, press the Call button on your bed that I showed you. I'll be just down the hall, checking on other patients."

When she walked out, Grandma huffed. "I still say it's 'cause I was cooped up too long. Y'all were acting a fool after that little TIA hiccup I had months ago."

"Grandma—"

"Don't you start," she cut me off. "I ain't gonna sit around that retirement home and stare at the damned walls. I've worked too hard to get to where I'm at to be sent off to pasture before I'm ready." She squared me, then my parents, with a look that brooked no argument.

"Well, no need to worry about any of that now," Mom said. "Gloria, are you hungry? Want me to go get you something from the cafeteria?"

"No, I'm fine. My stomach is tied up in knots over all this."

Mom nodded and went over and kissed my grandma on the forehead. "Since you've decided to stick around a little longer, I'm going to take your son downstairs and make sure he eats something nutritious. You know how he eats prepackaged garbage when left to his own devices."

Grandma chuckled for the first time since we came in. "Go on. I'm fine."

When it was Dad's turn for a forehead kiss, Grandma clutched on to his arm and held him close just for a moment—long enough for an instant lump to form in my throat. My grandma could say up and down how this latest incident was just another blip on the radar, but it'd obviously scared her too.

When my parents left, Grandma looked at me, and her face set back into the frustrated glare she'd given the nurse. "Don't you start on me, Landon."

I put my hands up in surrender and laughed. "I wasn't going to. Mostly 'cause you already know what I'm thinking."

"You're thinking I'm too old to be tending to my own business affairs, but you listen here—"

"Grandma, I don't think that, and you know it," I said as I sat beside her along the edge of the bed. "I *do* think I want my grandmother to stick around a while longer, assuming she's not too dang stubborn to slow down just a bit for her own sake."

"Pssh," she said, but I knew from her demeanor that she wasn't feeling quite as defensive. I read that as my opportunity to really get through to her about the seriousness of the situation, and I took it.

"I've decided to stay and help out for a while. We both know you've still got plenty to teach me about Carter Stores, so you best start pacing yourself."

Was I trying to bribe my grandmother into taking better care of herself? Absolutely. But I also spoke the truth.

I must've said the right thing, because a smile spread across her face. "All I had to do was have a little attack and you decided to come back home for good. Hot dang, it was worth it."

I shook my head. "You are something else, Grandma. Anyway, I'm not committing to forever, but I'm happy to commit to now—provided you don't keep up with these health-scare tactics. I'm serious about that."

She leaned against my side. "I was scared," she admitted. I reached over, took her hand, and held it while she talked. "I'm not ready to go yet. My sister died of the very thing that got me today. I know how close I came, even if I pooh-poohed it to your parents. I didn't want to worry your father more than he is already. He's just like his daddy. Love runs deep for Carter men, even if a person can't get two words out of 'em about it."

"I'm glad Mom was with you in the ER," I said, knowing my mother was the most level-headed among us in a crisis. "The doctors should've checked you over more thoroughly when you were in here before."

"That's the thing, Landon, they did. There was no evidence of anything like this happening."

"So you grow 'em quick," I said, trying to make light of a hard conversation.

"They're going to put me on blood thinners, but son, I honestly don't know how much time I've got left. I guess none of us do, but I'd like my grandson to be around for the rest of it. Phone calls and emails just ain't the same. I want you here where I can see you, regardless of all the business stuff."

Tears slipped out of my eyes despite my efforts to hold them back. I leaned over and kissed her on the top of her head. "I want that too, and I'd already decided to stay before today. I missed being home, just didn't realize how much until after I came back."

Grandma squeezed my hand, then leaned back. "I think I'm going to rest a bit now," she said.

I kissed her head again and slipped out of the room. Then I headed to the cafeteria to find my parents and let them know I'd just committed to staying. I had no doubt Grandma would tell them if I didn't.

They were happy to hear it, and I was glad to be able to deliver some positive news to offset the difficulties of the day. "Why don't you go on home. Your grandmother is not one to tolerate a bunch of people hovering around," Mom said. "The doctor told us she'll likely be sent home tonight or tomorrow."

I nodded. "Okay, but you promise to call me if anything changes or you need anything."

Both my parents nodded, stood, and hugged me. Dad hugged me the hardest, and I returned the embrace just as tightly. Grandma was right—still waters ran deep among the Carter men.

I began my drive back to Grandma's house and decided I shouldn't be alone. Luckily, being somewhat of a local now, I knew Wilcox Café was seldom, if ever, empty, despite the fact that the food sucked. Since no one knew Grandma had experienced another spell—word traveled fast here but not *that* fast—I wouldn't be fielding a million questions either. So I could have some pie mostly in peace.

Just as I walked into the café, I spotted Jason sitting alone in the back where we sat the last and only time we'd been here together. His head was down as he looked at papers spread over the table, so he hadn't seen me.

I knew there was a good chance that I'd see him here, but I hesitated, even though that might have been the real reason I came. I'd spent the past few hours fighting back tears, and all I could think of was how I wanted someone to hold me. I wanted that someone to be Jason, and it made my stomach hurt and swirl with butterflies at the same time.

Before I could overanalyze it, I waved at the lady behind the counter to let her know I would seat myself and walked toward Jason.

"Hey, can I join you?" I asked. My palms felt clammy all of a sudden, and I was glad I'd tucked my hands in my pockets.

Jason glanced up and looked startled, then smiled. "I'd love that, actually. I was just about to have dessert."

"That's what I came for as well," I said and sat down. Just seeing Jason was already making me feel better, which took me by surprise. My heart hurt from seeing Grandma in the hospital, and our little conversation and the weight of the day had left me feeling emotionally wrung out. I needed a friend. Jason had been that once, or nearly so, and perhaps he could be again.

The server brought our dessert, and the two of us ate as we shot the bull about town happenings. I welcomed the pleasant distraction from my worries. Finally Jason asked what I knew he was desperate to know. "So, how's the project going?"

I smiled. "Just put the finishing touches on the proposal this afternoon. I'm going to go over it one final time and then present it to my grandmother and my dad later this week." Mentioning Grandma out loud threatened to crack the false wall I'd put up to hide my emotional state, and I swallowed thickly. Despite wanting to cry, I bit back a chuckle. Grandma would approve of me not sharing her private business.

"I know you've got to be excited. But," Jason said as he leaned in and lowered his voice, "the ones who are aware of your plans are pretty excited too, especially after seeing Johney's drawings."

I'd already lost my grip on who knew about our project. Johney had asked if he could share the preliminary plans with Ellen, the county commissioner, and Mayor Polly, since the two women would have a big part to play in securing the appropriate approvals. He wanted to ensure that the city council would be okay with his plans before we got too deep to make changes. It was me who asked Johney to share the designs with Jason. I figured since Jason was a third party in all this, it might be easier for Ellen and Polly to express their real concerns to him than me or Johney.

When our conversation hit a natural lull, I discreetly studied Jason's technique of assembling the perfect bite of dessert—equal parts pie and ice cream. When I watched him lick the spoon, I nearly swallowed my tongue. "I've decided to stay," I blurted and then shoved apple pie into my mouth.

"Oh?" Jason said, sounding genuinely surprised. "I figured you'd end up going back to Chicago. That's where your grandmother told me you've been living."

I shook my head. "No, I-I let my ex have the apartment. I've still got a small storage unit, but to be honest, I think I was ready to come home. To *be* home," I corrected. And I could've kicked myself in the butt for blurting that out. What the hell had gotten into me? I should probably just get up and leave before I did something totally stupid. I probably would've if the pie didn't taste so damned good.

Jason sat staring at me for a long time and then asked, "You're taking over for your grandma?"

I shook my head, then nodded, then sighed. "I don't know, Jason. I'm trying to figure it all out."

Emotions swirled through me, and I had difficulty holding back tears, so I pushed my plate away. "I-I'm going to go. I've just had a lot going on. Sorry."

"Hey, let me walk you out." He quickly paid for both of us and led me outside. I know I would've said no at any other time, but right then I was just not myself.

Once we reached the parking lot, Jason looked around, and when he didn't see anyone nearby, he whispered, "Is there something else going on?"

The tears slipped past me then, and I quickly wiped them away. "Grandma had another attack. She's at the hospital in Eugene. I just came from there."

"Shit, I'm so sorry. Hey, come with me. You don't need to be alone right now." When we got to his office, instead of going in, he led me upstairs into what I assumed was his home. The moment we stepped inside, he hesitated and said, "I can call Marisa or Owen, if you want me to."

I let out a watery laugh. "I'm not a naïve teenager any longer, Jason. You aren't going to take advantage of me or anything." Despite what I said, I knew I was stepping in deep and really hot water. I needed to leave. My brain said that over and over and over, yet my heart blocked all common sense.

He nodded, went to his refrigerator, and pulled out two beers. "Want one of these?" he asked.

"Yeah, I really do," I admitted, because I could use some alcohol to take the edge off.

Jason handed me a bottle, then sat on the opposite end of the sofa. "I'm sorry to break down on you," I said.

"You don't need to apologize to me. I'm just glad I was there. I like that I could be there for you."

I felt the olive branch Jason had just held out, and I had to blink back tears again. I wanted to take it, to latch on to it like a lifeline, but I also knew I wasn't ready. So instead of jumping into that emotional minefield, I deflected with the most pressing one. "I can't imagine what I'd do without my grandmother. I've been gone too long, Jason. So many years have passed that I can't get back, time I could've spent with her. Now the grandmother I've always considered a woman of steel is getting older and facing, well, shit, she's facing the final years of her life."

"I remember when my grandparents died," Jason said quietly. "It was almost more than I could take, like losing a part of my heart. That feeling never really goes away, not when you truly cared about someone. So spending more time with your grandma is why you've decided to stay?"

"No, not entirely. I haven't felt like I've had a home in a long time. Chicago always felt temporary, even though I lived there several years. And I never liked Northport. It's too… I don't know, something, and always has been. But Wilcox feels right to me."

"I can understand that. Northport is not very welcoming, even to straight families. To people like us? Forget about it."

"Is that why you moved here?" I asked, hoping the change in conversation would prevent me from breaking down and bawling like a baby.

He shrugged. "Partially. I never wanted to leave the area, if I'm honest. I've always liked it here and didn't particularly enjoy living in a big city. When Tim Bradford offered me a position at his law firm, I knew it was the right move."

I sighed and leaned back against his very comfortable sofa. "Sometimes things change for the better. Other times, life can get fucked up so fast."

Jason didn't answer, so I let myself stay reclined with my eyes closed for a bit. Finally I lifted my head and saw him looking at me with eyes full of compassion. I wanted him to reach over and hold me, and he looked ready to do just that. Instead of leaning into what my heart secretly yearned for, my brain decided on the opposite. "Um, well, I should probably go."

Jason nodded sadly. "If you need me for anything, I'm here for you, okay?"

Before I got up, my phone rang. "Hey, Mom, what's happening?"

She paused, then I heard her sigh. "Honey, just letting you know they're keeping your grandmother for the night. They think there might be another clot, and if so, they want to remove it surgically."

That was it, the straw that broke the camel's back. Tears blurred my vision while I struggled to maintain some semblance of control. Mom must've known, because she didn't speak for a while. Finally, when I was able to get myself together, she said, "I'm going to stay with her tonight. She's resting comfortably now and being monitored very closely. You should come back tomorrow morning and be here when the doctors give us an update."

I nodded, even though she couldn't see me, and wiped my eyes on my sleeve. "Dad? What's he doing?"

"He's going home to sleep, but he'll be back early tomorrow too. Honey, are you going to be okay tonight?"

"Thanks, Mom. I'll be okay. I'll see you tomorrow." Then we hung up.

Jason had moved to sit next to me, and I inadvertently leaned into him. "The doctors think there's more clots," I choked out. "They're going to do surgery tomorrow."

Jason handed me a tissue. "Is it dangerous?" he asked, and I shrugged.

"To be honest, I don't know, but after the scare earlier… now there's more clots. I just… I'm not ready to lose her, you know?"

Jason wrapped his arm around me and pulled me to his side. "Shh, you're not going to lose her. Your grandmother is a hard nut to crack. I'm her attorney, I should know."

I smiled. "Thanks, Jason. I-I'll go."

"I wish you'd stay a little longer. I don't think being alone when you're this upset is good. We can watch some TV, or…."

He didn't finish the statement before my inner desires took over and I took his mouth with mine. I needed the closeness, needed to feel something other than heartache and worry. Jason didn't move, but he didn't push me away either. I pulled back, a little embarrassed. "I'm sorry, I-I feel so vulnerable, I shouldn't have…."

Jason's side hug turned into a full embrace, and he pulled me close. "I wasn't joking earlier, Landon. I want to be here for you. Even if it means sitting like this all night. It'd be my privilege."

I nodded into his shoulder and let him hold me. I didn't care at the moment if I would regret it in the morning. Honestly, I needed him… or someone, and so I let my reservations go and melted into his side. We ended up lying on the sofa, stretched out beside each other with our legs intertwined and me still wrapped in his strong arms. I rested my head on his shoulder and soaked up all the comfort he offered.

At some point I fell asleep nestled against him, feeling more safe and secure than I had in a very long time.

Jason

I watched Landon sleep for at least an hour. Then I had to move my arm because it had fallen asleep. Landon's eyes immediately popped open and met mine. "You sleep okay?" I asked.

The slight smile he gave me sent an electric current through my heart. "Thanks, I needed that. More than I knew. I-I should probably get going, though. Tomorrow's going to be a long day."

"You know you can stay here, right? To sleep, I mean."

He laughed, which was a welcome sound. "Jason, if I stay here, chances are we'd end up revisiting a past I'm not sure needs to be revisited." He rolled off the sofa and then bent over me and kissed my lips chastely. "Thanks for being a friend. I really did need this."

I sat up as he slipped his shoes on and pocketed his phone, then disappeared out my front door.

When he was gone, I leaned back on my sofa and whispered, "I needed that too." Should I call Marisa and tell her Landon made the first move? No. No, I needed this for myself, especially given what he said about not revisiting the past.

Maybe this was just a fluke. He'd just thanked me for being a friend, so maybe that's how he saw me. It was something I should've been when we were in high school—something I would be now, if that's what he needed. That's what mattered. He mattered.

Now that I knew Landon would remain in Wilcox for at least the near future, I was all about making his time here a good experience. If that meant friendship and never more than the occasional hug or holding him when he needed comfort, I'd take it. Like I told him, it'd be my privilege. I'd never again take his trust in me for granted.

I didn't sleep much the rest of the night. Mostly I stared at the ceiling, thinking about a future with Landon in it. Would he let me be a real friend? Could I call him when I just needed a guy to talk to? One who didn't have a nine-month-old and a wife who occupied all his thoughts?

Poor Owen. His and Marisa's lives were forever altered being parents, but even in the trying times, I knew they loved it. Of course I still belonged—I always would—but their marriage had caused an inevitable shift in our friendship. It wasn't bad; we just weren't the solid trio we'd been growing up. Now they were part of a trio again, only instead of me, they had Reena. That was natural and to be expected, but it also created a kind of gap for me that I could really use to fill with a buddy who wasn't married.

Just a buddy, though? I mean, it'd be nice if that void was filled by a romantic relationship, but it didn't have to be.

Not really.

Landon

I'D WOKEN up in Jason's arms. It still surprised me when I thought about it. I'd slept wedged against him, as close as two bodies could be while fully clothed, and he hadn't made a move on me. I knew without a doubt, had I initiated it, he would've been happy to go there. The feel of his hard cock pressing against my thigh made that abundantly clear.

But he hadn't taken advantage of the situation, and I had to respect him for being true to his word. What he gave me—cuddling, comfort, and reassurance—was what I'd needed the most. Even my ex was bad at showing care and support when sex wasn't involved. His own sexual needs would've won out over consoling me.

But there were so many other issues swirling in my head about Jason. Did I want him? The easy answer was yes, more now than ever before. Could I trust him, though? Should I maintain the boundaries I'd set so we could become friends? Would I be satisfied with friendship?

I got to the hospital early, just before they wheeled Grandma into surgery. The surgeon wasn't willing to wait when the clot could move again. With my mother and father, I waited in my grandmother's room, each of us ignoring the other. Thinking about Jason almost caused me to forget where I was, which wasn't necessarily a bad thing.

My relationship musings came to an abrupt halt when my parents practically leaped out of their chairs.

"She's out of surgery," I heard the nurse tell them.

"How did it go?" Dad asked.

The woman grinned. "The doctor will be out in a minute to give you the details, but she's doing fine. She's in recovery, and as soon as she wakes up, we'll get her settled back in here."

We all sighed with relief as the nurse left the room. My parents are wonderful people and have always supported me, but their lives were as tied to my grandmother as mine. We'd been on pins and needles all morning, knowing how much we all had to lose if this didn't go well, so we had no desire for chitchat.

Grandma's doctor appeared a short time later and recapped the surgery, which had gone perfectly well. There were two clots, one smaller than the other. He described the large one as a widow-maker. In other words, we're damn lucky they found it or Grandma wouldn't be with us any longer.

The surgeon assured us that, with adequate medication and periodic checkups, it was unlikely she'd be caught off guard like this again. That, more than anything, was a relief.

"Might as well tell me what needs to be done at work, 'cause your grandma's going to be worried the moment she comes out of anesthesia," Mom said after the surgeon left the room.

"I've called all the regional managers, and they assure me nothing is so out of hand that they can't manage it," I said.

Mom shook her head. "That's not going to be enough to satisfy her. Can you visit each of the main stores tomorrow, just to be sure? I'll call all the out-of-state reps and check on them now that she's out of surgery. That way we can give her a full report when she wakes up."

"Now?" I asked, surprised.

"That's exactly what she'd tell you to do." Mom smiled. Only then did I realize how tired she looked. The stress of the past couple days had worn us all down. "But I'm your mother, and I say you seeing her and then getting some rest takes precedence today. So we can let her know that you're going out first thing tomorrow."

"She's a tyrant even when she's not coherent," I said with a smirk.

Dad laughed. "But that's the reason Carter Stores is so successful. Just don't tell her I said that."

"How about you, Dad?" I asked. "What's going on with the building crews?"

He cringed. "Well, the one in Idaho got delayed, mostly because I had to be here instead of up there keeping them in line."

"What about the Washington store? Is it still on schedule?"

"Yeah, but I'll have to go check it out after I get back from Idaho."

"Why don't you have an assistant, Dad?" I asked, and Mom turned toward him and gave him a *yeah, explain that* look. "Seriously, why are you and Grandma working yourselves into early graves when you can simply pass some of the buck to reliable assistants?"

Mom snorted and, to be honest, I already knew the answer—neither trusted anyone enough to hand over that much power in our family business. "Son, you're doing the right thing because your grandmother and father are cut from the same cloth," Mom said. "They will never change unless someone like you makes them see reason."

Dad huffed, but when I glanced his way, he shrugged in agreement.

"Okay, after I run errands tomorrow so I can report my findings, I'm going to begin figuring all this out," I said. "Then maybe we'll be able to put a legit plan in place."

Just then they wheeled Grandma in, and seeing her in her post-surgical state shut down the conversation. I vowed to myself right then and there to do everything possible to lift as many day-to-day pressures off her and the rest of my family as I could. If Grandma's health scares had taught me anything, it's that time was precious, and so were the people I cared about.

Jason

It'd been three weeks since Landon spent that evening cuddled in my arms. I hungered for that again, but the fact that I saw him almost every day was a great trade-off.

We met at the café most evenings for dinner, just the two of us. Although we weren't exactly dating, we were more than what I'd consider just friends. There were too many small touches and sweet brushes of our hands to think otherwise, let alone the way he'd lean into me when a couple like Polly and Tim or Xander and Rhys joined our table.

Sometimes I'd walk over to the old filling station site when I knew he'd be there and we'd talk about my business or his—just getting to know each other again. More often than not, someone else would join us, so most of the small-town gossip had been diverted so far. That didn't mean the more hawkeyed folks had missed our lingering looks or how close we walked side by side.

But I didn't care about gossip. I did like Landon, and if the whole town wanted to speculate about that, then more power to them for getting something right.

I'd also been looped into Landon's weekly dinners at Marisa and Owen's place. The nights when we'd pass Reena between us were my favorite. Landon always made me laugh when the baby would nuzzle in like she was looking for a breast, and he'd say, "I know, sweetheart, these boobies are useless. Let's see if we can find your mama."

I'll admit, seeing him cuddled up with my goddaughter melted my heart.

It was just as we were leaving Marisa and Owen's one evening that Landon got his chance to return the favor from three weeks earlier. Aunt Kathy called me in a tizzy, saying my dad was over at her place, demanding she take my shit off his hands.

I rushed to leave when Marisa stopped me. "Jason, you don't go over there alone. Take Owen or Landon with you. In fact, take Landon. Your father is less likely to become aggressive if it's not one of us with you."

She was right. If my dad was over at Aunt Kathy's, he was spoiling for a fight. That'd been his way since I moved out at seventeen. It was rare for him to show up at all these days, but it was better to be safe than sorry.

"Do you mind?" I asked Landon.

"No, I don't mind at all. Lead the way."

I drove because I didn't want Dad to see Landon's car or license plate. Knowing my father, he'd start giving Landon grief for having helped me. "Hey, you okay?" Landon asked when we got into the truck.

"Yeah, I will be. He does this from time to time, and I don't like to leave him alone with my aunt."

"Has he ever hit her?" he asked.

"No, I don't think so. He reserved all that for me." I let out a pent-up breath and sighed. "I've never told anyone besides Marisa and Owen about him, but he was always abusive. When I came out, he went insane. Had it not been for Aunt Kathy, I'd have been taken into foster care… not that he'd have minded."

Landon reached over and took my hand. "Well, I'm here if you need me. I can also do a little karate, if he tries to attack you."

I burst out laughing. "You took karate?"

"Well, yeah. Self-defense is important, especially in a city as big as Chicago."

I squeezed his hand. "You never cease to amaze me, Landon Carter."

My dad was sitting in his big-ass pickup in my aunt's driveway. Fortunately, she was nowhere to be seen.

I parked along the street, waited for Landon to get out, and walked toward Aunt Kathy's house. I knew better than to approach my dad's pickup when he was having a hot spell.

Dad saw me and got out, calling my name. "I'm checking on Aunt Kathy first. Then I'll deal with you," I said loud enough for any close neighbors to hear.

My aunt poked her head out the door then and said, "I'm fine, Jason, and I've called Sheriff Jones. She's on her way over."

"For heaven's sake," my dad said behind me, "why'd you call the law?"

Aunt Kathy simply closed the door behind her, and I heard the lock click.

Dad cornered me on the porch and was about to unleash his typical tirade when Landon stepped up. "Jason, let's wait in your vehicle for the sheriff to arrive."

He literally stepped in front of my father, making room for me to pass while blocking Dad from reaching for me—at least, not without putting hands on Landon in the process.

Of course, my dad was a jackass, and I was willing to bet he'd been drinking. As soon as I walked past, he grabbed for me. I honestly don't know what happened next. One moment Dad was trying to get hold of me, and the next, he was lying face-first on the ground.

"No one is going to use violence today, Mr. Murrin," Landon said in a firmer tone than I'd ever heard him use before. "I recommend you get into your truck and wait for the sheriff."

Landon stepped over my father, grabbed my hand, and led me to my truck. Then he all but pushed me inside and slid in beside me. Dad slowly got up, dusted himself off, and appeared to be about to walk toward my truck when the sheriff pulled up behind us.

I got out to meet her, and Dad yelled, "That boy in there attacked me. Threw me down on the ground."

Landon climbed out then and sighed. "Sheriff, I believe Mr. Murrin is drunk. I'd prefer to talk only when we are assured he won't attack us again."

She nodded. "Lee, you been drinking?" she asked as she walked toward my father.

"No!" he bellowed.

"Okay, well, you won't mind a breathalyzer test, then, will you?"

Dad was about to protest when another patrol car pulled up. As soon as the deputy got out, the sheriff called, "Aaron, bring one of those breathalyzers here, would you?"

Unsurprisingly, Dad got belligerent with them and ended up in handcuffs in the back of the sheriff's vehicle. Only then did Aunt Kathy come outside, and she explained that my dad had come screaming at her to get all my "worthless shit" out of the back of his truck, so she'd called me and them.

"Did you attack Mr. Murrin, like he said?" Sheriff Jones asked Landon.

"In self-defense, yes. He went for Jason and ended up hitting me on the chin." Now that he mentioned it, I noticed the red mark on Landon's face. "I simply maneuvered him onto the ground, but not in a way that could hurt him."

"Sheriff, I've got a security system with cameras," Aunt Kathy said. "I'm sure the whole thing was recorded, and you're welcome to it."

Sheriff Jones nodded, and I could tell she was resisting a smile. She'd been a deputy back when my dad was using his fists on me. She was even the one who came to my aunt's place when children's services showed up. So the sheriff knew our situation better than most.

"I'll need a copy of that video," she said after she watched the footage via Aunt Kathy's phone.

"I'll see if I can't get one of those young techs to copy it and send it to you. Lord knows I don't know how to do it," Aunt Kathy replied.

The sheriff smiled and nodded. "Kathy, that's all I need. I'm going to take Lee in to dry out a bit. Then we need to have you and Jason speak to the county prosecutor about whether or not he needs a little more enticement to keep his hands to himself."

We both nodded. "Just have them call me," I said. "You should have my number."

She patted my shoulder and then turned to Landon. "Mr. Carter, you ought to consider offering self-defense classes. You displayed some pretty impressive skills."

Landon shook his head in a modest, self-deprecating way, and we watched as Sheriff Jones and her deputy drove off. "You okay?" he asked me as soon as they were out of sight.

"No. I haven't been okay with anything to do with my dad for a long, long time, but it sure made me happy to see him laid out like that. The sheriff was right. It was impressive."

Landon smiled. "One of the easiest moves in the book. It's best not to put your hands on people who know how to put you on the ground."

When Aunt Kathy came over, she was visibly shaken. "You boys come on in. We've made enough of a spectacle for the night."

We followed her inside and let her fuss over us, which was Aunt Kathy's way of handling stress. Once she'd served us both a large glass of iced tea, she found some cookies to put in front of us as well. "So, Lee said he and Mildred are moving to Florida once and for all, and the store could rot to the ground for all he cared," she said, still shaking. "He hasn't been that violent in years, not since you came to live here."

"I'm sorry, Aunt Kathy, but my parents moving away is a good thing."

"It is, and I want them gone and out of our lives for good." She looked over at Landon and sighed. "If your granny still wants me to sign off on the sale, I'm ready. My brother is a no-good low-life bully—always has been—and if selling that damned store gets him out of my life for good...." She looked at me and then reached over and took my hand. "Gets him out of *our* lives, then so be it."

Landon reached over and took her other hand. "There's no need for you to make a decision tonight. The offer stands, if and when you decide to take it. If you do want to sell, just let Jason know, okay? But right now, all that matters is that you and Jason are safe."

She nodded as tears slipped from her eyes. "You're a good boy, Landon Carter. All your people are good folks. I won't be changing my mind, though. We're selling."

Landon slid his chair closer and let her hug him while he rubbed her back. A little while later, Aunt Kathy said, "I prefer there be witnesses here in case your dad coaxes your mother into saying we did something to his truck." Then she called Mom and told her to come get Dad's damned truck out of her driveway.

"Did Jason get his things?" I heard Mom ask over the phone. Aunt Kathy then put the call on speakerphone.

"My things?" I asked.

Mom paused, and I heard her sigh. "Lee swore he wasn't going over there to cause trouble. Just to drop off your things, Jason. I told him to take them to Kathy's so he didn't show up at your place and cause a ruckus."

"Well, he caused it over here," Aunt Kathy said. "Has he called you yet? Sheriff Jones put him in jail."

I heard Mom whimper. "I'm sorry. I didn't know he'd still be—"

"Mom, honestly, I don't want to hear that any longer. No more apologies or excuses. And I don't care about any of the stuff. You can just toss it."

"No, Jason, those are things that belong to you—stuff from your grandparents, stuff you earned in school. I fought Lee over it, said I'd leave him for good if he threw it away. You should have it."

I couldn't resist the sigh. "Mom, what's so important about any of it?"

"It—it just is. For me, not that you owe me anything, but please, son, take it. There's not much there."

"Okay, Mom," I said. "But I don't want to hear Dad making up lies about us scratching his truck or anything if we unload it."

"He won't. I think he really is scared I'm about to leave him."

"As you should've years ago," Aunt Kathy said. "Okay, Mildred, I'll help the boys unload the stuff, but you need to get someone to come over and fetch his truck. I don't want my brother anywhere near this place again."

"I'll have D.L. drive me over later," she said.

D.L. was an old man who'd worked at the family store for as long as I could remember. The poor old guy was still having to clean up after my dad. It seemed to me someone as old as him should be retired by now.

We went out, removed the boxes from the bed of Dad's truck, and put it all in mine. I was sure none of it would make a hill of beans difference in my life at this point, but I'd rather take it than have to deal with my parents again. I was on the same page as my aunt—the sooner the two of them moved to Florida, the sooner we never had to deal with them ever again.

I hugged Aunt Kathy before we drove away and luckily before Mom and D.L. showed up. I had made my peace with my mother years ago. She stood by Dad when he was an abusive asshole. She was my mom, and I loved her, but that wasn't something I'd ever be able to forget. I'd forgiven her, at least enough that I wasn't eaten up by her betrayal, but I no longer thought of her as a mother. Aunt Kathy was that for me.

Even when we were young, my aunt was a better caregiver to me and Marisa. She was tough, strict, and wouldn't hesitate to lay down the discipline when needed. She'd always been my strongest ally and parental figure. I was lucky.

Landon and I rode in silence most of the drive, but he held my free hand the whole way. He was such a good, kind man. "I'll drop you off at Marisa's to pick up your vehicle," I said.

"You sure you're okay? I can stay for a while. Help you unload all this at your place."

I almost said no, but the truth was I wanted to have him there. "If you're sure you don't mind, let's get your car, and you can meet me at my building. I'm just going to stick this stuff in the basement. It's dry. In fact, when it was a store, they used to keep all the extra merchandise down there."

"I don't mind. I'll follow you, if that's okay. You can show me where to go to access the basement."

Despite the horrors of the evening, my heart kicked up a beat thinking about spending time with Landon at home again. "Friendship," I reminded myself out loud as he followed me from Marisa and Owen's place to the small parking area around the back of my building.

After tonight's events, I could really use a friend.

Landon

I HELPED JASON unload his pickup and stack the boxes in his building's basement, where pallets were already set along the floor in the unlikely event the dry basement might flood. Once everything was stored, he began looking through the boxes and chuckled a few times as he pulled out things from his past—a report card from his elementary school days, a set of photos documenting him as he grew up through the grades. When he came to a box containing his teddy bear, the emotions hit him. He sat down in an old chair off to the side of the boxes, across from where I'd hopped up on one of the counters. "Dad was always unpredictable. One minute, he'd be fine, the next, he'd be screaming and throwing stuff." Jason clung to the teddy bear as he talked.

"Mom left him once, back when I was still young. But some dumb-ass minister told her if she left, she'd go to hell, so she and I went back to a *living* hell." He stared out across the basement like he was seeing his memories on the opposite wall. "My grandparents were still around then, and they managed to keep him calmed down most of the time, sometimes by threatening to kick him out of the store. I even heard Grandpa tell him he would remove Dad's name from the will if he didn't shape up."

"Why did they leave your aunt in the lurch like they did, with the trust and all?"

"My guess," he said, looking over at me, "is they were afraid he'd become violent if they left her in charge. I'm sure that's exactly what would've happened. My dad was a ticking time bomb, and according to Aunt Kathy, he always had been. In their own way, I think they were trying to protect her from him."

"Do you think your aunt will really sign the paperwork to sell the property?" I asked. "Seems to me that might be the best solution, remove him from the area and your lives."

"Oh, trust me, we've discussed that before, but she held on for some odd reason. My guess is because that old store holds her childhood memories. I think that before my grandparents died, it was a happy place for all of them."

I let the silence lie between us since I could tell Jason was lost in thought.

"You know," I finally said, "the store could be all that again. Just because we'd be buying it doesn't mean it wouldn't still be a place for locals to gather. Some of the more rural stores are just the same, except cleaner and more modern. They still attract the same old men who sit around shooting the bull and telling old wives' tales."

"Dad pretty much drove all those people away. Hardly anyone ever comes to the store just to hang out anymore. Not that I've been there in years, but people tell me stuff, ya know. Like, somehow, they're tattling on my father or something. I… well, I do think they miss it."

"So let's give it back to them. A country store like that operates on its own time and with its own peculiarities. Even my obsessive grandmother never forces her will over the spirit of a place. Besides, your family's store is special to her. She says her dad used to take her there, and they'd buy peanuts and soda and sit in the picnic area watching cars go by."

Jason chuckled. "Lots of people used to do that. I don't understand the love of salty soda, but some do."

"Oh, it's a thing. Even I love it."

Jason just shook his head; then he stood up and invited me upstairs. "Let's go up to my apartment and have a beer."

I shook my head. "Better not. I don't think I can be as generous as you were the other day when I was feeling down."

A knowing smile stretched across Jason's face, and he took a step closer. "I'm okay with being taken advantage of, Mr. Carter," he said.

I laughed. "Even so, it wouldn't be good for either one of us." I jumped off the counter, closed the distance between us, and kissed him. Jason's hands settled on my hips, and I snaked my arms around his neck. Then I broke the kiss. "However, I've decided if you're interested in something more than a quick fuck, I'm interested in letting you court me."

"Do we need a chaperone?"

"Hell no. I'm done with three-ways. Too much work. Sorry, dude."

He laughed out loud. "Me too. And I'd like that, courting you. But this time, we do it right. No more me being an inconsiderate jerk and you not talking to me if I screw up."

"I'll try, but you know I'm not a very forgiving man."

Jason kissed me deeply, and the hands that'd been resting on my hips slid to my ass. "I'd say you're very forgiving if you're willing to give me another chance."

"Some would say that's not forgiving, just stupid," I said, a little breathless.

"Whatever. I'll take it."

It was my turn to laugh. "Okay, for real, date tomorrow, then. You can take me down to Roseburg to that fancy Italian place my parents keep going on and on about."

Jason kissed me again. Then he let me go and sighed. "I can do fancy if that's what you want."

"What I want is not having every person in this little town gossiping about when we're gonna get married."

"Smart man."

My heart wanted nothing more than to stay with Jason, to nestle into his warm embrace and make sweet love all night long, but my gut told me it wasn't the right time. I wanted this to work between us. I wanted something real and more than a quick roll in the hay. As I walked toward my car, I skipped a couple steps as a happy thrill went through me at the possibility.

I was acting like a lovesick teenager, but after all that'd happened in our past, it was nice to feel good about Jason again. It felt even better when I realized this was the most excited I'd been about going out with a guy in… well, ever.

THE DAY had finally come for me to present my business proposal to my family. I'd checked and double-checked the numbers, had one of the analysts I'd worked with in Chicago look it over, and I'd called Xander multiple times to make sure I didn't accidentally miss something that would cost more than expected.

I was ready… well, okay, not really. I doubted I'd ever be prepared to face Grandma and Dad with a proposal to change how they had done business basically my entire life.

Mom had invited us to the house in Northport to ensure I had room to spread out all my paperwork, architectural drawings, and projections.

I almost backed out when I came in and saw Grandma giving Dad the business about something regarding the Idaho build, but Mom saw me and smiled. "Y'all, stop your fussing and let Landon catch his breath. Honey, come on in here and get yourself a cup of coffee."

Surprisingly, Grandma and Dad stopped arguing and smiled my way as I dropped all my paperwork onto the dining table and went into the kitchen. I was so freaking nervous. I took a few sips of coffee, glad Mom still made it the same way despite being out of the business for as long as she had.

Carter Stores were known for their drip coffee. It was the best around and so good that it rivaled the top coffeehouse chains. Of course, that was part of my proposal.

I finally walked back into the dining room with my second cup of coffee. "I'm nervous because both of you are hard to please, so I'm gonna present this and ask that neither of you interrupt me or give me the third degree until I get through it all. Then you can smack it around or whatever you want to do."

When neither of them responded, I took a deep breath and dove in. An hour passed as I went through all the details. I should've known neither of them would sit still without asking questions, but luckily, they didn't share their opinions.

I purposely gave them my projections last. When I was done, I sat down, took a long swig of my now-cold coffee, and waited for them to shred my proposal.

Moments turned into minutes as both of them looked over the paperwork. Dad grabbed the architectural drawings and *humph*ed several times. Then he handed them over to Grandma, who did the same thing.

"How do you know these projections are correct?" Grandma asked. "I recognize the same things we're doing in our regular stores, but is the drive-through based on facts or is it speculative?"

"No, I based it on one of the stores in rural Illinois, not far from Springfield, which is comparable to Wilcox and its proximity to Portland. That's the revenue they make from their drive-through window."

"What about the park? There's one nearby. Have you considered picnic traffic on Sundays after church?" Grandma asked.

I shook my head. "Um, no. I wasn't aware we knew those numbers."

She scoffed. "Still got a thing or two to teach you," she said under her breath before she went back to perusing the papers.

They looked over the paperwork so long that the coffee caught up with me and I had to go pee. But I didn't want to leave them alone and risk missing their conversation. Finally, I had no choice. I stood up to go to the bathroom when Dad and Grandma looked up.

"Landon, this is good. I didn't expect it to work, but you've figured out things I didn't think about. For example, the drive-through and walk-up windows." Grandma looked at Dad. "We might have to think about this in our other stores, especially if it turns out to be as lucrative as this indicates."

I bounced up and down and smiled. "Okay, gotta pee, but hold that thought."

When I got back, I plopped down in a chair and listened to the two of them talk about the proposal. They were tearing it apart, looking for anything I might've missed. I listened for over half an hour before they both shook their heads.

"This is impressive. Okay, I'm in," Grandma said and looked at Dad expectantly.

"I agree. Ain't nothing to say no to. Let's do it."

I felt my eyes bug out. "Really? You… you're not just doing it 'cause I proposed it?"

Mom, who'd been quietly listening this whole time, laughed. "Son, that's a ridiculous question. They both love you like crazy, but we all know they'd never put the business at risk just because of that. I'm no longer in the business, and even I know you put together an excellent proposal."

I released my breath. "Okay. Okay, I'll let Jason know to draw up the purchase contract. Then we'll need to take this to the town aldermen, have them okay it. Then there's—"

"There's always something to do. Just take a moment to enjoy it." Dad smiled. "Your mom's correct—we're tough, and we already discussed how we were going to let you down gently. You gotta know you impressed us because we'd even consider it, let alone greenlight the project."

I had to take a moment to catch my breath. Not even when negotiating the Traguilla deal had I felt as good as I did about this. It meant more to me than I could say that my dad and grandma believed in me. And I knew Dad was telling the truth about letting me down easy. They were both pretty set against this project, and it spoke to how much they loved me to let me try.

"Now, not today, 'cause this is your time, but the next time we do this, it needs to be about you stepping into my place," Grandma said.

Both Dad and Mom froze, and I sighed. "Grandma…."

She put her hand up. "Son, it's time. We all know you're made for this job, and this proposal just proved that to be true. I need to back down some. I ain't ready to go, but both my doctors told me I would have to slow down or my body would stop on its own."

"Grandma, I…."

She smiled. "I know you love me, and you didn't want to take over, but I can tell you've changed your mind, partially by your work here and how excited you were as we went through it all. I'm not saying I'm quitting, and I'm gonna watch you like a hawk, but I need to slow down and you need to step up. Don't we all agree?" She looked at my mom and dad, who both nodded.

"Give me a few days to think about it. I'm not saying no, and you're right that something changed recently. I like the idea of continuing my work with Carter Stores. Just, you know, taking over operations is a lot to accept."

Grandma stood up, kissed my cheek, and headed for the front door. "Let's plan on doing this again week after next," she said and left the door open behind her. Mom grabbed her purse and followed Grandma out to drive her back home.

I leaned back in my chair like I used to do as a teenager after I'd eaten my fill of food. "Do you both think I'm ready to take over?"

"The job offer was our vote of confidence, but you need to answer that question for yourself," Dad said. "You were basically running Traguilla, weren't you?"

"Yeah, I guess so. Anyway, I'm going to take a few days off and let my head settle. Especially after all the time this proposal took to do. I'll let you tell Grandma I'm skipping town."

Dad laughed. "Better enjoy it now, 'cause once you step into her position, that won't be something she allows unless you're almost dead."

I nodded. I wasn't on the payroll yet, but the moment I was, the expectations would be fierce. And that was one of the main reasons I needed to think it through.

Jason

"Whatcha doing?" Landon asked when I answered his call.

"Just the same old paperwork I'm always doing," I said.

"Cool, can you play hooky?"

"Play what now?" I asked as I put my pen down so I could focus on him.

"Do you have time to run away for the weekend? I'm needing a break, and I've got good news too, but that comes after you agree to run away with me."

I laughed. Just last night it was *we're going to have dinner*, and now we were running off together? Not that I was going to complain. "Where are you wanting to go?"

"Gold Beach, Coos Bay, don't really care. Could stay around here too. Crater Lake? We could also go to Silver Falls. I haven't been there in a while. Up to you."

I looked at the pile of paperwork on my desk and sighed. Maybe I really should hire a legal assistant. I just kept getting further and further behind.

But I threw caution to the wind. "Count me in. But close is better, just in case I have to rush back home for a case or something."

Landon laughed. "Maybe you *have* changed. Your teenage self would've been all about playing hooky."

"Yeah, teenage Jason didn't have bills to pay," I said. "So, troublemaker, when and where do you wanna meet for this excursion?"

"I'm going back to Grandma's house to pack, so why don't we meet at your apartment? We can decide where we're going from there."

"So no plans, just hit the road?"

"Sure, why not?"

"Guess I'm not the only person who's changed since adolescence. Okay, see you in a few."

I stared at my wall for a moment and thought about how things were progressing in our relationship. I was ready to move to the next level the moment Landon was. I wanted him so much, and that need became stronger every day. So I got a bit of a thrill at the idea of spending the weekend with him.

Landon had said "the weekend," which meant we'd only be gone a few days. I quickly went through all my priorities, and once I felt confident I could get away without destroying my business, I flipped open my laptop and looked up Eagle Crest Resort in Redmond.

I'd discovered the area years ago when I was working too much and wanted to be close to home without being home. The resort was beautiful, but I could still get phone reception in case of a legal emergency—though that only ever applied to Adam's clients. I sighed as I pressed the Call button.

"Hey," Adam answered after the first ring.

"Hey yourself. I'm running away from home for a few days, but I'll have my phone on me if there's any emergencies."

"You're running away? What's really happening?"

"Dude, I have a life."

"Not that I know of, but good for you. I doubt there'll be anything I can't handle. When will you be back?"

"Not sure. Maybe Sunday evening, might even be Monday."

Adam laughed. "I'd like to see what or… wait, *who* is keeping you out past your bedtime. It's a who, right?" he asked.

"Not talking about that stuff, Adam. Oh, before I hang up, you've been giving me shit for years about getting an assistant. Well, here's your chance to help me fill that role. I need a legal assistant, someone who doesn't mind being in the middle of nowhere, and someone I can trust to handle some of this damned paperwork."

Adam woo-hooed, then laughed. "Okay, I have someone in mind."

"Cool, but Adam, not someone I'll have to spend copious amounts of time training."

"All right, and you did right by trusting me. I'll make a phone call, and if she agrees, I'll ask her to stop by your office next week. Now, who is this guy?"

"Bye, Adam," I said and hung up to his laughter. I loved Adam, I really did, but the man was gossip central.

I had nearly finished packing when the doorbell downstairs rang. I rushed to let Landon in, kissed him, and then returned upstairs to pack the rest of my toiletries. "Want some lemonade? I bought a few bottles of it in Salem when I was there for court earlier this week. In fact, why don't you pack them in the cooler that's above the refrigerator," I yelled from the bathroom.

I tossed the final stuff into my carry-on and leaned out the door to see why Landon hadn't answered. He was sitting on my sofa with his head laid back, staring at the ceiling. "You okay?" I asked.

"Yeah, just thinking."

I plopped down beside him and nuzzled in. "About?"

He turned his head and took my mouth with his. "About that," he said when he broke our heated kiss.

I didn't believe him, but Landon obviously wasn't ready to talk about whatever was on his mind. So if I couldn't lend an ear, I'd make him smile. Before I opened my eyes, I asked, "Um, so, no on the lemonade?"

"Damn, you're a card, Jason." He started tickling me, and before I knew it, he was lying on top of me on the sofa. We were both still panting from laughter when we locked eyes. My breath grew ragged as I waited for him to make a move.

"You okay with this?" he asked, rolling his hips.

I swallowed thickly as his hard cock ground into mine. "Yeah, really good, but if you're wanting to go somewhere, this isn't how to make that happen."

"What if *this* is what I want to happen?" He ground again and bit his lip.

"Happy to oblige," I said, smiling. Then I leaned up and took his mouth.

All my hopes and wishes were being fulfilled, though I knew it might be too soon. I should have pulled back, but I wanted Landon so much. I wanted my mouth on him. I *needed* to taste him, feel him, be a part of him.

I tugged up Landon's shirt with one hand and unbuckled his belt with the other while my tongue assaulted his abdomen. When I unbuttoned his pants and saw that he hadn't worn underwear, I almost came just from that.

With desire for him coursing through me, I dragged Landon's pants down to mid-thigh, and he responded with a needy whimper. That was all the confirmation I needed to explore his cock with my mouth. Landon moaned and began to slowly thrust against me while my tongue circled his head.

He whimpered again, this time in pleasure, as my tongue found his slit and played with it. We locked eyes just as I deep-throated him several times and then pulled back to gently suckle his head again.

"Jason. Oh my God! I'm going to come," Landon panted. "Oh my God, I'm coming!"

I fully engulfed his cock in my mouth right before his cum burst into it and hit the back of my throat with a force that spoke to how much he needed that release. I swallowed quickly to avoid choking on the sheer volume of it.

I licked up the last of his release and slowly kissed my way up his body to his mouth. His responsiveness was a turn-on. Seeing Landon relaxed and sated from the pleasure I brought him, I'd be damned if I didn't want to repeat it over and over.

Landon

I COULD TASTE myself when Jason ravaged my mouth after giving me the best blowjob of my life. Somehow, just that was enough to get me hard again.

I reluctantly broke our kiss and slid out from beneath him to strip out of my shirt and kick my pants the rest of the way off. Jason sat up and tugged his shirt off as well and was about to unbutton his pants when I put a hand out to stop him.

He gave me a quizzical look, and I could see the doubt and apprehension behind it, but when I winked at him, he relaxed back into the sofa. Maintaining eye contact, I sank to my knees and slowly removed his pants and underwear. I knew I would want to devour this gorgeous man's body with my eyes at some point, but first I wanted to watch him come apart from my touch.

When I finally broke eye contact and took him into my mouth, Jason moaned in the most delicious way. Now that I'd come, I had all the time in the world, and I took it to explore his beautiful and well-proportioned cock.

I knew I wanted to feel him inside me before the night was over. With renewed passion, I sucked on Jason's head, then moved down to his balls and pulled each into my mouth while my tongue explored the recesses below his sack. The thought of going further than oral led me to push Jason onto his back and lift his legs, which gave me better access to his ass as I climbed onto the sofa.

When my tongue lightly grazed his hole, he moaned with pleasure, enticing me to use my finger to play with it while I went back to sucking his cock. I moaned myself as erotic pleasure coursed through me from the intimate contact.

I wasn't a size queen by any means, but the size and smoothness of Jason's cock made exploring it that much more exciting. It'd been a long time since I'd seen him naked, and I didn't remember it being as amazing as now. Probably because I'd been so inexperienced when this last happened between us.

I quickly pushed those thoughts out of my mind. Tonight wasn't about the past; it was about him and me and what we had in the moment. And I wanted both of us to enjoy every second.

I continued to slide my mouth up and down his long, thick shaft, and lightly played with his head each time I found my way back to it. When I released him with a pop, I waited until he made eye contact, then said, "We're going to need lube."

It took a moment for Jason to understand, which made me all the more proud my actions had scrambled his brain.

"Um, yeah, in… in the bedroom."

I nodded and caught him off guard when I deep-throated him again in one gulp. I laughed around his cock when he cried out and rested a hand on the back of my head. Using my middle finger, I explored the soft insides of his hole until I found his prostate. Jason writhed with pleasure as I increased my movements. I sucked his cock and played with his hole until he pulled out of my mouth and came all over my face.

Then he leaned down and kissed me tenderly. To my surprise, he licked his cum off my face between kisses.

"Damn, that was hot," I said, thinking of how I had never been with a man who had a cum kink. I never considered I had one either, but if I'm totally honest, when I watched porn, I loved when men weren't afraid of licking up after their partner or themselves.

"You know," I said as we cuddled in each other's arms on the sofa, "I'm hard as a rock. I could come again, but I'd rather wait until we're in your bed."

Jason seemed to hold his breath, then nuzzled into my neck and licked under my ear, which just made me that much harder. "If I'd known that was an option, I'd have pulled you into the bedroom to start with."

I felt lighter than I had in ages. "There's no hurry. I seem to recall we planned to spend all weekend together."

MY STOMACH growled loudly, causing Jason, who was still curled into my side, to giggle. "You better put something in that monster before he gets hangry."

He leaned up on his elbow and looked at me. "You okay with what just happened?"

"Jason, I'm not a teenager any longer. I'm fine. In fact, if I weren't so damned hungry, I'd be pulling you into your bedroom for our next adventure."

"Well, let's feed the beast, then see what happens."

I leaned in and sucked on his delicious lips. I was ready to take what I wanted. The sex had been good, better than I remembered, which it should be since we weren't clumsy teenagers any longer. But my connection with Jason wasn't only about sex. My heart was involved now, just like it had been back then, and that scared me.

While it wasn't quite the same, I was afraid of forming a real relationship with Jason just like I was afraid of taking over the business from my grandmother. Both weighed on my mind.

I'd been truthful when I told Jason I wanted us to date, to go courting, yet here I was afraid of where that might lead… that I might give him my full heart and had to trust he wouldn't break it. I'd never done that with any man, and it terrified me. Maybe I needed to call my therapist again.

I quickly pushed those thoughts out of my head. I wanted to enjoy lots of great sex and copious amounts of cuddling before I let my overthinking brain take control again.

"Okay, let's eat," I said as I untangled myself from Jason and then pulled him toward the kitchen. "What have you got here?"

"Ham and cheese for a sandwich is probably your best bet. I usually nuke frozen foods or risk a meal at the café. When I'm really lucky, Marisa or Aunt Kathy will invite me over for dinner."

"Damn, you're such a typical bachelor. I'd say let's go to the café, but we're lucky we haven't gotten food poisoning yet as it is, and I wouldn't want to risk this time together."

Jason laughed. "Speaking of spending time together, I thought you wanted to run away?"

"Still do, but you know, we don't have to run just yet. I'm sure you've got a nice, comfy bed, after all."

"Have you ever been up to Eagle Crest Resort in Redmond?" he asked while he made me a sandwich.

"Oh, wow, not since I was little. Why?"

"'Cause I thought we could rent a suite. I used to go there when things were hairy at my last law firm. The beds are comfortable, and the rooms come with full kitchens, so we wouldn't have to go out to eat unless we wanted to."

"I'm game for anything, but I'm also happy to stay here as long as it's just us. I told my family I'm running away for a bit, so showing up at the café is a bad idea. Someone will tell Grandma I'm still around, and she won't hesitate to chase me down."

"Same, and if I stay up here, someone will come knocking. But I'm happy to do a staycation, especially if it involves time in there." He nodded toward the bedroom.

"Oh well, let's stay at my grandmother's old place. It's out of town, and you can park behind the house so no one will see your pickup. I'll pull my car into the garage."

"You got enough groceries?" he asked.

"Nope, I'm living the bachelor life too. Grandma moved into a nearby retirement home and has the house on the market, but there hasn't been one showing since I've been home."

"It's a unique property." He chuckled.

"I agree. So why don't we run to Northport and get some groceries?" I asked, getting into the idea of a sex-filled staycation with Jason. "I'll run by the butcher shop too, get some steaks to grill out."

"Actually, the Lopez family closed their butcher shop in Northport when they bought the old grocery store in Wilcox. They have great barbeque too. Let's get some to go from the store. Even if someone catches us there, we can say we're taking it with us on our trip."

Someone was bound to see us and report it to my grandmother and parents. "Before we go, let me just check in with my family."

I typed a group-chat message to my parents, then looked at Jason. "You're really okay with all this?" I asked, though I realized I was asking myself maybe more than him.

He stared at me for a moment and then nodded. "I like you. I mean, I *really* like you, and this time I'm not caught up in all my teenage abuse and stuff. I feel like this is a chance for you to know the real me, no games and no bullshit. How about you?" he asked.

I smiled as my heart warmed to his question. Then I leaned over and kissed him. "I'm happy… happier than I've been in a while. So…," I said, ready to push the conversation back from the emotional depths, "about that food, do you think you're up for grilling?"

Jason shrugged. "Let's grab what I've got here too—beer, lemonade, stuff for sandwiches, which, as you can see, is pretty good." He looked down at my now-empty plate.

"Hey, I haven't eaten all day, so I was hungry."

"Not saying anything, except you seemed to like it."

"Okay, but I don't want to do a lot of cooking. Mostly I want to watch TV, play some video games, maybe take a hike. I could even show you my dad's farm. It's pretty overgrown, but there's still some good trails and stuff."

"That all sounds great to me so long as you're there," he said.

By the time we got to my grandmother's house, we were both ready to relax. I stripped out of my clothes and threw on some shorts and a T-shirt. Jason followed suit, and we flopped down on the sofa Grandma had left when she moved.

We sat beside each other, blowing up aliens and messing with each other's controllers to make the other person lose until finally my avatar got the expected beating he had coming. "Wow, you still suck at this," Jason said with a smirk.

"Hey, man, I don't have time to practice. You see, I'm running a company. Even back in Chicago, I was too busy for gaming."

"I run a law firm single-handedly, and I still beat you."

I leaned back and laughed. "I just don't have the eye-hand coordination."

When I looked at Jason, he was frowning. "What?" I asked.

He sighed. "I was such an ass back then." I must've looked as puzzled as I felt at that, because he pressed on. "You said the very same thing that day I came over. I was so lost at the time, Landon, and for years afterward. But even then, I didn't want to hurt you. You've always been special to me. I just fucked up."

I leaned over, cradled his face in my hands, and kissed him gently. "I've begun to understand you, Jason, including how you were back then. Spending time with you, talking to Marisa and Owen, seeing how your parents treat you… I get it. If I didn't, today would've never happened. And I want more days like today."

He rested his forehead against mine. "I feel sad for that boy. The one I was back then. I felt unlovable. Fucking around felt good, so I did it instead of facing life. If it hadn't been for the wake-up call I got when I hurt you, I'm not sure if I'd have ever changed. It still took me a long time to come around, to figure myself out."

I leaned back and sighed. "I was just as confused as you were, Jason. I was just a baby gay who had no idea what it meant to *be* gay. I just knew I liked you a lot, and when I thought you had intentionally hurt me…."

"I know. I tried to make it right, but you weren't having any of it. You wouldn't even speak to me."

"My people aren't the most forgiving," I said with a half-smile.

Jason looked at me seriously then. "Why didn't you ever tell your family about us?" he asked.

"How do you know I didn't?"

"'Cause I'm still alive, and I also work for your grandmother."

I nodded. "I didn't want to out you or tell your business, so I didn't tell her why I was reticent. Just that you and I had a falling out when we were kids."

He looked me in the eye and smiled. "You know what she told me?"

I shook my head, ready for any number of things that could've come out of my grandmother's mouth.

"She said, 'When he comes back, you can make it up to him like the grown man you are.'"

So she'd known something was off after all. I'm not sure why I was that surprised. My grandmother was astute. Despite Jason's honesty, I didn't want to rehash the past. I just wanted to be easygoing and to enjoy Jason and our weekend.

I smiled. "That sounds like her. And you know what's really funny? She knew you and I had a falling out and yet she still planted me in front of you days after I got home."

"Fewer things are more conniving than the women who love us," Jason said.

"Got to love 'em."

"They don't care if you do or don't, as long as you do what they want you to."

I nodded. "No truer truth ever spoken. Now I'm done talking about the women in our lives. Let's go to my bedroom, and I can redeem my pride while making you moan."

Jason dropped his controller, jumped up, and pulled me up with him. "Yes, sir, lead the way."

Jason took his sweet time with me. We were both on PReP and had been tested since our last hookups and relationships, so we didn't use condoms.

"God, you feel so good," Jason purred as he thrust into me with long, languid strokes over and over again. Other than my uninhibited moans, I had to keep my mouth shut or I would've said something stupid about how I felt about him. My heart may have been ready to jump into the deep end with Jason, but my mind wasn't ready to go there. I just relished the freedom to feel and be with him. It was more than enough.

Jason

I FELT HAPPY and totally relaxed after spending three days of beautiful, toe-curling bliss with Landon. I guess I needed those days a lot more than I knew. When Monday morning rolled around, the phone began ringing before I got out of bed.

"Hey, Jason," Adam said the moment I answered. "I'm sorry, but it's Cody. He's in trouble again, and I need you to help me get him out so I can fire his ass once and for all."

"Ugh," I groaned. "Why didn't you already fire him so I can fire him as well?"

"'Cause he's young, gay, and stupid, and I thought maybe I could help him get a clue."

"Dude, you should've known better. He has to fall off the cliff a few times before anything will get through that blockhead of his."

I leaned over and kissed Landon, who was just starting to wake up. "I'll go make coffee," he whispered as he rolled out of bed.

As I watched his cute naked ass walk out of the bedroom, I was ready to be the one knocking sense into stupid Cody myself.

"Tell me what he's done," I said and let Adam fill me in on Cody's latest stupid act of drunken ignorance. I didn't have the patience for it, no matter how much money I made from a client.

"I think it would do him some good to sit in jail for several hours. Don't bail him out. I want to talk to him first." I usually wouldn't want that because, if a client went off admitting stuff while drunk or speaking too freely during questioning, it could be ugly. But in Cody's case, I knew that when he got arrested, he shut down like a clam in the ocean.

I drank some of the coffee Landon made and slipped into my clothes. I would shower in my apartment since I'd need to throw a suit on. Then I'd head to Portland, where Cody was currently being held. I was so firing that man as a client.

When I got to the jail, a police officer led me into a room where Cody and I could have a private conversation. He was sober, but the smile he usually had on his face wasn't there. Instead my client appeared somber and sad.

"What happened, Cody?" I asked.

He hesitated a moment, and then the tears started to fall, surprising me. "Cody?" I asked. "What's wrong?"

"You—you know I've got a brother and sister that live back East?"

I did remember something to that effect, not that I'd paid it much attention. "Yeah, why?"

"They told me they'd flown out here to see some old friends, and last night they invited me to meet them at this big shindig on their friend's farm. I knew they would be drinking, so I brought my bodyguard with me to ensure I didn't get in too much trouble again. I've been trying to stay sober, you know, since last time and… and you know, rehab and all. But…." He paused and wiped at the tears. "They said I was being a sissy faggot. Said I'd gotten my fancy pants so tight I'd lost circulation to my dick."

"Your siblings said that?" I asked, sorta shocked.

"Yeah, my brother said it, and my sister was laughing. They've always hated me. I don't even know why, just that I was the baby. They said I always got away with shit." He took a deep breath. "Well, the whole night was all a fucking setup. I went to take a piss, and some dude was hiding in the bushes taking pictures. I came out yelling, and both of them laughed, saying they would finally get some money for having to deal with me."

"So you hit your brother? That's where the assault charges came from?" He nodded. "Okay, well, I'm guessing you'll get to explain all that to a judge, but I'll see what I can pull up on your siblings, see if they have any priors. Cody, do you have a problem with me twisting their arms? If they went to these lengths to embarrass you, to get pictures to sell to the tabloids, I'm guessing they're hiding some pretty ugly secrets themselves."

He nodded, then hung his head. "They've both been hooked on meth. I thought they were done with it, but now I'm not so sure."

"Yeah, I suspected something like that." We sat in silence for a few minutes while I reassessed where I stood with my client. "So, I'm gonna be really clear with you, Cody. I came here today to bail you out and then resign as your attorney. I don't normally do this kind of work. I'm small-town, and I like a simple life. I also know what it's like to have shit for family, so I can understand how you were pushed to your breaking point. But this is your last shot. If I meet you at another jail, you'll be getting another attorney, understand?" He nodded. "Okay, they want to interview you. You can tell them about the pictures, and if they ask if you hit your brother, I'll handle it from there."

He wiped away his tears again. I shook my head as I went out to talk to the officer in charge. Why do so many families turn out like this? My own dad didn't do drugs but probably needed medication. Others, like Cody's siblings, were so strung out they'd take lewd pictures of their famous brother just for a couple of bucks, with no care in the world what impact it had on him.

I'd need to file an injunction to keep those damned pictures from seeing the light of day. It was going to be a busy week, and that didn't even include the pile of work I ignored to run off with Landon.

And there was the bright ray of sunshine I needed. The three days I spent with Landon were like our own private paradise. I couldn't say when I'd been happier. We had a hell of a lot in common—not just our roots but the games we liked to play, the things we liked to eat, even the same stupid TV shows we liked to watch. The more slapstick, the better. Not only that, but Landon made me feel whole.

I sighed as I listened to Cody tell his story and an officer asked him questions. For the most part, the officer was respectful. Only a couple of times did I have to redirect the questions, and only then because I didn't want Cody to get a felony charge even if he had knocked his brother's front tooth out. I learned that detail in the interview.

When it was all said and done, I released Cody into Adam's care. Adam had been waiting while I went in to see Cody, and hopefully my friend would give our client a piece of his mind as well.

On the drive back to Wilcox, I called Landon. "Hey, I'll be stuck with work stuff today and probably will be all week. But I'd like to have dinner with you. Can you meet me at the café in about half an hour?"

"Ugh no, let's do pizza. I can't stomach the food there again. If it's not pie, I'm out."

"Deal," I said.

"Oh hey, with you distracting me all weekend with sex and television, I forgot to tell you my news."

"Oh? What's up?"

"Well, Grandma and Dad agreed to my proposal. They're on board. The downtown project is a go."

I pulled my truck over and stopped. "Really? They went for it? I mean, I should've known they would. You're a genius."

Landon laughed. "I don't know about that, but we can go over the details at dinner. I'll leave you be this week, but next week we're going to need to dive into this and make sure to cross all the t's and dot all the i's."

I could've listened to Landon's voice the rest of the drive home. Our lives were about to get very busy with work matters. I was terrible with the whole work-life balance thing, but I'd never had the incentive to actually balance it until now. I wanted to spend as much time with Landon as possible, and I hoped he felt the same way.

"So, just so we're clear, you're leaving me alone this week only applies to my office hours, correct?" I asked, feeling playful. "You're not cutting me off from my Landon hours, right? Not sure I could go cold turkey."

Landon chuckled. "Not a fan of cold turkey, hmm? Well, I could probably ensure you have a slab of fresh, hot meat on the regular."

I burst out laughing. "My God, your dirty talk is the worst. I appreciate the valiant attempt at puns, though."

"Screw you," Landon said through giggles.

"For you, sunshine, anytime. I'll see you soon," I said and ended the call as I took the exit toward Wilcox.

Landon

I STILL HAD too much to think about regarding taking over Grandma's business, so I spent a few more days just hanging out, playing video games, reading a book I'd been meaning to read for over a year, and calling a couple of friends from Chicago to catch up—stuff I never just let myself do. I'm not sure why I could do it now, except three days of amazing sex with Jason seemed to relax and unwind me in a way nothing else ever had.

I went to Dad's farm and drove along the old roads, which left me feeling sorta sad that nothing was happening out here. I reminded myself to talk to Dad about it. It just seemed such a waste that it was so overgrown.

I took a different route back to Grandma's house, spotted a winery, and pulled in. Dang, how could this have been hiding back here? An old farmhouse had been transformed into a visitor's center with art adorning the walls from floor to ceiling—beautiful, museum-worthy art. I sure as heck didn't expect to see all that.

"Hello, welcome. Can I help you?" a young woman asked when she saw me perusing the artwork.

"Um, yeah, I'm sort of shocked to find you out here. My dad owns some land down the road, and last time I came through, I'm almost sure this wasn't here."

She laughed. "We've only been open a few years, but our wine has already won awards. Would you like to sample some?"

"Oh yeah," I said and followed her to a bar area.

"This is the wine we produced two years ago," she said and poured me a sample. I noticed the bottle featured the old farmhouse on the label.

It was rich and creamy, dry but not bitter. I shouldn't be surprised. Oregon had amazing wine, but most of it was grown farther north than here. "Wow, that's unexpected."

The woman smiled. "We're just starting our new vintages, but we carry wines from other Oregon vineyards. Would you be interested in sampling those?"

I shook my head. "No, I'm more than happy with the one you gave me already. It's delicious. I'll take two bottles. No, give me three. I'll take some over to my parents too."

"Yes, sir. I can have those ready for you at the front desk," she said.

"Thank you. I'm going to wander around. The art is amazing."

"The work currently on display is by several of our resident artists. The winery's owner is an art connoisseur of sorts. You're welcome to go upstairs and see some of their other works as well."

I looked over her shoulder and saw a stunning oil on canvas of my grandparents' old home down the road from here. "Wow, who is the artist who created this?" I asked, pointing at the painting.

"It belongs to a sweet couple who live about a mile away. They just bought that house and moved their family here from Portland. The artist painted it for his husband, and it's not for sale. I had to beg him to let me display it while they had some renovation work done on their home. It's beautiful, isn't it?"

"Another married gay couple?" I asked, and I could see the woman stiffen behind the counter. "Please don't take that the wrong way. It just seems every gay man that comes to this county ends up married. I'm afraid I'm going to be bitten by the hitched bug before long too."

That made her laugh, and as I sipped my wine, I enjoyed listening to her chat more about the artist, as well as several other gay couples she'd met in and around Wilcox.

BY THE following Monday, I was ready to get back to work. Jason was pulling all the contracts and legal paperwork together for the Wilcox project, as I was calling it now, so I just had to go herd cats for my grandmother.

Things were in utter chaos for several Carter Stores. I picked Grandma up at her retirement home, and we drove to put out one fire after another. Some issues were bigger than others, but all of them required our attention. I hadn't noticed how the lack of an official headquarters impacted the workflow until now. There were a lot of outdated processes and old ways of doing things that needed to change, especially if I were going to step in to replace Grandma. My dad and grandmother needed to see where the inefficiencies were costing us money and time, not to mention energy.

I lay awake Wednesday night pondering the problem. "We need a central office where we can consolidate all our resources and get the regional managers all in one area so I can keep the flow moving efficiently, especially if we're going to expand any further out of Oregon," I told myself.

I was beginning to form a plan, and I knew it wasn't going to be one Grandma or Dad would be happy about. But this was nonnegotiable for me.

I was confident I'd be able to figure it all out; I just needed to show it was good for business. I was just about to doze off when Jason called. "Hey," I said, and the stress of the day left me as soon as I heard his voice.

We chatted until I almost fell asleep, and even after we hung up, I dreamed about him. They were vivid dreams of his strong hands stroking up and down my body at a lazy pace, setting every nerve ending ablaze. I woke up with a raging hard-on and no one to share it with. Not for the first time, I lamented not waking up in Jason's arms. I had it bad for him. And for the first time in many years, I was okay with that.

Jason

"I miss Landon," I whined to Marissa. Owen was working late, so she and Reena had dinner with me.

"Jeez, how long have you two been bumping uglies? Less than a week, and you're already a blubbering mess?"

"Hush up. You got your man. I've tasted the good life, and now I want more."

Marisa just chuckled and switched Reena to the other breast. "Honey, listen, you're both grown men with busy lives. You're going to have to make time for each other, though. When are you getting together to go over the projects again? Take him out for dinner, or better yet, make him one of your famous bachelor meals, the one that gets you laid."

I pinned her with a glare. "I don't have a get-me-laid meal," I said, although we both knew I did.

"Regardless. I'm sure he'd appreciate the gesture. Show him you're suave, not just a pri—um, I mean, a jerk wanting to have sex. Romance him a little. I'm sure a man like Landon would love that."

"Yeah, it's a good idea. I've got court on Friday morning in Portland, but that shouldn't take long. Then I've got to interview someone Adam is bringing over as a potential assistant 'cause I've finally relented."

Marisa laughed. "Adam gets what he wants most of the time. But for real, you've needed help for a while, and your clientele are used to someone answering the phone when they call."

I sighed. "I know. Adam still acts as a go-between. That's not fair, especially since he brought me most of those clients. It's time. Anyway, gotta run. Oh, tell Owen he needs to stop by the office. I've got some paperwork he needs to sign for the county."

"No problem," she said through a yawn. I'd bet it would only be a few minutes after I left that she would be asleep.

I texted Landon from Marisa's front porch.

Me: *Friday night, after we're done with project business, let's have dinner. I'll cook.*

Landon: *Sure, sounds good. What do you want me to bring?*

Me: *Do you really have to ask? LOL*

Landon: *Nasty-minded man. I keep that with me all the time. I'll bring wine. I found a sweet little winery outside of town.*

Me: *Awesome place, isn't it?*

Landon: *Best ever! Gotta go. Later!*

I practically skipped to my truck. It was turning out to be a shit week and wasn't showing signs of stopping, but I was happy. By the end of it, I'd get to see Landon.

Landon

I ASKED XANDER to meet me at the dilapidated buildings next to the filling station to discuss my latest idea. I didn't ask Polly, Jason, or Johney, because where the filling station had been a long shot, getting my dad and grandmother to open a centralized office here—or anywhere—would be a freaking miracle.

Xander assured me he could get the keys without Polly getting too excited. I wasn't so sure. I didn't know Polly well, but I doubted many things got past her.

The buildings were a mess, which wasn't a shock. "Xander, these are both tear-downs, right?" I asked as we walked through the less water-logged of the two.

He nodded. "You can't rebuild this. It's gone. Worst two structures left in Wilcox. But the good news is, new construction is cheaper than rebuilding, and the exteriors are in pretty decent shape, so it's not like that would cost too much to salvage."

I sighed. "Okay, tell me your estimate off the top of your head."

"You could save money by combining the reconstruction with building the filling station, but it's still not cheap."

I staggered a bit at the number he hit me with. "Yeah, that won't fly. Oh well, it was a long shot."

"Wait, there may be other options. If we did a total teardown, the city could finance that. It's already budgeted, anyway. We'll salvage the bricks like we did for some of the old buildings we restored downtown, along with the other decent materials I pointed out. If we do that, you could probably shave a full hundred grand, maybe more, off the top of that estimate I gave you."

I nodded. "Okay, that's a lot to think about. I'll have to do some hard talking to convince my grandmother and dad, but I'm one hundred percent sure your last suggestion is the only one that'd work for us. But Xander, please don't let this get out, even to your mom or Rhys's parents. I'd hate for us to lose the filling station just because I had a harebrained idea about doing this too."

He nodded in understanding, and I thanked him before we shook hands and left the building.

I'd parked my car in front of Jason's, hoping I might run into him on my way to or from meeting Xander. Jason and I had an appointment that afternoon, but I really missed him. Even if I just got a quick kiss, that'd be enough to tide me over until later.

I could tell someone was in the office with him, and even as I walked toward his door, I chastised myself for bugging him. But that didn't stop me from doing it.

I walked in, making sure I clanged the bell so he'd hear me and I didn't disturb his meeting too much.

I heard talking as I came in and walked toward the lobby, thinking I'd simply wave at Jason and leave.

I stepped around the corner just in time to see someone launch into Jason's arms and lay a big kiss on his mouth. I stood stock-still, remembering the last time this happened. It was a repeat of the past. "Fuck, I never learn," I said.

Jason saw me and froze. "Shit, Landon, stop, it's not—"

"It's exactly what I think. Don't lie to me, Jason. And is that fucking Cody Evans? For real? Fuck." I turned to go.

"Dude," I heard Cody's voice behind me. "Dude, wait up. No, you don't understand."

I ran out of the door toward my car and was stopped by Cody. "Wait, man, I was just thanking him for what he did for me today. He—"

"Save it. I don't want to hear any more. I've already given that man two chances too many," I said and slammed my car door in Cody's face. I pulled out onto the street with tires squealing.

I banged my steering wheel as I drove toward my grandmother's house. Shit's my luck. Of course today, of all days, the Realtor would have a showing. "Now what?" I asked myself and immediately thought of Dad's land. I drove too fast down the backroads and reached my family's old farm in short order.

I wanted to cry. Probably needed to, but I was so pissed off I could scream. So scream I did. I leaned into it, then collapsed on the ground and let the tears come. Was I more upset at Jason for betraying me yet again or at myself for believing he'd changed? Did it even matter now?

What the fuck was I doing trying to make a happy life for myself here? Why did I think I could? I needed to return to Chicago, rent a little studio apartment, and live my life as a single gay man, just like I'd planned to do before I came down here and let my family fill my head with thoughts of running the family business and building innovative, history-inspired Carter Stores.

I leaned back against one of the trees that'd sprung up over the years. Fuck Jason. I loved that filling station project. I might suck at picking boyfriends, but I'd hired excellent staff when working for Traguilla. I wiped angrily at the tears. I was a great judge of character in business; I just sucked at picking men for myself.

No, I wasn't going to let Jason Murrin drive me out of my hometown again. "Fuck him and fuck him again, and never ever fuck him in real life again," I yelled into the void.

I returned to the car, found my phone, and dialed the mayor. When she answered, I forced myself to smile. "Hey, Polly, my grandma and I are supposed to meet with Jason this afternoon to sign some final paperwork about the filling station project. Can you be there too? I want to get your thoughts on how to present this to the aldermen."

I could tell she was surprised. I'd worked hard to keep her at arm's length while I figured out the project details, and I probably still should, but I'd be damned if I let Jason get in the way of this deal. My grandma was like most grandmothers… or mothers. She wanted me married off with kids. Now that I suspected she'd played matchmaker with Jason, I wasn't going to let myself be in a situation to be pressured by either one of them.

I would probably bow under pressure. I liked Jason too much. Infatuation, lust, desire for something that would never be? I didn't know why I liked him so much, but from now on, I'd keep people firmly planted between that player and me.

Jason

"MAN, I'M so sorry," Cody said again. "Seems I mess things up wherever I go lately."

"Listen, Cody, I appreciate you trying to fix it, but I'll worry about my own shit later," I said, though seeing the shock and disappointment on Landon's face had gutted me. "As I was saying before all that happened, your brother and sister agreed to delete the photos of you to avoid having a restraining order placed against them both. But you listen to me, Cody, until they get straightened out, you need to stay away, hear me?" He nodded. "You also need to stay sober. If you hang out with people doing drugs or drinking, you're going to do it too, and you're going to blow your career. There's nothing Adam or I can do to save it if you do."

He nodded again, and I could tell he was still feeling bad about Landon. And he should. Who fucking kisses their attorney as thanks? My most problematic client ever, apparently.

"Should I go find your boyfriend and try to explain? I don't want you to break up over me."

I laughed bitterly. "Cody, that's just my shitty luck with men. I'll find Landon and see if I can work all this out."

He saluted me like he was in the military or something and left. I crashed down in my office chair and resisted the urge to cry. Fuck my life. I finally fixed things with Landon, finally had a romantic partner I wanted to build a future with, and he walks in just as my idiot client lays a thank-you lip-smacker on me.

I didn't want to kiss Cody Evans. Lord only knows where that mouth had been anyway. I wanted to kiss Landon and only Landon. "Shit, shit, shit!" I said to the room.

"Well, I haven't had that kind of greeting in a long time," a woman said, and I looked up. She was standing in my office doorway with Adam. I recognized her from around town, but we hadn't met yet.

"Sorry, dealing with an interesting client. Come in."

Adam grimaced because we both knew which client I was talking about. I stood and shook the woman's hand. "I'm Jason Murrin, and you are?"

"Dawna McDonald. Adam tells me you're looking to hire a legal assistant?"

"Yes, I'm just beginning my search, and he said he had someone who might work."

"I believe that someone is me." She handed me her résumé, which I quickly looked over as they both sat down.

"Your experience is impressive. After working at these large firms in Salem, why are you wanting something here, in small-town Oregon?" I asked.

She laughed. "Well, I live here with my wife now. We moved when my wife got a job working on a local agritourism farm. Have you met Dalton and Pierce? They hired my wife, who is a vet tech, and they got a volunteer babysitter in me as a bonus. Anyway, sorry, I'm rambling. It's just I'm ready to be working somewhere again."

"Oh yes, I know them very well," I said, the lightbulb finally switching on. "I'm sorry we haven't met. Every time I've been over at Dalton and Pierce's, you've been gone. I did meet your wife, Laurel, though."

"I've been traveling back and forth to Salem the past few years. My former boss had separation anxiety." She chuckled.

I nodded. "Totally understandable, especially since this résumé speaks to your being a highly capable employee. So, I haven't had a legal assistant in a very long time. I'm afraid if you take on the position, you'll be helping me learn how best to utilize you as much as anything else. But," I said, pointing to the piles on my desk, "you can see I've got my hands full, and our buddy Adam here seems hell-bent on increasing that workload."

Adam just chuckled. I looked over Dawna's résumé again and smiled. "Can you start next week?" I asked.

"Monday works for me," she said. Then she shook my hand again and left with Adam. A few moments later, he walked back in.

"So, Cody."

"Don't even start, Adam. That man has done nothing but make my life miserable." Adam's eyebrow shot up like it did when he wanted to question you. "Don't give me that look. That idiot laid a big smackeroo on me just as Landon walked in."

"And?" he asked, and it was my turn to cock an eyebrow at him. "Oh, Landon is the one you've been shacking up with."

"Don't cheapen it like that. He means a lot more to me than some weekend fun. Landon is the one I want, and I've fucked things up with him before. Now stupid-ass Cody might've messed it up for good."

"Over a little kiss? Were you giving him tongue or something?"

I glared at Adam until he put his hands in the air. "Okay, no tonsil hockey with Cody, but I don't get it. Why would Landon be that upset, especially after you explained our client was just being overly Cody-like?"

I sat back in my chair and explained my teenage faux pas. Adam shook his head. "Yeah, that's shit timing then, huh? But you're all adults now, not some snot-nosed horny teenager."

"Landon has a legitimate reason to be upset. It's basically history repeating itself, at least in his eyes."

"But this time you weren't participating in the kiss or anything else. You were practically an innocent bystander to Cody's mouth."

"He ran out on me the same way he did back then, thinking the worst before I could get a word in. The only difference is this time, I deserve the benefit of all his doubts. So tell me, Adam, how do I convince him of that?"

Adam shrugged. "You let him choose. Either he's willing to trust you, or he's not. You can't get around that. You want to know the truth? If I found someone kissing Joey, I'd be devastated because I trust Joey with my heart. But I'd also give him plenty of chances to explain because I love him with all that heart."

"I get it. I'll have to think on how best to approach Landon without him shutting down. Anyway, I'm kicking you out. I've got to finish up these contracts before he and his grandmother get here to sign them."

"Good luck, my friend," Adam said and came over to pat me on the back.

I skipped lunch and ignored the hunger pangs to get the paperwork done. If his grandmother thought I wasn't on top of my job, she'd send me packing no matter what her grandson thought of me.

Landon

I DECIDED IT was best to ride with Grandma, so I drove my rental to her retirement home and swapped it for her Lexus. My grandmother spent most of her life in her car, as she'd said years ago when Dad needled her about the fancy rides she bought. So she wanted some luxury around her. Whatever I could do to keep her content and comfortable, the better.

She met me outside her door, purse in hand and looking as spry as a calf on a spring day. "Grandma," I said when I saw her, "what's got you all chipper?"

"Never you mind any of that." She slapped gently at my hands and pulled me down the hallway. Of course, she wasn't fast enough that I didn't catch sight of an elderly gentleman slipping out of her room.

"Grandma, you have a boyfriend?"

She stopped in her tracks, turned, and gave me her most menacing glare. "I don't butt in your private affairs, now do I?"

"Oh, I'm stopping you right there. You butt in my private affairs as often as you can."

I thought she would blow a gasket, but instead, she chuckled. "Well, I'm your grandmother. That's my job."

I kissed her cheek, and then nudged her with my elbow. "He's a dapper-looking man," I said.

A hint of a smile played on her lips. "You leave my man alone and tend to your own. Come on, we've got papers to sign."

I sighed and shook my head as we walked out. She had no idea how much I didn't want to deal with my own man at the moment. Not that Jason was ever mine.

I teased her all the way to Wilcox, which she mostly ignored, but I could tell she was enjoying it. "I want to know more about him," I prodded.

"Well, there's not much to say. He came for breakfast is all, and I tried to shoo him out before you got there, but he's rather… attached," she said as she pulled the visor down on the passenger side to check her makeup in the mirror.

I reached over and took her hand as soon as she stopped preening. "I'm happy for you, Grandma. I wish you could've found this sooner."

"Pishposh," she said, using one of the old-fashioned words she seldom used and only when she was putting on airs. "I was too busy for a man. Listen to me, Landon. I was so in love with your grandpa, I couldn't see up from down, but when he died, it left me alone and miserable. This business gave me what I needed to work through the grief and discover what it meant to be a modern woman, but I never stopped missing him."

She sighed, flipped the visor back up, and leaned back in her seat. "It's hard giving up the reins. Even now I'm struggling, but there's more to life than working. You've said that yourself. I think I sort of forgot that. So when Gerald came courting, I didn't say no. I'm still a woman, after all."

"So his name is Gerald."

She looked at me and shook her head. "That's all you took from that?"

I winked at her. "Grandma, anyone who knows you understands what you did and why. You're a powerful woman, one I've always admired. But I also know you need to give yourself some happiness too, and if this Gerald gentleman makes you happy, then by God, you should let him court you till the cows come home."

Grandma gently slapped at my shoulder and chuckled. "Anyway, talk to me about this paperwork. Anything I might need to be aware of?"

I told her I'd invited the mayor over just so we could begin buttering her up, which wasn't really the truth, but I figured it was good to have Polly working with us instead of against us. Thank goodness I hadn't told Grandma or my parents that Jason and I had been spending time together, because, Lord, that would've made this awkward as all get-out. Even more than it was going to be already.

We pulled up in front of Jason's office just as Polly walked over from the town hall. She opened my grandmother's door for her and helped her out. "Gloria Carter, you look stunning today."

"Don't you go attempting flattery, Polly. Pretty words don't work on me."

"Now, Gloria, I was just making an observation."

Grandma smiled at her and replied, "Well, you can keep those observations to yourself."

Polly laughed out loud. "I do adore you, Gloria Carter, and I can't tell you how excited I am that we'll be seeing more of you in town."

She didn't correct the mayor or tell her that I was likely to be overseeing this project and our other business prospects. One thing you could say about my grandmother, she seldom let her private matters leave her mouth.

When we walked in, Jason visibly stiffened. I ignored him, and once Grandma was settled, I sat next to her. "Jason, the mayor is joining us so we can discuss some of the particulars about getting approval for the project, and she can let you know what concerns the city council might have that we need to work through."

Jason stared at me but nodded. "Why don't we get started?" I said instead of giving him a chance to launch into his false apologies.

We signed all the documents, which weren't many, just the purchase agreements and paperwork regarding the estate that Jason would need as the probate officer.

Polly didn't have a lot of concerns, saying we'd addressed most of them when Johney designed the building to look historical while hiding most of the modern elements. Her face lit up when she saw the plans, saying it was ingenious to have the walk-up as well as the drive-through, since we were bound to attract as much foot traffic as vehicles.

I'd thought of that too, but being so close to the main park in town was just another of those lucky elements of the project. "Well, if there's nothing else…," I said and stood to go.

Jason hesitated, then said, "There is something else. Polly, I'm sorry, but this is going to be awkward. I need to speak about a private matter with Landon and his grandmother."

"Um, no, you don't," I said quickly and hovered in the doorway, trying to get Grandma to follow me. Neither she nor Polly moved an inch.

"Jason, this isn't appropriate. We are in a professional meeting."

"No, we've just concluded a professional meeting," he countered.

I stood awkwardly. "Why do you need to do this, Jason?"

"You misunderstood what you saw earlier today. Mrs. Carter, Polly, I did something awful when Landon and I were young. I seduced him, although I barely understood what that even meant at the time. Then he saw me with another guy. Even though I was a screwed-up kid, I knew I'd messed up. Landon refused to talk to me for years after that. Now

I had a second chance, and we were enjoying each other's company. I've always had feelings for Landon," Jason said, his eyes never leaving mine. "Now, because an overzealous client of mine laid a kiss on me that I didn't ask for or want, Landon thinks I'm still that young boy who did him wrong. Landon, I'm not. The only person I want is you."

I took a long breath and held it, my eyes closed. When I let it out, I was ready to do this.

"Jason, I'm sorry. I don't want this. I want to help my grandmother expand and grow her business. I want to ensure the store we're building in Wilcox is the best it can be. I want a lot of things, but this…," I said, waving my hand between us, "I just don't want to keep going through this. I'm done."

I did leave then, paying my grandmother no mind. She could sit there all damn day if she wanted. I could go to the café and wait. Hell, she could drive herself home or have Polly give her a ride. I'd walk back to her house if I needed to. Even if these Italian loafers were most certainly not designed for long-distance trekking.

I made it to the café, ordered a cinnamon roll as big as my head, and sat down on the opposite side of the restaurant from Jason's favorite table.

My mind was spinning between internal emotional outbursts—intensely heavy grief at losing something I was really enjoying and hoping would become more, and anger for letting myself be fooled once again. I was almost done eating when Rhys Healy walked in, saw me across the café, and headed my way.

"Hey, Polly called and said you might need a ride back home."

I scoffed. "I'm assuming my meddlesome grandmother left me in the dust, then?"

He chuckled. "Well, let's just say Polly and your grandmother are cut from the same cloth. May I sit?"

"Suit yourself. I'm having dessert. Want something?"

"No, thanks, I ate at home. Wanna talk about it?"

"That would be a hell no," I said in a whisper. I sure as heck didn't want to get kicked out of the best dessert restaurant I'd ever eaten at because I was cursing in public.

"In that case, when you're done, I'll talk, then take you home."

I didn't know Rhys that well. We'd hung out several times when Xander or his stepfather Johney and I were going over plans for the new build. He was certainly nice enough, but I was in no mood to play the nice guy. Mostly just to be a jackass, I also ordered blackberry cobbler, although I was almost sick from eating too much as it was. I was mad, and I just wanted some fucking comfort, even if it meant I might puke on the way home.

I fully intended to ignore Rhys, but my curiosity won out. "Why you? Why did Polly send you?" I asked, trying but failing not to sound like an ass.

"'Cause you and I have a lot in common."

I dreaded another lecture, even if he meant well. Instead of responding, I dug into my cobbler. But Rhys must've misread my cold shoulder as a sign I was listening.

"A few years ago, I fell in love with the big lug you've hired to build your store. I almost lost him, and we're talking just by the skin of my teeth, because I was too frustrated and overwhelmed to hear him out."

Curious now, I put my spoon down.

"I was all small-town. I had renovated my Aunt Helen's place and was prepared to settle down here in Wilcox and be a bachelor for the rest of my existence. Then Xander managed to work his way into my life and sent me totally over the edge in love with him."

Rhys stared into the cup of coffee he'd ordered, and I wondered how much of his story he was reliving. "We ended up moving to live in my dad's house in Portland, but I was building Cliff and Brandon's barn at the time and started making assumptions about Xander's long-term plans. I thought he was about to sell a property we were thinking about building out together. I thought he was making plans without me."

"What did you do?" I asked.

"I began making plans to dump him for good and never look back."

"But you're married to him and run one of the most successful companies in town."

Rhys laughed. "That didn't happen overnight. It took a lot of healing and some serious talking on his part for us to get through it. Ultimately we wanted to be together, and deciding to improve our communication was a major step. That's the best decision we ever made."

I felt my eyes narrow into slits. "So you're here to tell me to forgive and forget? Well, I'm—"

Rhys held his hand up to stop me. "No, that's sure as hell not what I'm doing here. Listen, Landon, you and I have different stories and likely want different things, but where we're the same is that, like you, I pushed the man I love out of my life. Nearly for good. One wrong move and I was done with him, at least that's what my brain told me to do. My heart knew better, though."

I looked away from Rhys then and stared down at my half-eaten cobbler, but he pressed on. "The truth is, I'm not sure how you feel about Jason. That's not my business, nor anyone's, not even Polly's or your grandmother's." He waited for me to make eye contact again, probably to make sure I was still listening. "But if you have real feelings for him, don't throw away an opportunity for true love. I know that sounds hokey, but I almost lost the best thing to ever happen to me. Sometimes we have to be reminded that the men we love are not perfect. They make mistakes, and the same goes for us."

We sat in silence a moment as I digested his words and the growing lump settling in my stomach.

"Now, are you going to eat the rest of that cobbler?" he asked.

I chuckled. "No, I've stuffed myself to the max."

"Then pass it over here. Peggy will skin you alive if she sees you wasting that much of her homemade food."

Rhys polished off the cobbler so quickly, I sat amazed. Of course he worked in construction and had the body to show for it. I guess he could afford to eat like that and not worry about weight gain. Maybe I should walk home just to burn it off… and to think.

Rhys took some cash out of his wallet and tossed it on the table. "Come on. I'll take you home," he said.

I followed him to his construction truck and climbed in. "So why did you decide to listen to Xander?" I asked. "Did he make some big gesture that let you know you could trust him again?"

Rhys shrugged. "No, not really. I just knew." He looked over at me as he started the truck. "What does your heart tell you? Can you trust Jason?"

I didn't respond. I didn't know if I *could* respond. Rhys started the truck and left me to my thoughts as he drove. *Could* I trust Jason? Did I already trust him? My mind said no. Bitter thoughts played on repeat in my mind. *Once a cheater, always a cheater. Players are players.*

Then I let my heart lead. I had to dig past the fresh layers of hurt, humiliation, and rejection that had settled upon the old scar tissue of those feelings. What did my heart tell me about Jason? Could I trust him?

The answer surprised me with how quickly it came. Yes, I could trust him. His teenage self, absolutely not, but Jason wasn't that teenager any longer. He was a grown man who kept his word. A small town like Wilcox wouldn't be very keen on him if he didn't. And he had built up a reputation as a respectable attorney, one who represented my grandmother no less, which also spoke volumes about his good character.

I sighed deeply and looked over at Rhys. "How long did it take before you stopped second-guessing him? Xander, I mean."

"Several months. We took it slow, which would be my only advice if you decide to give Jason another chance. You need time to get to know him as an adult, not the kid you remember. I'm not the same person I was back then; none of us are. And okay, one more piece of advice. Don't just assume he's cheating on you. I always thought Xander was a better catch than me. I mean, the man does look like a freaking supermodel, but I had to force myself not to think of him as a player. If I had, well, it wouldn't have worked." He smiled over at me.

I sighed and let out a long, beleaguered breath and said, "When I'm not so overwhelmed with all this, you and Xander need to invite me over and give me all the details of your relationship. I sorta feel like I'm invested in the story now."

Rhys laughed. "Oh, I'm sure if you want the gossip, anyone in the town could fill you in. Our relationship was a public affair, still is some days."

"Oh, sorry," I said, feeling genuine sympathy.

Rhys just laughed again. "It's part of living in paradise, Landon. That and our mothers are among the biggest gossips around, though they'd never admit to it." He parked at my grandma's retirement home so I could get my car. "You can reach out anytime to chat, okay? You've got my number."

I would probably never take him up on the offer, but I was pleased he made it anyway. "Thanks, Rhys, for the relationship advice and the ride back here."

"Anytime," he said, and I closed the door and walked toward my car. I wasn't ready to make a decision about Jason, but Rhys had helped me get beyond my own anger and, yeah, maybe some stubbornness.

I drove back to Grandma's house, downed two delicious shots of Jack Daniel's Tennessee Honey, brushed my teeth, and crawled into bed. The Jack gave me a comforting glow as I pondered the mixed-up mess of my life. For God's sake, why in the hell did anyone think romance was worth all this?

I didn't tamp down my feelings, even though I already felt wrung out from the past several days. Instead, in a move totally unlike me, I let myself war with all my conflicting emotions. By the time I drifted off to sleep, my heart yearned for Jason.

Could I simply forget and forgive? Forget? No. I was too much of a stubborn overthinker for that, always had been. But thanks to Rhys, I had gained a new perspective. As for forgive? Yes, otherwise it'd eat me alive. But I didn't have to forgive Jason… he'd done nothing wrong. I knew that in my heart. No, I needed to forgive myself for my rush to judgment. I could only hope *he* could forgive *me* for that.

Jason

I CRASHED DOWN on my sofa and let misery engulf me. Both Gloria and Polly sat with me after Landon left my office. Of course, there was no sympathy for me. Both of them gave me a piece of their minds—especially Gloria.

In the end Polly said she'd do me a favor—what exactly, I didn't know—but said if she ever heard of me fooling around on that boy, she'd personally take me behind the shed.

Although her threat might've been idle, the meaning behind it wasn't. This town protected its own. Yeah, I was part of that, but so was Landon. In the short time he'd been here, the people of Wilcox had quickly accepted him as part of our community.

No surprise, really. Landon was good, in a bone-deep sense. He was also smart, savvy, and quick to lend a hand to anyone who might need it—not to mention as stubborn as the day was long and just as protective. And I'd fallen in love with him. Honestly, that happened long ago. I was *still* in love with him.

Fucking stupid Cody Evans, I thought.

That wasn't really fair, though, even if Cody needed to learn some damn boundaries. But if it hadn't been him, it would've been someone else. Some other innocent gesture or look or offhand comment that would've caused Landon to doubt me. The reality was our past hung like a dark cloud over our heads. Maybe I just needed to give up and let go. The thought of that ripped at my heart. I didn't want to, but for his sake, I would if he needed that.

A week passed. Gloria called a couple of times to check on things, but I didn't hear from Landon.

The meeting with the Carters and the aldermen was set for the following week. Had I not been the attorney, I would've bowed out, but not only was I tied to the Carters, I was also tied to the land. I needed to be at the meeting.

I released a heavy sigh and smiled as Dawna came into my office. "I've finished up the paperwork for all the clients on the to-do list," she said, referring to the tracking spreadsheet she'd created when she first arrived. "Since it's after five, I'm going to call it a day, unless you have something else for me to do."

"No, you've already helped in more ways than I can say. I have to admit, it's nice to have someone reliable and capable who can actually stay in the office and get stuff done."

Dawna chuckled. "Well, I've known a lot of attorneys, and unless they're part of a large law firm or new grads, being pulled from one task to the next is pretty much how they live their lives."

"Which is why I needed you."

"Now that I'm here, though, you can take more on. And possibly bring in another attorney."

I looked at her with a cocked eyebrow. "Dawna, we talked about you being Adam's spy."

She laughed. "I'm not, I promise. It's just I see a lot of folks come in with smaller issues that our office could easily handle if we had more capacity, and it'd prevent those potential clients from having to hire someone from Northport or Eugene."

"You should talk to Tim Bradford or Henry Erickson. They're both officially still on the books, although I haven't seen either one take a case in months. Besides them, I'm not anywhere near ready to have another attorney in my space. But ask me again once we get through our current cases. Organization is a good motivator for growth."

"On it, boss," she said, and I laughed. As in almost any profession where there was an assistant, the boss was seldom the boss.

By Monday morning, I was wiped out. I'd spent too much time drinking coffee, ignoring sleep, and burying myself in work to have a restful weekend. It'd all been an excuse to avoid dwelling on Landon. Every inch of my apartment held some heartache-inducing memory of him—the bedroom and sofa being the worst—and even the basement wasn't safe. Neither were my dreams.

I rubbed my eyes and kept them closed as I leaned back in my chair, hoping for a quick catnap. I heard the front doorbell chime and figured it was my assistant, seeing as she arrived at exactly the same time each morning. "Dawna, can you come chat when you've got a second?" I called out without opening my eyes.

When I heard a man clear his voice, my eyes popped open. "Landon?"

He moved with a little embarrassment. "Sorry, your assistant isn't here yet, and I didn't want to disturb you, but...."

I stood up and rounded my desk. "Hey." I stopped a couple of feet away from him, not wanting to make him bolt.

"Hey," he replied and rubbed at the back of his neck. He was clearly nervous. "So, I've been thinking about what you said."

I groaned and rubbed my hand down my face. "I'm sorry, Landon. I shouldn't have put you on the spot—"

"No, you did the right thing. I was never going to give you a chance to explain, and I needed more than just the voices inside my head to be involved. Did you know Polly sent Rhys to talk to me?" he asked.

"No, but I'm not surprised. Maybe surprised Rhys did it, but not surprised Polly asked him to."

"He talked a lot of sense."

Dawna came in behind us and waved at me to let me know she was up front. Then she disappeared back to her desk. Landon looked her way and sighed. "I should let you work. Let's talk later when you have time, okay?"

"I've always got time for you, Landon. Just let me go tell Dawna something, and then we'll be free to talk."

I filled Dawna in on the work I'd finished over the weekend and asked her to file it away. "Do you mind holding down the fort for a couple of hours?" I asked her. "I'll just be around town and will have my phone on me if you need anything."

"No problem, boss. If you and Mr. Carter head over to the café, I wouldn't oppose a slice of Peggy's homemade apple pie to go."

"Yes, ma'am. Marching orders received." I gave Dawna a little salute, and I was smiling when I returned to my office and found Landon staring out the window.

He smiled when he saw me, but still looked uncertain. "Have you eaten at our donut shop?" I asked.

Landon chuckled. "No, I've been avoiding it. I had a bit of a Dunkin' Donuts obsession in Chicago. I was trying to avoid the same pitfall here."

"Well, you're in for a treat, waistlines be damned. Come with me." I resisted the urge to place my hand at the small of his back as I led him toward Roland's. The donut shop was just a few doors down from my office, so I could smell their fresh-baked donuts almost every morning.

Landon groaned when he drew in a lungful of the mouthwatering scent as we stepped inside. "Polly needs to campaign for a fitness facility or gym in this town. I swear, between the café and now this place, I don't know how I haven't gained a hundred pounds since being home."

"That's a good idea. Maybe you can build one next to your filling station."

Landon laughed as I led him into donut heaven. They were busy this morning, which wasn't uncommon. They usually sold out of donuts long before lunch, and Monday mornings were one of their busiest times.

We waited in line for a while, then took our donuts and coffees across the street and into the park. "You know, I actually haven't walked around the park before. It's so pretty," Landon said. "The old trees, picnic tables, the little covered bridge that spans the river. It just screams small town."

We sat quietly then, each of us picking at our food. "I wasn't exactly honest with you," Landon finally said.

I turned toward him, willing him to continue. "I told you I don't want this, that I don't want you, and that's a lie. I do want it, and that's the problem. I want it, but I can't handle being cheated on."

I opened my mouth to respond, but Landon shook his head to stop me. "Listen, okay? Just let me finish. I need to get this out while I still have the nerve."

I nodded, and he sighed. "I broke up with my last boyfriend because he wanted an open relationship. That was a hard no for me. I know that sounds old-fashioned, and in many more ways than I like to admit, I *am* old-fashioned. I don't want to share with other men. I know there are plenty of gay men out there who wouldn't care, and that's cool, but for me, it's what it is." He looked me in the eye, and I didn't dare blink. "It's me and only me, if you want that kind of relationship. I'll never be willing to share you."

I itched to grab his hand, to touch him in any way I could, but I kept my hands to myself. Right now, my words were what mattered the most. "Landon, my wild days are over. I've probably fucked half the gay and bisexual men our age in the Pacific Northwest. Well, that's an over-exaggeration, and I'm not trying to sound like a braggart or conceited, but you deserve honesty. I'm not going to lie to you and pretend like I regret that, because frankly, I don't. For better or worse, it's my past, and that's where it's going to stay." I stared out over the park to gather my thoughts rather than risk a glance at Landon. I could only imagine what he was thinking. "You know about my childhood, you know my dad is a royal jackass, and you know I used sex to work my way through my issues. It might not be the best method, but it's what I did. I can't regret it because it's led me to who I am now. And Landon, I like who I am now."

He smiled, took my hand in his, and nodded. "I like who you are now too, but I need you to understand where I'm coming from. I never needed or wanted meaningless hookups. And I don't mean to imply yours were meaningless. I just have a harder time hitting and quitting, you know? I mean, I've slept with more than a few guys myself, and I don't regret that either, although some were definitely losers from hell." He chuckled, then took a deep breath and let it out slowly. "Mostly, I just want a simple life. I want to spend time with a man I enjoy. I want the same kind of love and friendship I see in my parents' lives and in couples like Marisa and Owen. Hell, like over half of this damn town. There're happy couples around every corner here."

The way he looked around, as if expecting another happy couple to randomly pop up, caused me to laugh. "Honestly, Jason, I'd like to be one of them, but only with someone who is fully committed to me. Not someone who'll fuck someone else when we're on the outs or when opportunity strikes, even if they are famous or some sexy new piece of tail that's swept into town. Don't get me wrong. I'm not asking you to propose or anything. I don't need a ring to be in a relationship, but I do need my partner's full commitment. Can you handle that?"

I reached over and cupped the back of Landon's neck, then hesitated to give him a chance to pull away. When he leaned into me, I took his mouth with mine. He smiled against my lips as I pulled back. "I was already fully committed to you, so yeah, I can handle that. For as long as we're dating—sorry, courting—I belong to you and no one else. And if and when I put a ring on it, well, that just makes it legally binding."

Landon sighed and leaned into my side, then stuffed a piece of donut into his mouth. The moment he swallowed, he moaned. "This is so damned good. Oh God, I'm going to be the size of a truck. Will you still love me when I'm fat?" he asked. I laughed and kissed him again.

"Let's talk about opening that gym," I said, and I dodged the piece of donut he threw at me.

Landon

The weeks flew by after my heart-to-heart with Jason. Grandma worked my butt off during the day, and when she wasn't showing me the ropes, Dad took me under his wing. Even Mom talked to me about management and ensuring our local and regional managers felt supported.

Evenings and weekends mainly belonged to my man. I barely had a minute to myself, and I liked it that way. I felt embraced, wanted, and needed—things I'd felt when working for Traguilla Industries, at least in the professional sense. It was a bit of an epiphany to realize that's why I loved working there so much. It was hard work, and I often came home exhausted, but I liked how I felt when I lived a full life.

I was delightfully surprised to learn that working for Carter Stores filled me with similar feelings. The building project in Wilcox took up a lot of my time too. I had a new respect for my father after working on this project.

When time permitted, I would stop by Jason's office. Finally, after his assistant Dawna had enough of me taking over the lobby area, Jason put a desk for me in one of his spare offices. I knew I was annoying, but I liked working alongside Jason. Even if we were both busy, I loved having him close so I could steal a kiss from time to time.

My favorite days were when Jason and I could steal a couple of morning hours to lie in bed making love or just sit in his apartment drinking coffee and in no rush to be anywhere. Grandma's house was under contract, and the couple buying it were artists from Southern California. The closing date was set for October, which meant I'd lose my living space soon.

Mom and Dad said I could move back home, but that was less than ideal. I wasn't quite sure I was ready to move in with Jason either. I'd talked to Rhys and Xander about renting one of their model homes this winter, but they ended up selling it before I could move in. Luckily they also owned an old home that sat back across the river from one of their construction projects. It was a dump but adequate for my needs.

I'd become as much of a bachelor as Jason. Not that we acted like bachelors any longer, with all the time we spent together, but I seldom ate at home. Most of the time, I would grab a salad from one of the service stations we were visiting or eat at Wilcox Café when I was in town.

A small house with a tiny kitchen would work fine. But the best part was Jason being just across town, a quick walk away. The filling station project was even closer, literally down the street. Life was treating me right.

Well, mostly. I was still struggling with the disorganization around Carter Stores. Now that Grandma was taking more time off, things were falling through the cracks, especially since I'd put my foot down about working ten- and twelve-hour days. I needed to figure out a solution, the sooner the better.

I vacillated about talking to Grandma and Dad about the centralized office. One minute I was convinced we needed it, and the next I'd hear my grandmother talking about overhead and I'd be persuaded to keep things as they were.

The tipping point for me came when one of our regional managers needed surgery and had to be out for two weeks. The managers in those stores weren't equipped to deal without her or Grandma. I ended up having to rent a hotel room in Eastern Oregon, where the stores were located, and spoon-feed the managers.

When our regional manager returned, I sat Grandma and Dad down at my parents' dining table and said I'd had enough. "You can't run a business, at least one the size of ours, without managers who can fend for themselves," I said in a huff. "Listen, I know I'm new, still green and all that, but what happens when two regional managers have to take off at the same time? We'd be screwed. There's no support in place to manage a crisis, and no, it can't be just me or you who rushes to fix every problem that comes up."

I leaned back in my chair and let the last of my frustration out in a whoosh. When I looked up, I saw resignation on their faces. That's exactly the reaction I'd hoped for. "Okay, I have a proposal," I began.

I didn't have all my papers in front of me as I had when I unveiled the Wilcox Filling Station plan. Instead I talked from the heart and explained how we needed training programs to teach regional managers how to prepare their store managers to handle problems—big and small—that cropped up.

"Our profit margins are incredible. Growth is not the problem. It's not letting ourselves grow that'll kill us."

Grandma sighed. "You can fix that?"

"Yes, I have a viable idea, but it's costly." I grabbed my laptop from my bag and opened the spreadsheet I'd created when I talked to Xander about the derelict buildings next to the filling station.

"These are some numbers I drew up a few months back. I was looking at the two buildings that border our downtown property. Utilizing them doesn't come cheap, but they come with price breaks that don't exist if we move into an existing building or to another town that isn't quite as popular as Wilcox."

I expected a lot more pushback regarding the costs, but both Grandma and Dad nodded. "I think we both already understood this," Dad said. "But we just weren't sure how to make it happen. Neither your grandma nor I have business degrees, you know."

I laughed. "I have two, and I can tell you they don't teach you *how* to centralize a growing business, just that you've got to," I said. "If you're both on board, I'll reach out to some of the folks that helped build Treguilla's centralized system. We're going to need some help."

Grandma studied the numbers for a while, then asked, "So you think we should build our offices in Wilcox? Give me your best pitch."

"It's a small town, and there's a lot of advantages, including some financial incentives. Polly and Jason could speak more about that. It also makes sense since we're rural based. We'd want to centralize in a similar place. Not to mention, the three highest-ranking employees in our family business already live here."

Grandma nodded, and for the first time since we sat down, she smiled. "It's a lot of money, but long overdue. Test out the options, talk to your architect and builder friends, and make sure those nosy folks in Wilcox won't cause us too much trouble. Then let's get a formal proposal from you on the table that we can approve."

I nodded, relieved they saw things the same way I did. "I can and will, but if you and Dad could do me a favor? Try to figure out how much money you want to dedicate to this. We could blow a budget quickly if we aren't careful."

Grandma and Dad shared a look. "I think that's something you should be involved in," Grandma said. "It's your project, after all."

When Grandma left and Dad went back to his office, I stayed seated at the dining table and let my head fall into my hands. "You okay?" Mom asked as she took a seat beside me.

"I'm fine, just overwhelmed. It's been a tough week."

She nodded. "How are you and Jason doing?"

I couldn't help the silly grin that about split my face when she mentioned him. "We're doing great," I admitted.

"Then why are you still here and not over there? Let your man help you navigate these tough times. They're always going to crop up, and spouses are the ones we lean on when they do. If you have a good one, that is, and I think you do."

I laughed. "Jason isn't my spouse, Mom, he's my boyfriend, but I get your point." I kissed the top of her head and yelled bye to Dad. Then I headed out and climbed into the Jeep I'd purchased a few weeks back. Mom was right about leaning on Jason. Especially when just hearing his name made me feel better.

Jason

I FOUND NOTHING funnier than watching my nearly unflappable legal assistant pretend to be upset when my boyfriend took over our office lobby for his work. It'd been her suggestion to give him his own office.

Landon and I were getting close, and I loved having him nearby. I was pondering that when my phone rang and pulled me out of my thoughts.

I smiled when I saw who was calling. "Hey, I was just thinking of you."

"Really? I was thinking about you too," Landon said. "Got a moment?"

I glanced at my desk and the piles of paperwork I hadn't gotten to yet. "Of course, I always have time for you."

"I need a shoulder, and yours is the one I want to lean on."

"Meet me in the apartment. I'll make us some coffee," I said. He agreed and said he'd be there soon.

I let Dawna know I was headed upstairs and asked her to lock up if I wasn't back by closing time. Landon came in about half an hour later and plopped down on my sofa. I brought a cup of coffee over, doctored up the way he liked, and joined him. "So, what's up?"

"Work and cornering my family into making some hard and expensive choices. It's just a lot, and Mom said I should be leaning on you for support. She was right, so here I am," he said and literally leaned into my side.

I laughed and wrapped an arm around him. "Your mom is so traditional, but I don't disagree. Not to pile on more, but that reminds me, I need your grandma to sign the paperwork for my family's store. Dad and Aunt Kathy finally came to terms."

"Didn't hurt that my grandmother said decide or she was out, I'm sure."

I chuckled and drew Landon into my arms. "My shoulder is yours anytime you need it, along with the rest of me," I said, and I meant it. I loved holding Landon close, had from the first time he let me. I couldn't imagine that would ever change.

"Wanna tell me about it?" I asked.

We cuddled while Landon explained his hopes, worries, and plans for the derelict buildings near the filling station site. I marveled at his ingenuity and drive to improve his family's business, let alone our adopted hometown as a whole.

"Have you talked to Xander?" I asked.

"Yeah, he gave me an idea of how to do it and still keep some historical elements in place. When they tore the buildings down, he convinced the city to preserve the bricks and some architectural elements that weren't as far gone. That's important, 'cause if we do this, we'll want to incorporate those into the new design."

"Well, I doubt the town will have a problem with your approach. I know more than a few people are upset that the buildings couldn't be saved, but that ship sailed a good twenty or thirty years ago."

Landon nodded. "They were in horrible shape. Worst I've ever seen that are still standing."

"Xander explained that to the aldermen. Doesn't mean it's not sad."

"True," he said and snuggled deeper into my side. We sat like that for a long time, and then Landon wiggled free, drank his cooling coffee, and got up. "Okay, time to work. I'm going to make a few phone calls and see if I can't figure out how to do this without financially bankrupting our business."

He leaned over and kissed me. "You mind if I work downstairs? I'd prefer to have a desk to spread out on."

"Don't even have to ask," I told him as I watched him leave.

I loved what we were creating together and that his mom thought of me as the person to console him. I didn't go back downstairs to work right away. Instead I called Marisa.

"Wow, you're alive," she answered without her usual greeting.

"Don't be a jerk. I've been busy."

"Busy getting nookie." She laughed. "What's up?"

"You're so crude, but you're also not wrong. What's up is I'm just wanting to find out how you are. Maybe set up a time to see my goddaughter and, you know, her parents."

"We're fine. Reena is great, although that child can get into anything these days. How can a toddler get through childproof locks? I'd blame you if I could figure out how."

"I'm sure you blame me anyway."

"True, so what's on the agenda tonight?" she asked.

"Well, Landon is downstairs working, so we'll probably spend the evening together. Work is kicking his butt and mine too, but how about Friday?"

"Sure. We don't have a life outside dirty diapers and the never-ending debate between apple sauce and mashed peas."

"Oh what a wild life you lead," I teased her.

"So, how's it going with Landon?" she asked. Knowing she'd pose that question was probably why I called her.

"I love it. I never thought domesticated life could feel so good."

"Ahh, you're in that disgusting mooning-over-each-other phase. Enjoy it while it lasts."

I snorted. "Well, since we won't be accidentally making a cousin for Reena, domestic bliss will last longer, I'm sure."

"Ugh, I so need to go back to work. I'm about to go domestically insane."

"What's keeping you from it?" I asked her.

"Mom not wanting to leave Reena with a sitter, Mom—"

"You're a grown woman, Marisa, and Reena will be happy if you're happy."

She sighed. "Let's talk about this later. Reena needs to wake up or she won't sleep tonight."

"Okay, but seriously, Marisa, if you're ready to go back to work, go."

"Yeah, we'll see," she replied. "Talk to you later."

I hung up and thought about what a life of domestic bliss might look like with Landon. We'd never talked about marriage or having kids and had barely broached the topic of living together—discussions that all felt sudden and overdue at the same time, but all ones I wanted to have at some point. That said a lot about how I felt about him.

Landon

I STARED AT my phone, trying to work up the nerve to make the call. I'd already talked to several colleagues from Traguilla Industries, except Orion, my ex. Unfortunately, he was the one I *needed* to talk to.

Orion had worked at Traguilla as assistant to the chief operating officer before he went to work for a large manufacturing company as their COO. If I was going to expand Carter Stores properly, I needed advice from someone with his experience.

I would send him an email, except that's how I'd ended things with him, and I knew I'd been a jerk to do that. He hadn't reached out to me again after that, and now here I was, about to call him. *God, this better be worth it*, I thought as I hit the Call button on my phone.

"Hello," he answered on the second ring.

"Um, hey, Orion, it's Landon."

"Oh, hi," he said, then paused. Hearing his surprise answered my question about if he'd erased my number. "Hey, good to hear from you."

"Yeah, thanks. I'm calling because I need some advice."

Again, there was a pregnant pause. "What kind of advice?"

I shook off the desire to just hang up, and plowed forward. "I'm taking over my family's business, and we're having growing pains. I need advice from someone who knows how to develop a good operations system."

"And you called me?"

God, this was a mistake. "Yeah, is that okay?"

"Sure, why not. Ask away."

I spent a few awkward moments explaining what we needed, and he finally said, "I charge a hundred seventy-five an hour for consulting. You can send me your company portfolio, and if I can help, I'll send you a contract."

"Um, great, thanks. I'll send an NDA over too, 'cause my grandmother won't work with anyone without one."

"That's not a problem," he said. "Send me your stuff. You've got my email."

Then he hung up. I knew that last statement was a *fuck you*, and I guess I deserved it.

I saw Jason hadn't returned downstairs, so I went to Dawna's office. "Hey, can I have you or Jason send an NDA to someone? I need to use him as a consultant and didn't want to send him our information without the NDA in place."

"Sure, I just need his email and I'll send it now. Same as you used for the folks here in town?"

I nodded and thanked her. Maybe it was best Dawna was handling this one anyway, considering Orion was my ex. I went back to the office and sent an introductory email to Dawna and Orion, explaining that Dawna was the legal assistant to my attorney and that she'd be handling the NDA and contracts.

Then I sat back in my chair and cursed the fact that the only person I knew and trusted to consult about Carter operations was someone I'd once dated.

THE PLANS for our new offices were simple. Johney had designed a structure that paid homage to the two old buildings but with a few clever, modern twists.

The lower level was Dad's domain. We built in several desks, storage for supplies, and a drafting area for his needs. The first floor also sported a kitchen that Johney convinced me we should have to test food products for our stores. He also placed our administrative assistant offices down on the first floor, for ease of dealing with the public and any walk-ins for regional meetings.

The top floor was where all the high-level administrative offices were located, including mine and Grandma's. Regional managers and other administrative staff would occupy the open area, which spanned the rest of the top floor and included restrooms, a meeting room, and a small kitchen. All in all, the space was very efficient and modern.

Johney assured me that, from the outside, it'd look like it was a hundred years old, roughly the same vintage as the buildings that'd been taken down. It was perfect, and with Grandma and Dad's final approval, we signed a contract with Xander. Jason drew up the paperwork, just like he'd done with the filling station, and as soon as that was done and the aldermen gave us the thumbs-up, construction would begin.

It seemed inconceivable that so much was happening in such a short amount of time. But as work began to get more hectic, I began to think it wasn't short enough.

Orion ended up giving invaluable advice, and I felt more and more like a heel about how I'd ended things between us. Not that I'd admit that to him. No, our current relationship—if one could call it that—was professionally courteous but strained.

Regardless, I began to put his advice into practice, and already our regional managers were making improvements and managing many more of the fires without calling in the cavalry—aka me or my grandmother. Even Dad had taken Orion's advice and finally hired an assistant for himself, which Dad now admitted should've happened years ago.

Grandma was less and less involved as time went on. She was intrigued by Orion and the other consultants we worked with. She often shared her opinions, especially when she pointed out differences between our business and the businesses our consultants came from. But she was no longer as obsessed with Carter Stores as she'd been when I arrived.

I knew it meant she would soon need to hand power over to me officially, but that was more so I could sign documents without having to track her down.

Regardless, I wasn't quite ready to take the reins. I wanted our projects in town wrapped up and the new organizational systems in place before I took it all on. Otherwise I could imagine the whole thing imploding, which none of us wanted.

Jason was invaluable as we went through the growing pains. He supported me and listened while I bitched and moaned, or just let me snuggle when I felt overwhelmed. With Christmas just around the corner, I was determined to do something special for him.

With all the rigmarole with our company, any forward momentum on acquiring the store from Jason's family had stalled. So I decided that would be my gift to him. Even though his dad mostly left Jason alone, I could tell Jason was upset with all the shit that'd been coming his aunt's way.

Besides, Grandma still wanted that store more than any other we'd talked about, so it felt good to make it a priority, especially with things so topsy-turvy on all our other fronts.

One week before Christmas, my grandmother and I met Jason's father at the title company in Northport and officially signed the document. He was cold when he saw me, and I understood. I had put the jerk on his face and would do so again in a heartbeat.

Luckily he didn't say anything, just signed the paperwork and pushed it over to his wife, who did the same. Then, when the title officer said it was all clear, he stood, thanked my grandmother, didn't look at me, and left.

"What was that about?" Grandma asked.

I chuckled. "Well, let's just say Mr. Murrin thought he could push the queers around and learned the hard way some of us don't budge so easily." Grandma gave me a questioning look, and I said, "Remember those karate classes Dad put me in when I was bullied in middle school? Those moves still come in handy sometimes."

She shook her head, thanked the title officer, who was trying not to laugh at my story, and stood to go. "Please have those sent to Jason Murrin's office," I told the title officer. "Kathy Long is going to sign her paperwork at his office."

"It's all been set up," the woman said. "I'll have them couriered over today, and I believe Mr. Murrin's aunt is going to sign this afternoon."

I thanked her, and we headed out. "Did you really use karate on Jason's dad?" Grandma asked when we got in the car.

"Only when he manhandled me and made a move for Jason, and before you ask, I didn't hurt him. I just gently laid him down on the ground. On his face."

"I'm surprised he agreed to the sale, then."

I shrugged. "Grandma, I'm not going to let a bully put hands on me or Jason. That man is a brute and has caused all sorts of grief for his family. Even if it cost us the sale, I would never let someone threaten me or those I care about with bodily harm."

"No, you were taught not to suffer fools. I wasn't saying different. I'm surprised, is all."

"He wants to run away to Florida, thinking people will like him down there."

Grandma shrugged. "They might, but most of us are happy to see the back of him up here."

"Hear! Hear!" I agreed.

We left the title company, and Grandma looked at me funny when I took the old country road back toward Wilcox instead of heading for her retirement home. "Where are we going?" she asked.

"To celebrate. You told us at Thanksgiving you could still have wine. Is that still the case?" I asked.

"Yes. Doctor didn't say I couldn't."

"Then I want to introduce you to a new place I found."

She sat back to enjoy the ride. When we pulled up at the winery, she sat up with a shocked look on her face. "This is the Monroes' old place. I used to bring ol' Cleo food after he lost his wife. Dang, when did they do all this? Did he sell it?"

I shook my head. "I know nothing other than it's an adorable winery now, and you and I deserve a little celebration. You finally got the store you said you've been chasing for years. Let's go make a toast to that."

She winked at me as I climbed out of the car and came around to open her door. When she saw the old house, she gasped. "I can't believe they saved it. Did you know this house was one of the first to be built in the region? I always thought it should be preserved."

"And now it is," a man said as he came out of the front doors. "Hi, I'm Will. We received your reservation, Mr. Carter. If you two would follow me inside, we've set out our award-winning wines for you to sample, as well as some local cheeses and other items we believe pair well with our selections."

"What happened to the owner of this farm?" Grandma asked as we walked inside.

"Well, if you're talking about the older man who used to live here, unfortunately, he passed away a few years ago. However, his grandson is my husband. We run the winery and vineyard together now."

Grandma's eyes grew big. "Little Duke Monroe is responsible for all this?" she asked.

Will chuckled. "Well, with my help, yes. Do you know him?"

"Yes, really well, at least when he was young. We owned the property cattycorner to this one, me and my late husband."

At hearing that, Will's eyes grew just as large, but I couldn't tell why. "We do love to entertain our neighbors. Freda will make sure you get settled in."

The woman I'd met when I was here before came over and escorted Grandma and me upstairs as Will took his leave. I loved this place so much and I was glad I got to experience it with my grandmother.

The place was amazing, from the gleaming old oak floors to the minimalist décor that felt so natural. What was most remarkable, however, was the artwork on the walls.

"This art, Grandma, it's so beautiful."

She nodded happily as she sipped her wine. "We have a lot of talent in our little area. I'm glad someone had enough sense to take advantage of it."

"Well, I can't disagree." I raised my glass. "Here's to finally closing the deal on your country store."

"And here's to my grandson finally stepping into his place as the head of our company," she added.

I sighed but smiled as we clinked glasses, ate our cheese, and talked a bit about our plans for the store.

We were just walking around the main showroom when Will and another man approached us. "Well, I'll be, look at you," Grandma said. "Little Duke Monroe, all grown up and just as handsome as can be."

The man laughed. "It's such a pleasure to see you, Mrs. Carter, and yes, it's been a while."

"Well, I probably should've checked up on your grandpa more, but once we moved, it wasn't as easy to get over here as it had been back in the day. I'm so sorry to hear about his passing. He was such a good man."

Duke nodded. "He was. If the two of you have a moment, Will and I have a proposal for you and your property across the road from ours."

Grandma gave the men a calculated look, and I knew her business mind had kicked in. "Well, we have some of your delicious wine left to enjoy. Why don't we go back to the table and share a glass."

Both men nodded, and I followed them, excited to see my grandmother back in her element.

As soon as we were seated, Will began to speak. "We want to expand the vineyards, but not just anywhere will work. You see, our grapes do as well as they do because they have southern exposure. This protects our grapes in the winter and ensures adequate sunshine in the summer."

Grandma listened patiently as he explained about his business.

"Your property is the only one close to ours with the same southern exposure. Have you considered selling?" Will asked.

Grandma shook her head. "No, that was given to my son shortly before I moved off the farm, but you could certainly broach the subject with him. I'm sure some of this fantastic wine would go a long way in helping to convince him," she said as she lifted her glass.

I almost burst out laughing as Duke jumped up, dashed over to a cabinet built into the wall, withdrew two bottles, and presented them to her. "These are compliments of the house," he said.

Grandma smiled sweetly and took the bottles. Talk about a masterful dealmaker at work, even when it wasn't technically her deal. We all talked a bit more about the property. Then I asked the guys about the art that was for sale.

Duke looked hesitant, then nodded. "We really don't sell the art that's consigned here. Wilcox doesn't have a good art museum, and we can't afford to build one, so I talk our local artists into displaying their artwork here. But I do have pieces I know the artists want to sell. Did you have something in particular you were looking for?" he asked.

I nodded. "Jason Murrin has a painting in his law office downtown. It's done by a local artist. I don't know anything about it, but it's something I happen to know he treasures. If you had something similar, like a companion to that piece, I'd be very interested in purchasing it."

Duke pondered for a bit before asking, "Is it the one with one of the covered bridges and an old, dilapidated barn in the distance?"

"That's the one."

Duke smiled and stood up. He walked over to the far wall, removed a painting, and returned to our table holding it. "This is the companion to that piece. See, here's where the other painting stopped and where this one begins," he said. "The artist has lived in Wilcox for well over half a century and has recently stopped painting."

When I recognized the old Murrin Country Store, my mouth fell open. "There was a covered bridge that crossed the river near Jason's family store?" I looked over at Grandma. Despite her usual collected demeanor, she was clearly as overwhelmed by the sight as I was. She nodded.

"Okay, wow," I said, directing my attention back at Duke. "If you're willing to speak with the artist, to find out how much he'd sell this for, I'll speak with my father about your interest in the property."

Duke thought for a bit. "Jason is a good guy and managed to talk me out of the other painting before I started displaying work in the winery. The two paintings were always meant to be together, so I'll speak to the artist for you. I'm sure he'll sell, though."

When Duke told me how much Jason had paid for his painting, I almost swallowed my tongue, but I wasn't going to let its companion piece go to anyone but us, not considering its subject.

"Deal." I reached out my hand for a shake. I didn't even look at my grandmother, because I'd get an incredulous look for paying that much for a painting.

I think the bit of wine Grandma had drunk made her more chatty than usual, because she started to share her memories about the old bridge and going to the country store with her father.

I enjoyed getting to know Duke and Will a bit as well as we all finished our wine. Grandma's house had sold right before Thanksgiving, and the buyers were also artists. I wondered if Duke and Will had met the couple yet.

When we left the winery, I dropped Grandma off at her place and returned to my rental house. I had no more than climbed out of my Jeep when I got a call from Duke saying the artist had agreed to the sale and asking if I could stop by to make the payment. I'd already decided it would be my Christmas gift to Jason.

He and I had agreed to have Christmas breakfast with his aunt and cousin, since little Reena was less likely to be grumpy in the morning than the evening. Then, for Christmas dinner, we were going over to my parents' house. It just made sense to have the painting delivered there for our gift exchange.

After a quick trip back out to the winery to get all that settled, I went back to my rental, lay down on the sofa, and let the amazing day sink in.

My ringing phone woke me from a catnap. "Hello," I answered.

"Landon, hi, it's Orion. I'm going to be in Portland the week after New Year's and wondered if you had time to meet me."

I sat up and could feel my forehead crease. "Um, I guess, but why are you going to Portland?"

"Just some business. I'll text you the date and hotel details. See you then."

He hung up, and I had to resist a shudder. I'd made sure he knew I had a boyfriend, even if Jason and I hadn't discussed labels, so surely Orion wasn't coming to Portland with some false hope of us getting back together. After the initial awkwardness, we'd gotten along okay working together, but….

I quickly texted him.

Me: *Orion, you know I'm dating someone seriously, right?*

The dots that told me he was typing came and went several times before I got a response.

Orion: *Get over yourself. I'm coming for work and thought I could meet with you is all. Maybe even charge you for the pleasure.*

Okay, that sounded like Orion. I let out the breath I'd been holding and sent him back a thumbs-up emoji. I rolled over, ready for a real nap before I went over to Jason's to pick up the finalized paperwork for Grandma's country store. For me, that was my greatest accomplishment thus far.

Things were falling into place.

Jason

A SENSE OF relief settled over our holiday meal. This year felt different, and not just because Landon and little Reena were joining us around the table. For the first time since my grandparents passed, the store no longer cast its shadow over our family.

Mom and Dad had moved to Florida, as far as we knew. Their home sold shortly after the store sale went through. I counted their leaving the area as an early Christmas gift for the rest of us.

The store was being taken over by Landon's family, and they'd closed it down for remodeling. They told everyone it'd be open again after the first of the year. I didn't remember much about store operations, but if memory serves, the timing made sense considering business could be painfully slow over the Christmas holiday.

We had a huge breakfast cooked mostly by Aunt Kathy, who said she was happy to have avoided the whole mess of a big evening meal this year.

After breakfast we opened gifts. Landon had bought everyone something, and each present was sweet and thoughtful, just like him.

We finished around noon, helped my aunt clean up, and got the dishwasher running. Reena was already irritable, so Owen and Marisa left early, leaving just Aunt Kathy, Landon, and me.

When she came to sit in the living room with us, she smiled. "I got you two something special." She reached into her pocket and pulled out a box I recognized. She handed it to me, and I opened it immediately.

"Grandpa's old watch?" I asked.

Aunt Kathy nodded. "And this belonged to my mother," she said and pulled out a beautiful hand-carved pen that she handed to Landon. "It's what Mom used when she'd write her correspondence. She believed using something beautiful helped her write beautiful letters."

Landon gently set the pen on the coffee table. "I can't accept this. It's a family heirloom."

My aunt smiled, took his hand, and placed the pen back in it. "You can. My mother had several pens, but this one was special—the one she saved for signing the really important documents or writing really important letters. It's also the pen I used to sign the contract giving you and your family the store."

Landon's breath caught, and I could tell this meant a lot to him. "Thank you, Kathy. I'll take very good care of it."

She patted his hand and then looked at me. "You boys helped heal a wound in our family. I've worked hard not to speak ill of your father, Jason, but I haven't felt this free in many years. I didn't realize just how much holding on to that old store was binding me to him. I...."

Aunt Kathy's voice cracked, and it took her a moment to regain control of her emotions. "I'm very grateful to you both for helping me break free, and I can't wait to see what your grandmother has planned for it, Landon. Oh, I do hope it's like the one in McMinnville. They have the best fried chicken. I have visions of bouncing down there on occasion just to see the place and sit with my good memories like the old-timers used to do. It's going to be excellent."

Shortly after that she gave us both hugs and kicked us out of the house. I put my grandpa's watch on, and nostalgia filled me. I'd loved that old man and had forgotten just how much until I felt that tangible connection to him on my wrist.

I loved beyond words that Landon had a piece of my history as well. Hopefully, he'd have my future too.

Landon

GIFTING ME the pen was a beautiful gesture, and I felt honored to have it. Jason couldn't stop sneaking looks at his grandpa's watch, which was adorable, and I knew receiving it had touched him deeply.

I was eager for him to see my gift of the painting and was having a really hard time containing my excitement. When we arrived at my parents' house, Grandma was already there, as was her gentleman friend, Gerald. I gave Grandma a teasing look when she introduced him, and she smiled and looked away.

"Gerald, it's a pleasure to meet you. Too bad my grandmother didn't let us know you were coming or we'd have gotten you a gift to open."

Grandma gave me the side-eye, but Gerald just laughed. "Trust me, son, I've had more than enough Christmases. I don't need any more stuff, just good food and delightful company."

We played games when we weren't helping Mom put together the meal. Fortunately for all of us, Mom had figured out many years ago that she was the only real cook in the family. So, while she called the shots with meal prep, we all fully accepted our roles as her helpers and clean-uppers.

We ate around five. Then Jason helped me clean up the kitchen and we all descended on the presents. When Jason wasn't handed one, he winked at me and whispered, "Do I get my present later?"

Of course Jason would take not having a present as an invitation to sex. I just laughed and shrugged. "You'll have to wait and see."

He'd gotten everyone something small and local—a pretty glass bobble for Mom made by a glassblower in Northport, for Dad, a goofy carpenter figurine with its pants falling down that was almost obscene. Of course my dad howled with delight when he saw it and passed it around so everyone got their fill.

For Grandma, Jason had found an antique hairpin. My grandmother was truly one of a kind, and on more than a few occasions, she would tie her shoulder-length hair up with something that looked like it was from the 1800s.

This one was real fourteen-karat gold, with tiny gemstones. "I found it at a thrift store down in McMinnville, if you can believe it. I knew immediately that it was more than just costume jewelry."

Grandma was speechless, which was rare. She kept staring at it, turning it over and examining the back, then the front. "It's… it's beautiful, Jason," she said, then kissed his cheek. "Don't you worry. I'll leave this in my will for Landon's and your daughter."

I almost choked, and Jason grinned. "We are so not going there, Grandma," I said once I recovered, which caused her to laugh in the naughty way she did when she pulled something over on someone.

While she rushed into the bathroom to put the pin into her hair, I ducked into my old bedroom to retrieve the painting. When Grandma came out sporting the beautiful pin, I followed behind her.

"One final gift." I handed the gift-wrapped package to Jason.

He looked at it, then back at me. "You got me art?" he asked.

I just shrugged. "Open it and find out," I said. "But be gentle."

He nodded and slowly removed the packing around the painting. The moment the painting revealed itself, he gasped. "You didn't… how? How did you talk him out of this?" he asked. "You've got to be kidding me. I begged Duke to part with this piece. I *begged* him." Jason stared dumbfounded at the canvas, now fully unwrapped and propped up for everyone to see. "I will never question your negotiating skills ever again."

Then without warning and right there in front of my entire family, Jason pulled me into the most heartfelt, toe-curling, passionate kiss I'd ever experienced in my life. When he pulled back, I was feeling more than a little giddy. "Remind me to buy this man artwork more often," I said to everyone's laughter.

Jason couldn't stop staring at the painting the rest of the evening, and Grandma couldn't stop touching her hairpin—all signs that we had a great Christmas. When Jason finally went to get his coat, he pulled out an envelope and handed it to me.

"What's this?" I asked.

Jason just smiled and waited. I opened it and found two airline tickets to Hawaii. "We can use them anytime over the next twelve months," he said. "We just have to let them know a couple of weeks in advance."

"Hawaii?" I asked. Now it was my turn to be shocked. "I mean, I've always wanted to go, but you know, never had time." I looked at my grandmother and shook my head. "When will I ever have time?"

"For something like this, Grandson, you make time." She patted my hand and then reached up and played with her new hairpin again.

"My goodness, this has been a good year for presents," I said to the applause of the entire room. "Gerald, next year, you get two from each of us," I said, and he looked at my grandmother and winked.

"Well, son, if this one doesn't boot me in the meantime, I'll accept."

Grandma laughed a little too loudly, telling me she'd been threatening to do just that. God, I loved her, and I loved watching her all goofy with love too. I looked over at Jason and realized I was feeling exactly the same way.

Jason

Work continued to pull Landon away more and more after the New Year. My own business was becoming busier too, especially with Dawna's help. I was able to get through most of my backlog of paperwork, meaning I had more openings, and with her encouragement, I took on more local clients who had minimal issues.

Dawna was right. I was a small-town attorney, and working with local small businesses and individuals should be part of my repertoire. It made a hell of a lot more sense than representing Adam's famous clients, though they also helped pay the bills. But having a busier practice meant what I dreaded most—I needed to hire another attorney.

I really didn't want to share my practice. But growing pains are part of a growing business. So, as part of my New Year's resolution, I put my concerns aside and called Adam to ask him to meet me for donuts and coffee.

"To what do I owe the honor?" Adam asked as he came into the shop and sat across from me.

"Well, as much as this pains me to say," I said, "I agree with you that I need to hire another attorney." He looked about ready to jump up and whoop, so I put my hand up to temper his excitement. "Before you get started, I need someone new, a new graduate or someone with one or two years of experience."

Adam sat back and grinned. "And you think I already know who could fill the position?"

"You usually do. Since you've been pestering me for going on two years now to add another attorney to my practice, I figured you should at least know I'm looking."

Adam thought for a while. "I've got some ideas—attorneys I've worked with in the past—but at the very least, they'd want partner status."

"That's a hard no, which is why someone more recently out of law school is probably a better fit. I like my life as it is right now. I only want to grow enough to provide more local folks with good legal representation. Simple as that."

Adam nodded. "I told you Dawna was the right fit. I wish my brother was further along in his studies. But he won't graduate for a few more years."

"He'd also have to get into law school. What is he now? A junior?"

Adam smiled, looking proud, and nodded. "But I already know he wants to work for you."

"I'll trust your judgment, but for real, please don't refer people to me that are dedicated to the hamster wheel. Let's try to keep everything small-town if we can."

By the time I got back to the office, I was feeling proud of myself. I didn't want to grow, and I already made enough money to keep me happy, but I felt like I was doing what was right for Wilcox.

I guess it had been stupid to resist as long as I had. There was plenty of business for another attorney to survive here. My only competitor had been Henry Erickson, but when he retired from being a county judge based in Northport, he nominally joined my firm and then mostly retired from practicing altogether.

When Landon came in, he waved and returned to his makeshift office. We spent almost every night together these days, though I was ready to move in with him or let him move in with me. But when I tried to broach the subject, he shut me down. "I'm happy with where I'm at. You and I are new, and we need more time making all this work," he said.

I worked for a few more hours, until my stomach started to growl. "Landon, Dawna," I called out. "Do either of you want to go with me to the café?"

Dawna called up to say no, she was too busy and trying to get done early so she could take kid duty over at Dalton and Pierce's place.

Landon came out scratching his forehead. "Yeah, I want to talk to you anyway," he said, and his uncertain expression concerned me.

"About?" I asked.

"Oh, I was just talking to my ex, and that's always a pain. Come on, I'll buy lunch," he said and led me out the door.

We got a couple of hamburgers, since that was about the only thing decent that wasn't dessert, and sat down just as Peggy brought us our usual iced tea. "Thanks, Peggy," we both said at the same time, which earned us a grin.

"So, what did you want to tell me?" I asked.

Landon sighed. "I began working with my ex, Orion, a few months ago. He's one of the most knowledgeable operations experts I know, so we took him on as a contractor. I didn't bring it up because, frankly, I didn't think our interactions would ever be anything other than emails and phone conversations."

"And now that's changed?" I asked.

Landon nodded and took a sip of tea. "He asked if I'd meet him in Portland. He's apparently going to be there and wants to see me."

"Does he know you're dating someone?" I asked, suddenly having to manage my jealousy.

"Oh yeah. I've made that abundantly clear, but I didn't feel right meeting him without you at least knowing."

"So when does this meeting happen?" I asked.

"He wants to meet on Thursday. I feel like I should go. I dumped him pretty hard, Jason, and he still agreed to help us develop our organizational plans and structures. I mean, we're paying him, but still, he could've said no."

"How hard did you dump him? Give me details," I said, smiling.

Landon laughed. "You're incorrigible."

He told me about the breakup, and to be honest, I was a little concerned that the guy wanted to reconnect. I trusted Landon; why wouldn't I? And his being honest about this helped me feel even more confident. But that didn't mean I trusted his ex.

"Thanks for telling me." I reached over to take his hand. "I'll try not to be too jealous."

Landon's smile was naughty. "It seems fair that you should be at least a little jealous since, you know, it's only been me having that emotion up until now."

I squinted my eyes at him and ignored the comment.

Landon laughed as he stood up. He leaned over and kissed me and then put on his coat. "I'm driving over to Cedar Falls to check on our store. I have no idea what I'll find when I get there. I'll probably be home late tonight."

"I can keep the light on if you want to come by. You won't disturb me."

"If I get back before midnight, maybe. Otherwise I'll just go back to the rental. I'll let you know either way." Then he kissed me again and left.

Landon

I'D DEBATED telling Jason about Orion's visit. It was just business; I'd make sure of that. But when Orion sent his hotel details, it became a real thing. I couldn't not tell Jason, so I bit the bullet.

I was glad I did, as I would've wanted Jason to do the same for me. I was getting more attached to him every day. Love? I was nervous to admit that.

We'd only been dating, like *really* dating, for a few months. Even so, I felt more committed to our relationship every day. Was that love? Why did we need to define it?

Of course I was deceiving myself. Of course I was fucking in love with Jason Murrin. That's precisely why I was going to keep my mouth shut and just let things happen the way they happened.

I ran like a crazy person from store to store all week, putting out the same stupid fires that all our recent work with Orion sought to avoid. I made a point to ask Orion whether he thought renting out hotel conference rooms would be the best way to restart our training processes.

Having things to discuss helped me feel less stressed about our meeting. I still thought it was odd that Orion was coming to Portland. To the best of my knowledge, he'd never been there, but I purposefully didn't ask for details about his life.

I called him Thursday morning to ensure we were still on. I didn't want to drive all the way to Portland if he wasn't going to be there.

"Yeah, I flew in last night. I'll meet you at eleven thirty. Is that okay?" he asked.

"Sure, that's fine. I have the hotel details you sent me, so I'll see you then."

I hung up just as Jason came out of the bedroom, his boxers hanging low on his hips. If I didn't have to run over to Grandma's before I headed to Portland, I'd have marched that half-naked body back into the bedroom and had my way with him before I left.

"What's wrong?" he asked.

"Oh, with your sexy ass standing in the doorway like that, I was frustrated about not having time to do naughty things to you."

"I don't mind you being late," he said as he sauntered over to me on the sofa and lined his crotch up to my face.

"You're evil. No, I still have to get a shower, then go to Grandma's, then go to Portland. I wish I'd just canceled."

Jason pulled me up and pushed me toward the bathroom. "Come on, I think I can help you kill two birds with a couple of stones," he said as he reached around and groped my balls.

I laughed, but damn, it'd been a couple of days since we'd made love, and I was hungry for his touch. The hurried but glorious blowjobs we exchanged in the shower would be the only reason I'd be smiling on my drive to the big city.

Jason

I didn't have to be at the office for another hour, and I'd worked late last night, so I didn't rush to get ready. When Adam called, I answered lazily. "Hey, I've got an issue with the hotel Cody used, well, abused. Their email is rejecting the contract I sent them for Layla's baby shower. Can you try to email it to them?"

I thought for a moment. The Layla deal was one of the main reasons the hotel agreed not to sue, and Cody had been doing much better since the incident with his siblings. I didn't want to risk them going back on the deal.

"I'd rather someone hand deliver it to them at this point. Is your assistant not available?" I asked.

"No, she's moved here now too. I don't have anyone left in Portland, but I could probably hire a courier."

"Or… hold on, Adam."

"Landon," I called back to the bedroom where he was getting dressed. "Would you be willing to take a contract over to a Portland hotel for Adam and me? I don't think it's too far out of the way."

"Sure, can you print it for me before I go?" he asked.

"Do you have a copy in print form?" I asked Adam.

"Yeah, why?"

"'Cause Landon said he'd take it for us. He's going to be in Portland today."

"Oh, cool. I trust him more than a courier, anyway. I'll have my assistant run it over to your office now."

"Can you text the hotel's address to Landon too?" I asked, and Adam agreed before we both hung up.

Sure enough, Landon's phone lit up with a text. I picked the phone up to double-check and Adam's text was there, as well as another message that mentioned Royal Hyatt. I'm guessing that's where he would be meeting his ex.

I got up and took Landon's phone with me to the bedroom. "Adam texted you the address to the hotel. Thanks for doing this. I'll run down and grab the contract from Adam's assistant. That way we won't make you late."

I rushed downstairs just as she arrived. "I'm so glad you're doing this. I'm swamped, and knowing Adam, he was going to make me deliver this in person," she said.

Just as she left, Landon came down the stairs, and I handed him the manila envelope. "Thanks again, honey. We all appreciate this."

"No problem, but you and Adam owe me," he said as I walked him to his Jeep. "Tell Adam I want my steak medium rare with his magic rub all over it."

I chuckled. "Careful, you don't want the gossipmongers to hear you talking about Adam's magic rub. I can only imagine the field day they'd have taking that out of context." We'd all been invited to Adam's home for a cookout before the weather got bad. He definitely cooked the best steaks of anyone I knew.

Landon smirked and playfully swatted at me. "You're terrible. Anyway, I'll text you when I reach Portland."

We shared a long, sensual kiss, and then he climbed into his Jeep and drove off. I wanted more mornings like that with Landon. I wanted *every* morning with him, and all the time in between. As his vehicle disappeared out of sight, I resolved to do everything I could to convince him to move in with me permanently.

Landon

BY THE time I'd picked up the paperwork for Grandma and signed a few things, I was running late. Even though I quickly texted Orion to let him know, I still forgot to turn my ringer back on. Grandma had been getting testy lately with my phone going off when we were "supposed to be doing business."

I stared at the manila envelope I'd agreed to deliver for Jason and Adam. "Sorry, that's going to have to wait," I said. They hadn't told me it had to be there by a specific time, so I guessed I'd be fine.

The trip from Grandma's place to Portland was beautiful. This part of Oregon had lovely rolling hills. Nothing as dramatic as they were in Eastern Oregon, but the understated beauty was something to admire.

I was really happy to be back home, and the impending meeting with Orion made me think more about my life in Chicago. A city that size was great for me when I was still starting out. I loved going to the clubs and meeting with friends. But now I truly preferred the quieter life I had, tucked deep inside the rural countryside.

Not to mention Jason. He was Orion's opposite. Orion was high-strung, always striving for the next accomplishment. Jason was successful but worked hard to keep it from overtaking his life. Although I hated comparing lovers, it was hard not to. Orion had been an aggressive lover—pulling and tugging—and although that was exciting at first, after a while, it began to feel like he was acting and not really feeling it.

With Jason, I felt everything. Sure, we had our hot and heavy times where we couldn't get each other naked fast enough. But more often our lovemaking was sweet, gentle, and passionate on an emotional level. I loved that and craved it more and more.

Traffic increased the closer I got to my destination until it was stop-and-go. Not for the first time, I was happy I no longer had to deal with this daily. Rush hour for me now consisted of getting through all the locals who wanted to talk to me as I walked from one end of our little town to the other.

The thought of that made me smile. Yeah, it was irritating when I was in a hurry, but it was also endearing. Thank you, Grandma and Dad, for agreeing to put our headquarters in Wilcox. I'd never been happier to have a hometown.

I arrived at Orion's hotel just past eleven thirty and had to cringe since my grandmother's sense of punctuality was so ingrained in me that being even one minute late was horribly rude. I handed the keys to the valet and rushed into the restaurant to find Orion sitting comfortably, reading a newspaper.

I hesitated to let myself take in the sight of him for the first time since we broke up. He was handsome—slick and polished—and unlike when we dated, that smooth exterior looked fake and put on, like our sex life had felt.

I walked over when he lowered the paper and saw me. "Hi, Orion. Sorry I'm late," I said.

He glanced at his watch and had a perplexed look on his face. Of course, being a minute or two late wasn't something to apologize for in the world we shared in Chicago.

He stood and greeted me with a bro hug, which was weird. I hadn't bro hugged someone in a long time. I sat down, ignoring the strangeness of us being anywhere together, and picked up a menu. "I haven't had breakfast yet, and that sounds good. What are you having?" I asked.

When I looked up, Orion was staring at me. "I'm fine, and how are you?" he asked, sarcasm dripping from his tone.

I put the menu down. "I'm sorry, Orion. I rushed all morning to get here. How are you?"

"Good. Portland is quaint. Are you enjoying it here?" he asked.

I nodded. "I'm not really in Portland. I'm living a few hours south of here. But yes, I'm enjoying it."

We exchanged small talk for a while until the waiter came to take our order. "I'll just take an omelet, chef's choice," I said, knowing that was the easiest way to order without having to answer a bunch of questions. Now that I was here and dealing with my stoic ex, I was ready to be done and get back home.

Orion ordered, then sat back and stared at me. "You've gained weight," he said.

"Excuse me?" I asked, then chuckled. He was either trying to be an ass or funny. I wasn't quite sure which.

"You have, but you still look good. I'm guessing it's all this greasy food. You'd have never ordered a whole omelet when you were living in Chicago. You'd have asked me to split it."

"Orion, I'm not interested in your opinion about how fat I've gotten. You said you wanted to meet, and I assumed this was about business."

He nodded, but I could tell he was angry I didn't take the bait and argue with him. In the past, we'd argue and then have make-up sex. It was a stupid way to keep things moving along with us, but anger was a good aphrodisiac. Again, I couldn't help but think I'd done well by snagging a man like Jason. Our sexual relationship didn't need all that crazy to be good.

"Do you remember Gordon Industries?" he asked. Gordon had been a competitor of Traguilla's.

"Of course. Why?" I asked.

"They're looking for a new financial officer. Since I've accepted their chief executive officer position, I thought of you."

I immediately reached over and patted Orion's hand. "Ori, that's amazing. You've been working your way up to CEO for years. Oh man, so this is a celebration."

That caught him off guard, and although I knew he'd been trying to resist it, he smiled. "Yes, it's good," he said, his voice remaining formal. "But I really would like to have you join us."

I patted his hand again and then turned toward the waiter, who brought our food. "That was fast," I said to no one in particular.

I took a bite and was pleased it tasted good. When I looked up, Orion was staring at me. I sighed and put my fork down.

"I'm sorry, Orion, but if you came all the way here to recruit me, you've wasted a trip. I've begun taking over Carter Stores."

"You can't possibly compare running a small country business with that of Gordon. We make a billion dollars in sales every year, and with my leadership, I have no doubt we'll double that."

"I'm very happy for you, but I'm not interested. However, I am very pleased with all you've done to help Carter Stores grow. We're going to be expanding."

"Stop. I don't give a damn about Carter Stores. You don't either. I know you better than that, Landon. We were lovers, for God's sake," he said rather too loudly, and several heads turned our way.

I'd just picked up my fork to take another bite, but with his vile words spewing at me, I put it back down. "Orion, what the hell is wrong with you?" I asked, keeping my voice low, hoping he'd follow suit. "You know I'm committed to my family business now. Why are you so… so angry?"

"Because you left me without provocation. We were in love, and you left because you didn't want to share me. Well, I've been honest with you. I told you the truth, and you tossed it all aside. Now I bring you a deal of a lifetime, and you're going to throw that in my face too? This is personal, isn't it? You just can't stand to see me succeed."

I put my napkin down and stood up. "This is over," I said. "Orion, thanks for your help, but I won't let you attack me. I hope you find real contentment in your life like I have."

I walked away, trying not to let my nerves get the better of me. Finding the waiter, I pulled out enough cash to cover the food and a nice tip, and said, "Keep the change."

Having seen the exchange, which was embarrassing to say the fucking least, he just nodded as I made my way out the main entrance.

The shakes came over me then. I was ready to rush out before my emotions overtook me and I started crying like some baby in a public hotel when I spotted, of all people, Jason. I whimpered, not knowing why he was here, but so fucking happy he was. I was just about to run to him when a hand gripped my arm and twisted me around.

Before I could resist, Orion's mouth came down forcefully on mine. It took a second for my brain to register what happened, but as soon as it did, I pushed him off me. "You touch me again and I will lay you flat," I yelled, anger spewing from me.

Of course Orion was an idiot, and he came at me again. This time I grabbed his arm, flipped him around, and shoved him away from me. Moments later, security was there, and I explained that I was leaving when Orion tried to stop me.

One of the guards nodded. "You're free to go," he told me.

"You're making a fucking mistake, asshole," Orion yelled at my back. I searched for Jason, but even before the tears hit, I knew he was gone. Maybe I hadn't actually seen him. Maybe he'd been a figment of my imagination.

I held back tears while waiting for the valet to return my Jeep. The moment I was behind the wheel, the floodgates opened. I was still shaking when I reached a service station.

My nerves had gotten the better of me, and it took me a minute to get myself together. Then I noticed the manila envelope I was supposed to deliver sitting on the passenger seat.

I grabbed a tissue, wiped my eyes and nose, and then opened my text messages to get the hotel's address. I noticed then that Jason had texted.

Jason: *Hey, Adam's assistant sent the wrong contract. I've tried calling but can't reach you, so I'm going to drive the real one over.*

Then about an hour later, he sent another.

Jason: *Can we meet for dinner, maybe do something in Portland since we're both going to be there?*

I really had seen him at the hotel. He must've come to find me when he couldn't reach me via phone.

I immediately called his number. No answer.

"Jason," I said, sniffing. "I… can… can you call me back? I think it was you who was there when Orion accosted me. I need to see you. I'm sorta fucked up right now and could use a shoulder."

I hung up and leaned back in my seat. I waited about half an hour, and when he hadn't called back, I rang again. "Jason, where are you? Were you at the hotel earlier? Call me back."

Then I texted him.

Me: *Can you call me? We need to talk about what happened.*

I waited another half hour, then went inside the service station and got myself a breakfast sandwich. I already knew it would taste like crap. Mostly I was biding my time, hoping to connect with Jason before I left Portland.

He still hadn't responded when I got back in the Jeep, so I texted him again.

Me: *I'm headed back home. Call if you get this message.*

I knew, at that point, he wasn't going to call. I was vacillating between being angry about that because Orion had basically assaulted me and Jason must've misread the whole thing, and being nervous that I might lose Jason.

Now that my head was finally clearing, the irony of the situation didn't escape me. This was a repeat of when Cody had kissed him, only in reverse.

I'd blown a gasket and jumped to conclusions. It only made sense that Jason did the same. But I had made it clear I'd never cheat on him. I'd never done it before in any relationship, ever. That had to count for something.

The tears were dried up now. Not that Orion gave a damn, especially with his new high-powered position with Gordon, but I didn't want my family speaking to him again. I called Grandma and Dad and told them what happened. Then I asked them to ignore any phone calls or emails they got from him.

"I'll send Orion a letter severing our relationship when I get home," I told them both.

I was a bit concerned that Orion might try to sue me for breach of contract, but I hoped the hotel had gotten everything on camera. I'd need to call and verify that later today. I'd also need to get an attorney involved.

Could that be Jason? Maybe, but if he was avoiding me, then maybe not. Damn, fucking Orion. I should never have agreed to meet him. Shit, I shouldn't have ever called him to begin with. I'd been an idiot.

However, Jason was being an idiot too. I was supposed to trust him, but he wasn't going to give me that same trust? Where was *my* benefit of the doubt? *My* chance to explain?

Where was *my* strong shoulder to lean on?

Jason

Damn, fucking damn. I'd gotten a frantic call from Adam telling me his assistant had brought over the wrong contract. He tried to reach Landon himself with no luck and asked me if I could track him down.

"I'm afraid if we give the hotel the wrong contract, they'll blow their top. We can't afford to screw this up, especially with Cody doing so well now," he said.

"I'll run it up to them myself," I assured Adam, and I picked up the correct contract from him on my way out of town.

I'd called Landon several times, even tried to reach Gloria, but she said he'd left several hours earlier. I figured even if he dropped the contract off early, I could exchange it with this one without much of an issue.

I made it to the hotel, and when I asked if someone already dropped off a contract, I was assured no one had. It was a relief, if not somewhat anticlimactic. With that crisis averted, and since I was in Portland, I decided to go find Landon.

I remembered the name of the hotel where Landon was meeting his ex, so I headed that direction. Besides, I was more than curious to know what his ex looked like. I can admit I was also a little jealous.

It only took me a few minutes to travel between hotels. I'd already texted Landon, letting him know I wanted to meet for dinner. I probably should've texted that I was coming over too, but since he hadn't responded to any texts since this morning, I figured either his phone was off or silenced.

I found parking close to the entrance, which I took as a sign of good luck, and dashed to the front doors. I was checking my phone to see if Landon had responded when I looked up and saw his face. Panic. I saw panic. I was just about to rush to him when some man grabbed him and twisted him around, kissing him hard.

I was stunned. Fucking stunned. Landon didn't pull away at first, just clung there. So this was why he hadn't responded to me all morning? He must've looked panicked because he'd seen me pull in and park.

I turned without looking back, got into my truck, and drove away. Fuck if this was okay. I drove straight back to Wilcox in a daze. My nerves were jumbled. I couldn't have seen what I saw. Landon had said he was a one-man man, a serial monogamist—faithful. He wouldn't cheat on me. He couldn't. Not the man I'd fallen in love with.

I couldn't shake off all the doubts that threatened to creep in. I tried not to get a ticket, but my foot kept pushing the gas like it had a mind of its own. I needed to get home, hide, lock the doors, turn off all the lights, and crawl into bed. I needed to get away from whatever the fuck I just witnessed.

I knew there had to be a reasonable explanation, but I'd seen his panicked expression. I'd seen him being kissed. How could I dispute what I had seen? Logical-attorney me knew the foolishness of even thinking that, but gutted-boyfriend me wanted to scrub that vision from my brain.

Deep down, I think I knew a happily ever after for Landon and me was a pipe dream. But I thought it would be me who shattered it, to unwittingly fuck it up somehow, not Landon. Not my sweet, honest Landon.

By the time I got back home, my phone had rung multiple times. I ignored it. I didn't care who was calling, and I didn't have it in me to talk to Landon. Not yet.

I double-locked my apartment door, even the top lock that had no key, which meant no one could get to me. I turned all the lights off, stripped down to my boxers, and crawled into bed. I felt exhausted and wrung out, but sleep never came.

Landon

I'D GONE directly to Jason's office when I got home, but Dawna said he hadn't checked in. I'd called repeatedly, but that'd been ignored as well. As the day wore on, I didn't worry. He was avoiding me, and I got that. But when nightfall came and the light from his apartment never came on—yes, I looked—and I couldn't find his pickup parked anywhere, I got nervous. Had something happened to him?

I waited until eight in the evening before I called Marisa and told her what happened. "He's not home, and I'm getting worried," I told her.

She sighed. "He didn't even try to confront you?" she asked.

"No, he was just there one minute and gone after, well, after the incident."

I heard her say something to Owen, which I couldn't make out, and then she came back to the phone. "Okay, I'll see if I can locate him, but Landon, you know if he saw you, he'll be heartbroken."

"Trust me, I know how he's feeling. But if he doesn't let me talk to him, I can't make it right."

"That's a good lesson for both of you to remember. Okay, I'll see what I can do," she said and hung up.

I paced the room, and when I couldn't stand it any longer, I put on my coat and paced the streets of Wilcox.

I saw Marisa knocking at his door, and when he didn't answer, I had to force myself not to freak out. Finally I walked over to her. "How worried should I be?" I asked. "Should we get the sheriff involved? Could he be hurt somewhere?"

She pulled a key out of her purse and tried to open the door. It worked, but for some reason, it was still locked.

"No, don't call anyone. He's in there," she said with another long sigh. "He's bolted the interior lock. He just doesn't want to see anyone."

"What?" I asked. "Do you have a key for that?"

She shook her head. "No, he joked when he renovated the building that he was going to leave the old lock in place so he'd be able to lock it when he needed privacy. I guess he's actually using it now."

I wanted to cry. "Marisa, what the hell am I supposed to do?" I asked.

She shrugged. "Go back to your place, get some sleep if you can, and then tomorrow, tell him what happened."

She turned to go, then looked back. "Do you remember when this happened to you? When you thought he was cheating?"

I nodded, and she continued. "He's never dated anyone longer than a month or two. I know from how he talks about you, how he lights up when he sees you, that he really cares for you, Landon. Imagine how you felt back then, compounded by a lot of big emotions. Give him a minute to deal with all of that, okay?"

I wanted to cry again. Instead I bowed my head in agreement. Marisa hesitated, then pulled me into a hug. "You'll get through this, and when you do, the both of you need to come up with a plan for how to deal with your shit together without completely shutting each other out."

She was right, and I knew it. Yeah, he fucked around on me when we were both still teens. I'd assumed the worst when I'd walked in on Cody kissing him. Now he'd done the same with me. I'd never given him reason to question me, but incriminating was incriminating. I couldn't blame him if he felt betrayed.

I didn't sleep well that night, and although I had to be at my grandmother's early to go over some details for the business, I was sure she'd let me off the hook to try to manage things with Jason, especially when I gave her all the details of what happened.

She already knew I'd had a falling out with Orion, but I hadn't told her Jason had witnessed it. When I spoke with her, I was still hoping that he'd been a figment of my imagination.

I met Grandma early the next morning, and then of course she let me go, and I got back to Wilcox around noon. I was beyond exhausted—not just tired but emotionally drained.

When I walked into the waiting room of Jason's office, Dawna was there to greet me. "I'm sorry, Landon, but Jason has requested not to see you."

I had to tamp down my anger. "He couldn't tell me that to my face?" Dawna looked conflicted. "Okay, make sure he knows this. I didn't do anything wrong. If he stops hiding from me, he'll find that out, and when I was in his place," I said, knowing he could hear me, "I gave him a chance to explain things. I think I deserve the same courtesy." I turned to go, then stopped. "I'm sorry you got caught in the middle of this, Dawna."

I drove my Jeep to my rental and parked it. I'd normally have left it in front of Jason's office and walked, but now that I was angry, I was ready to give myself some distance. If Jason was done with us, then so be it. *I* was the injured party here. Until Jason would hear that and believe it, there wasn't much else I could do.

Next I went to my room and fell on the bed. I didn't even resist the angry tears, because I needed to let it all out. I couldn't be with a man who didn't trust me and never gave me the chance to make things right. No matter how much what he saw hurt him.

Jason

"WHAT THE hell is wrong with you?" Marisa asked the moment she came through my office door. I was on hold with a client and pointed to my phone. So she plopped down in the chair across from my desk and crossed her arms.

Luckily the client came back on shortly after and gave me the information I was waiting on. I made my notes, hung up, and turned to Marisa. "What do you mean?' I asked.

"You know fucking well what I mean. You're throwing away your relationship with Landon, and why? 'Cause you saw his ex basically assault him?"

I cringed. I'd been told the story the day before when Marisa called me, but I was behind on work after my dash to Portland and let that be my excuse for not calling Landon.

"I've been busy."

"Bullshit. Don't you dare bullshit me, Jason Murrin. Now tell me what the fuck is going on."

Marisa was clearly mad, but letting the f-bomb loose that many times gave me a clear picture *how* mad. I wanted to rage back at her, but that would end up with me not speaking to my best friend, and I needed her now more than ever.

"I'm going to break up with him," I said quietly, not wanting my business all over the freaking town.

"Why?"

"'Cause, Marisa, I can't handle all this… this drama. He and I are always struggling with stuff. Him with Cody, and now me and his ex. I'm not cut out for being in a relationship."

Marisa stared at me and stood up. "No, you nitwit, you're being a fucking coward. This has nothing to do with you seeing him kiss his ex. This is due to your fear that you might love someone enough that you're afraid you could lose him. Well, cousin, you *are* going to lose him. And it'll be your fault, no one else's. So get your head out of your ass and clean this up before that happens."

Marisa turned, and I expected her to stomp out of the office, but her hand came up and she held on to my door frame. She looked out the main window, away from me. "Jason, you've never been happier than I've seen you these past few months. Landon didn't cheat on you, and we both know that. Please think twice before you throw this away. You're not going to get a third chance with him."

I nodded when she looked back at me, to let her know I'd heard her. Then she left, and I sat there working through all my jumbled emotions. I knew she was right. I was running scared. But I was so afraid—afraid I'd lose him if I tried to make this work, afraid I'd already lost him, afraid he had actually been cheating. I was beyond rational thought.

I put my head on my desk and considered going back upstairs and hiding away again. "Want to talk about it?" Dawna asked from the doorway.

I laughed bitterly without lifting my head. "About as much as I want a root canal," I said.

"Well, if you change your mind, I'm here," she said. Then she left me alone again.

I didn't have it in me to work anymore. It was almost lunchtime, but my stomach was in too many knots to do the café, not to mention I didn't want to deal with people. I opted for some fresh air and walked to the park, knowing I could hide away in the back corner closest to the river.

I realized it was the wrong decision the moment I sat down in the swing set facing town. I could see all the work being done on Landon's projects. The filling station was almost complete, and now footers were going in along the area where the two buildings had been taken down.

Landon had been so smooth with the city council. They voted unanimously to sell the vacant lots to Carter Stores and even readily accepted Johney's preliminary drawings. Unanimous agreement was something that rarely happened among Wilcox's governing body.

The Carter family business had been readily accepted into Wilcox. Now folks loved Landon like he'd always been here. I sighed. Landon was easy to love—kindhearted but strong. He didn't suffer fools, which, to be honest, is another reason people loved him so much. Respect was required, but the folks here liked someone who stood up for himself when the times called for it.

Marisa was right. I was going to ruin my chance at a happy life with the man I loved if I didn't get out of my own way. But I could also use a little help repairing the damage. I picked up my phone and called Gloria.

"Well, you've got some nerve calling me after how you treated my grandson," she answered without her usual hello.

"And that's exactly why I'm calling."

"You ought to be calling him, but you've piqued my interest. What do you want?"

I held back a chuckle at Gloria's typical no-nonsense manner. "I want to apologize, then whisk him away to Hawaii before he's taken over everything from you. We both know when he does that, he'll be unable to get away for months, if not years."

Gloria sighed. "Son, I would just love to box those ears of yours, but the truth is I love you like you were one of my own. The reality is my grandson does too. If he didn't, he wouldn't be sulking around here like someone just kicked his puppy. I'll do it, but you listen here. You clean this shit up right now, you hear me?"

"Yes, ma'am, I intend to. You can't tell him, but I plan to propose while we're in Hawaii. We love each other, and now that I've got my head out of my ass, as my cousin says, I'm going to make it official."

She *yeehaw*ed, then paused. "Son, go on, make your plans. We'll keep the fort locked down. I want video footage of him telling your ass off, though, and of him saying yes. I want them both."

"Yes, ma'am," I said, smiling. I wouldn't record him telling me off because he had the right to say what he wanted when he did it. I had crow to eat, and I knew and accepted that as fact.

As for proposing, I'd already been thinking about it before things went down in Portland. This whole mess had proven to me how much I loved Landon. I'd been stupid to let my fears about losing him nearly cost me everything. *He* was my everything.

Landon

GRANDMA WAS acting goofy when I showed up. She kept smiling at me. Then she'd shake her head and say something about kids these days. I figured it had to do with her and Gerald. I wanted to be happy for her, I really did, but my heart was still so broken over Jason. I was trying to be strong… trying and failing miserably.

I continued going through the motions for the company as I set up the training schedule for my regional managers.

It had been Orion's idea. I wish I could've kicked his ass right then and there, but even if I had, it didn't change the fact that Jason didn't trust me, didn't even give me the same courtesies I'd given him—and not once but twice!

"Stupid men," I muttered and looked up to see my grandmother chuckling across her dining room table from me. *Whatever*, I thought, *sit over there and be happy with your dapper granddaddy man. Forget your grandson is going through the worst breakup of his life.*

The bitterness in my thoughts surprised even me. "Grandma, I'm headed home. I can finish all this there."

"Whatever you need, dear," she said, bringing me up short.

"What's gotten into you today?" I asked.

"Never you mind me. You got plenty to tend to over there. Go on home. I'll finish up what I can, and then you can do the rest tomorrow. No need for you to burn the midnight oil when I'm still here to help."

I cocked my eyebrow at the woman who was transforming in front of me. "You sure I don't need to call the doctor? You may need your medications checked or something."

"Out with you. Shoo!" She waved her hands toward me.

I ended up laughing, and it'd been so long since I smiled, it felt weird on my face. "Okay, but they say personality changes are a stroke symptom. You call the doctor if you get the urge to be any nicer than you're being now."

Grandma squared me with a look, and I knew I'd gone just a little too far. It felt good, considering I was annoyed to see anyone happy or think they would have a good relationship when I probably never would.

I felt guilty and walked over to kiss her on the cheek. "I'm sorry I'm a grump. I'll check my attitude and be better tomorrow," I said. Then I told her I loved her and left.

I considered driving somewhere else, maybe going to the winery or cruising the backroads, but nothing sounded like much fun. So I took my bad attitude home, looking forward to a hot bath and a glass of wine from the last bottle I'd gotten at the winery. A soak and a sulk was about all the bandwidth I had left.

Jason

Xander let me into Landon's home, evidently because he wasn't aware we'd had a falling out. Very few people had figured that out, and I sure as hell wasn't going to tell him. I'd picked up food from the grocery store. They had the best smoked brisket in all of Oregon, and I remembered how much Landon liked it. When I told Justin, one of the owners, I was doing this for a romantic dinner for two, he added containers full of all sorts of sides. He also sent enough of their signature dessert to last for several days.

Once I got everything set up, I reclined in the chair and waited for Landon to get home. This part of town was quiet. You couldn't hear the traffic, and since I'd slept like shit since the Portland incident, I fell asleep.

When I finally woke up, Landon was sitting on the end of his bed, staring at me. "Um, sorry, I fell asleep."

Landon didn't speak, and when a tear slipped out of his eye, I rushed to him. "I'm…. Landon, I'm so sorry. I…."

"Me too, but I don't know why. I didn't think I'd ever… I thought we'd…."

I pulled him into my arms as his tears wet my shirt. "Shh, you have nothing to be sorry for. This was all on me. But baby, I was so scared. I thought I'd lost you, and then I was afraid I'd reacted so badly you would leave. I've been a fucking mess."

He nodded and leaned into my arms. "Landon, I've never been in love before. It's fucked with my head. When I saw your ex, it… I didn't know what to do. I should've knocked his lights out, especially now I know he accosted you, but all I could think was that I was going to lose you. Lose…." I breathed deeply a couple of times, and the tears spilled from my eyes. "I was going to lose myself."

We held each other like that while our emotions poured out. In front of anyone else, I'd feel like a proper fool with all my feelings leaking everywhere, but with my sweet Landon, I knew I was with the one man who'd let me be myself.

Finally we pulled apart, and he wiped his eyes. "Today hit me the hardest. Just before I came home, I thought my heart would be ripped out. I barely made it home, and then, inside my rental, there you were, asleep in the chair. I wanted to scream at you and hold you all at the same time. But… but we have to talk about what happened. What didn't happen."

"No, I know. I knew then you didn't want that. Wouldn't do that to me."

"I don't understand. Why wouldn't you talk to me, then?"

"I was paralyzed by fear. Irrational fear—fear I'd lose you, fear I already had, then fear that I couldn't trust you, fear that I'd die alone. I can go on and on, 'cause my brain wouldn't stop. It kept going around and around. I… fuck, Landon, I was barely functioning."

"And you couldn't come to me?" he asked.

"No, not until today. Not until I worked it all out in myself first. But please don't let that be a reflection on us. The reality is you mean everything to me. That's why I was so fucked up. That's why this hurt so bad."

He stared at me for a moment and searched my eyes, then nodded. "I get it. I don't want to, 'cause I'm still mad at you, and I have a right to be." He pulled farther away.

"You do. No doubt you have every right to be mad at me."

"Good, we both agree on that, but God, Jason. I love you so much. I hate that we're telling each other this now instead of the other day when we were snuggled up together. My asshole ex doesn't hold a candle to you or how I feel about you. It's important to me that you know that."

"So, did you flip him like you did my dad?" I asked, hopeful.

Landon paused, then shook his head. He smiled. "I didn't put his ass on the ground, although I should've, but I did move him out of my way. The hotel security handled the rest. I'm so sorry you saw that, but," he said, cupping my face and looking deep into my eyes, "I hate it much worse that you left and didn't let me explain. I hate that you even thought that son of a bitch could hold up to you. Nothing can, Jason, nothing. You get that?"

"I do now, yeah," I said and nuzzled my face into his palm. "I brought dinner. I told Justin at the grocery store it was a romantic dinner, so he sent enough food to feed an army."

Landon laughed, then pulled me close. "Come here. I need to be held for a little while before we eat, okay?"

"Yeah. Me too," I said, and we both lay back on the bed and cuddled face-to-face.

"Oh, um, I told your grandma I was gonna do this," I said and felt myself blush. "I want to run away with you to Hawaii before you take over for her, and she agreed. It was spur-of-the-moment, but yeah, I'd like it if we could… maybe next month?"

Landon's eyes grew wide. "That's why she was so weird all day. I thought maybe she was all gooey over Gerald. Um, I don't know about getting away. A lot is going on right now," he said, and I could feel my face drop.

"Then again," Landon said, leaning over to kiss me, "you're right. This might be the only chance we get for a long time. I'll talk to Grandma and Dad tomorrow and let you know."

"Perfect," I said as I rolled on top of him and began to kiss every bit of skin I could reach.

Once I got him all hot and bothered, I said, "This whole rental house thing is bullshit. It's private, I know, but it's time you moved in with me." I ground my cock into his. "It's time, and you know it."

Landon laughed. "We just had our biggest argument, which included you locking me out of the apartment for days. I think it might be too soon."

I sighed and sat up on my knees, straddling Landon, and looked down at him. "I know, but I also know I'll never do that again, 'cause I'm ready to commit to you, to commit to us. No more just two guys dating. You're my boyfriend, my lover, however you wanna define it. And I want you with me, okay?"

Landon nodded, and I could see his eyes get glossy again, so I leaned back down and devoured his mouth. "So, you moving in?" I asked when we came up for air.

He nodded. "Yeah, you idiot. Even though it's probably too early, I want to spend as much time together as possible. Now kiss me again."

And I did, all night long. I almost proposed then and there, but I didn't want it to be an apology and proposal in one. I knew one honest conversation wasn't like an automatic restart button. I still had a mess to clean up, and my head was still a little fucked up about it all. But I figured that with some tough-love chats with Polly, Adam, and Marisa, and real, open discussions with Landon, I'd work it out by the time our Hawaii trip came along.

Landon

HAWAII WAS stunning, just like I knew it would be—sandy beaches, sapphire seas. We saw sea turtles up close and went on more than one whale-watching tour. The babies were mesmerizing.

We saw plenty of sharks too, but after we went snorkeling a few times and most of the sharks darted away, I realized my fear wasn't worth ruining the incredible underwater sightseeing.

Grandma had agreed to two full weeks in the latter half of February, and then she seemed to get ridiculous about it because it's all she could talk about. "When you get to Hawaii, I want pictures of…" and she'd talk about things she'd looked up on the internet. I'd already decided that I'd be booking her and Gerald their own trip in the near future.

We'd been here a week and had done a little island-hopping. Now we were in Maui, one of the most popular islands. We'd just finished eating when several men came to our table wearing grass skirts and playing ukuleles.

I reached over to hold Jason's hand, wanting to enjoy the romance of it all, when he stood up, winked at me, and then got down on one knee.

He paused for a moment and smiled up at me as my brain slowly began to register what was happening.

"Landon Carter," he began, the smile never leaving his face, "I love you with all my heart. Waking up to your sweet face every morning and falling asleep every night in your arms has been the highlight of my life so far. I want to spend today, tomorrow, and every day after that by your side—loving you, supporting you, and being your shoulder to lean on, for the rest of our lives. Would you consider becoming my husband?"

I sat slack-jawed and stared down at him and the ring he held out to me. I wanted to shout yes, but instead, my stupid emotions got the better of me again, and tears slipped out of my eyes while I tried to catch my breath. Jason remained on bended knee, giving me time. I finally drew in a breath and then launched myself into his arms and kissed his face. "God, yes," I said between kisses.

The folks around us cheered, and I pulled back, blushing now because the scene had almost gotten pornographic. In the excitement of the moment, I'd forgotten Jason and I weren't alone.

As soon as we settled back in our seats, the waitstaff brought us each a glass of champagne, and Jason took his phone back from someone who'd apparently filmed us. "Your grandmother will skin me if I don't send this to her," he said, and I laughed.

"Really? Grandma knew?"

"Sorta. I kinda bribed her with the proposal so she'd let you come with me."

I chuckled and admired the engagement ring now adorning my finger. Of course my overbearing grandmother knew Jason was going to propose to me. I guess I shouldn't have expected anything less.

"Well, she's going to be your grandmother too," I told Jason, who beamed at me. "Don't say I didn't warn you."

Epilogue

Landon

GRANDMA, MOM, Dad, and Jason laughed when I said I wanted a small, private wedding.

"Oh, son, you should've thought of that before building our business in Wilcox," Grandma said.

I sighed. "You really think they'll care?"

Jason nuzzled into my side. "Folks in town will never let us live it down if we don't make the whole thing a… thing," he said.

I sighed again, and this time I dragged it out with as much drama as possible. The truth was, Wilcox had become my home and the people my extended family, so they were right and I knew they were. "Okay, but I don't want all the pomp and circumstance. I hate weddings," I said, then quickly turned to Jason. "But you know, I'll do whatever you want."

Jason chuckled. "I'm flexible too. Why don't we have a small ceremony at a church in town, and then we can have the reception in the park? The Lopez family can cater it, which means the food will be delicious and there'll be plenty of it."

"Great idea. Can we have Peggy supply the dessert, though? She makes the best in town," I said, which brought another snicker from the family.

"Your dad and I will manage the cake, if you'll trust us," Mom said.

"Jason?" I asked, and he shrugged.

"Baby, the only thing that matters to me is that, when this is all said and done, you'll be my husband. Then I'm going to take you back to Hawaii," he said, giving my grandmother a look, which she mysteriously didn't complain about, "for our official honeymoon."

I sighed happily. "That sounds perfect." What actually made it all perfect was the man I was about to marry. Sometimes I had to pinch myself because the guy I'd had a crush on when I was a kid was the man who'd chosen me to walk beside him through life.

Our wedding was in late September because the downtown Carter Store would be up and running by then. Like it or not, even the big life moments had to be scheduled around work. But there were advantages to having an autumn wedding. The weather was blessedly cooler, and I loved the pumpkins, the bright seasonal flowers, and the beautiful fall foliage and falling leaves that provided a lovely backdrop for our wedding photos.

I stood staring at myself in the mirror. Grandma, Mom, and Dad were helping me get ready while Marisa, Owen, and Jason's Aunt Kathy were helping him. He'd broken down and invited his parents, but they never responded to the invitation, which I was secretly happy about. I had no love lost for his parents.

"You ready?" Mom asked.

"Fuck yeah," I said, then blushed. "Sorry, Mom."

"Oh, I think we can look the other way this time," she said to the chuckles of Dad and Grandma behind her.

Jason and I met at the back of the church, and although I wasn't supposed to, I stole a kiss before we walked together down the aisle with our families close behind us. The symbolism brought tears to my eyes. I'd come to love his people as much as it seemed he'd come to love mine. Even fussy little Reena, who was closing in on the terrible twos, had won all our hearts and was currently putting on a show as both our flower girl and ring bearer.

It was hard to keep my hands off Jason as we stood before the altar with Adam and Marisa on his side and Rhys and Owen on mine.

Reena, with a lot of help from her mom and dad, gave us the rings, which we exchanged.

"With this ring, I promise," I began, "to do all the love and cherish stuff we're supposed to say, but my sweet, soon-to-be husband, I also promise to give you the benefit of the doubt. Jason, you are my rock, my shoulder to lean on, and I'm grateful every day that we got our second chance. From now until the end of time, I'll love you."

Jason smiled, and although he was a thousand times less emotional than me most days, he wiped a few tears away. "Landon, you and I have had a long and bumpy ride getting here, and I caused most of the bumps," he said, which drew some snickers from the crowd. "But there's never been anyone I've loved as much as I love you." He didn't hold back the tears that slipped from his eyes and streaked down his cheeks. "I'm the luckiest man alive because you took a chance on me, and I promise you everything I have to give—my heart, my fidelity, and the rest of my life. I promise to be yours forever."

"Then by the power vested in me by the state of Oregon, I now pronounce you husbands. You may kiss," the minister said to the loud applause of the packed church.

Jason's kiss was all I needed to make the day complete. He wrapped me in his arms and dipped me for our kiss in what had to be the most swoony moment of my life.

When he set me back on my feet, he leaned in and softly whispered, "Husband."

I nodded. "Husband."

He wiped away the tear that slipped down my face and then kissed my hand. Then we walked hand in hand down the aisle.

We left the church and led a procession down the street toward the park. The minister had kindly allowed everyone to leave their vehicles in the church parking lot. Considering the church was packed, I was glad they'd given us that option.

During the hours-long reception, I think every single person in town and then some filtered through to wish us their congratulations. My heart felt as full that day as it ever had.

It wasn't lost on me that Jason and I could now count ourselves among Wilcox's plethora of happily married gay couples, most of whom we considered close friends. That realization warmed my heart too. There really was something special about this little Oregon town that had become the center of my universe. My home.

Marisa's announcement that she was pregnant again was cause for massive celebration, although it was clear she hadn't planned on baby number two. I don't think she was ready to become a mom again, at least not quite yet. Handling a precocious two-year-old was already a lot.

Owen convinced her that once the baby was born, he'd take paternity leave and be a stay-at-home dad for the first few months. Even Marisa's mom seemed to agree that was the best plan.

By the time the baby was on its way, Jason and I had settled on a house plan. The piece of Dad's property we chose was on a mountainside with a creek running down it. That picturesque part of the property was no good for growing grape vines, which made our decision even easier. I'm sure it made our new besties, Will and Duke, happy as well.

We were out at the property with Marisa, Owen, and Reena when I looked across the creek and an idea struck. "Why don't you all build over there?" I asked Marisa. "It's a perfect house site. We even considered it before we chose this side of the creek."

Marisa looked at me, then over at the spot I'd pointed out. "Um, why?" she asked.

"You know, I don't know. That thought came out of nowhere, but now that I've said it, I think you would like it out here. Jason wants kids, and maybe someday that'll make sense for us, but even if it never does, having you all right next door does. We could help look after your kids, and they'd have all this to play in as they grow up." I waved my hand around to illustrate my point.

Marisa looked thoughtful. "Maybe, but you should ask your dad. He sold you this property, but he might not want to sell off more pieces."

"Dad doesn't own it anymore, Marisa, we do. He sold us the entire thing. See those stakes?" I asked. "That's the boundary of our property. Jason and I own the entire mountain."

Her jaw dropped, and she blinked at me a few times. "I'll talk to my husband, you talk to yours, then we'll need to have a real heart-to-heart about it."

I smiled. Whatever she needed to convince herself, but I knew like I knew my own name that this was happening. Something serendipitous had caused me to blurt out the idea before I even really thought about it. The universe wanted us to all be neighbors.

I felt like my personal and professional lives were both on a pleasant upswing, or maybe I was just getting used to my good life. I loved running Carter Stores, although it was a lot of work. Fortunately, the training and internal structures we'd put in place had been extremely successful. Grandma mainly focused on two stores now—the downtown location and her beloved country store that had belonged to Jason's family.

She'd planned and organized the latter almost entirely on her own. Grandma spent copious amounts of time planning to restore the picnic tables outside. Carter Stores's signature fried chicken and drip coffee were also at the top of her priority list. One major detail required the help of Xander and Rhys, though, and it was my gift to her.

It took some doing, but I talked Grandma into letting me fund the rebuilding of the old covered bridge that'd been near the country store. Since the land the bridge was built on had reverted back to the store's deed, that belonged to us as well.

I couldn't think of a better way to celebrate our new store than with a new covered bridge to honor the legacy of Jason's grandparents and my own, as well as the legacy bridges around Wilcox.

The store would be my grandma's final major project for Carter Stores, which saddened me, but she and her new man were having a great time exploring the world and building their relationship. I was happy knowing Grandma was feeling the same for Gerald as I felt about Jason.

Jason and I were curled up in our favorite spot on the sofa and had just turned off the TV when I brought up my idea for Marisa and Owen's new home. "I asked your cousin to think about buying and building a house across the creek from us. What do you think?"

"You want my family that close? I thought you wanted the privacy that came with living out in the sticks."

"Honey, we're both town boys. We're going to go stir-crazy out there by ourselves. Besides, I want family around us. Don't you?"

"I do, and Marisa and Owen would be good neighbors."

"And we can help raise the kids," I added.

Jason leaned over and kissed me. "It's a good idea, but let's see if we can perform a miracle and make a few babies ourselves tonight."

I laughed as he pulled me into our bedroom. "I love you so much, Jason Carter." I smiled. No matter how often I heard his new name or said it to myself, the sound made my heart sing. Just like the man himself.

Keep reading for an Excerpt from
Bridging the Divide
By Greyson McCoy!

Prologue

I DROVE THE ATV across the freshly harvested side of the wheat field, keen to surprise my boyfriend with lunch and a make-out session. I was almost giddy, knowing how surprised he'd be.

When I pulled up alongside the combine, I kept a safe distance and waited for Donny to spot me. When he did, he slowed the huge machine and stopped.

I climbed up the side of it and crawled into my boyfriend's lap. "I brought you lunch."

"Um," Donny said, "might be too much of an audience."

He nodded his head to the side, and I glanced over to see Ben smirking at us through his truck window. The guy was as straight as an arrow, but since Donny brought me to the farm almost two years ago, he'd been nothing but supportive.

Undeterred, I kissed my man deeply and heard the truck door creak open and then slam shut. "You two need to get a room," Ben hollered as he walked toward us.

I leaned back and yelled, "You're just jealous, Ben."

I crawled off my boyfriend and back down. "I brought sandwiches and chips."

Ben immediately attacked the bag on the passenger seat of the ATV, making me laugh.

"Hey, for goodness' sake, clean your grimy hands first. There's wipes in the bag. You two can be so freaking nasty."

Donny climbed out of the combine and popped me on the ass. "*You* are such a princess."

"So that makes you either an ogre like Shrek or a cursed frog prince who needs a kiss?" I replied, and he smirked as he hauled me in for a deep kiss. "Thy curse is broken, though you'll always be my frog."

Donny chuckled as we all settled around the ATV for lunch. I deliberately wiped my hands before I grabbed a sandwich, which earned an eye roll from both men.

I watched Donny and Ben cut up with one another while we ate. I still couldn't believe the direction my life had taken. All this was a total fluke, thanks to my uncle.

Donny and I graduated together from a university here in Iowa. I took a bad-paying part-time job working for a catering company in Des Moines. Donny was working for a farmer outside of town. After a while, a commute on top of long workdays was too much for Donny, so we relocated from the city to his family's farmstead to help Donny's parents. Even though I was broke and Donny made next to nothing, I didn't want to return to central Oregon.

For the time being and with no full-time job prospects on the horizon, I worked as a house husband/boyfriend. There wasn't much my history degree would do for me career-wise unless I went back to school, which I couldn't afford to do.

Regardless, I knew my gifts lay in the kitchen. Heck, before my paternal grandparents died, my grandmother had put me in charge of meals while she helped manage the cattle with my dad and grandpa.

I still think it's interesting that she knew I fit better in the kitchen than the pastures. I was eleven when Grandpa died and almost thirteen when she did, so I never found out if they'd have accepted my sexuality.

Of course, as strict religious people, even to the point of being teetotalers, I doubt they would've. But they tolerated boys in nontraditional roles and vice versa, with Grandma running cattle while I ran her kitchen being a prime example.

The sound of a contented sigh pulled me from my thoughts. "Thanks for the grub. It hit the spot," Ben said as he stood up and headed back to his truck. "You two get your kissin' done so our boy here can get back to work. Got a lot to get done, and we still have to get through the gulch."

Donny moaned. "I hate the gulch. Tell me again why we keep planting that area?"

"'Cause your dad says money is money."

I understood why it was an issue. The gulch was a bizarre canyon that swept through the Dougherty farmland, and Donny's dad farmed right up to the very edge of it. I wouldn't have worked equipment next to it, and I didn't understand why Donny didn't just refuse. It's not like his dad paid him enough to do dangerous work. It's not like his father paid him much and often didn't pay at all. His parents were the most entitled people I'd ever met, and they just expected him to work for free because they let him live in his grandparents' old farmhouse, which was empty and falling apart when we got here.

I kissed my boyfriend and left before I said something offensive about his parents again. There was no love lost between them and me. Donny's family took advantage of him, but he was loyal to a fault. Of course that was also one of the reasons I loved him so much.

I drove back to the farmhouse and began prepping dinner. Ben would join us like he usually did when they were working the fields together. I liked that, actually. Truth was, I liked my role. I wasn't really a house husband. I thought of myself more as support staff, but I did tend to do all the jobs a traditional farmer's wife would.

That left us uncomfortably poor. But when you're in love, who cares if you have money? Not like I ever had much, being from a farming family. Oregon had been cattle, and now I was in Iowa it was all grain, but a farm was a farm, and if there was money in farming, I'd yet to see it.

My phone rang just as I finished adding the onions to the pot. Seeing it was Uncle Henry, I hit Answer. "Hey, Uncle Henry, to what do I owe the honor?"

"Don't play coy with me, Justin. You know why I'm calling."

"'Cause you love me so much?"

My uncle chuckled. "That I do, although I often wonder why, especially when I have a probate case still on my desk that needs to be put to rest so I can get paid, for goodness' sake."

I sighed and plopped down on a kitchen chair. "Tell me again why you can't just send me the papers and let me sign them here."

"'Cause, as I said last time, you need to come home. Both Jeff and I want to see you."

"So this is about you missing me and not legal papers that need to be signed."

"It's about both," my uncle said, and I could hear the smile in his voice.

"You know I don't want to come back there. The memories...," I admitted, feeling the conversation turn somber as my words trailed off.

"He was a son of a bitch, Justin. You deserved more, but you know there's a lot more to come home to than bad memories. Besides, we wanna meet that strapping midwestern farmer you speak so highly of."

"Oh, trust me, Donny wants to come too, but if I bring him there, I'm sure he's gonna talk me into keeping the land and farming it. I'd rather deal with his parents than go back."

Uncle Henry sighed. "Well, son, like I said, your uncle Jeff and I miss you something awful. And you do gotta get this paperwork signed. I'll overnight it to you if you're sure you won't be coming home."

Just then, movement out the kitchen window caught my eye. Ben's truck was barreling down the road toward the house. "Hey, Uncle Henry, I've gotta go," I said as a knot formed in my gut. "Something's wrong."

AN EMPTY and endless void of darkness overtook me in a way I never knew was possible. At least Donny's parents hadn't forced me away from his grave. I lost track of how long I remained at the cemetery after the service, sitting on the ground next to the fresh mound of dirt, feeling utterly alone and adrift. I hadn't just buried my boyfriend; I'd also buried our future together.

Ben startled me when he placed a hand on my shoulder. If not for him, I'd probably have stayed at the cemetery all night. Without a word he helped me stand and practically carried me to his truck. It was then that Donny's brother Jake, who must've been waiting in his car for me, approached and told me I had a week to vacate the family's property or they'd have me removed by the sheriff.

That would've hurt if my heart wasn't already numb, even if their callousness was expected. What I couldn't process was the loss of the man I'd loved so much. Every hair follicle hurt, every fiber of my being missed him, and I was left with nothing.

Well, not exactly nothing. Donny had taken out a five-hundred-thousand-dollar life insurance policy on himself and me earlier in the year. Why? Well, according to his insurance agent sister, who'd sold us the policy, "You need to protect your loved ones, and you're young and healthy, so it's not that expensive." Donny only got a small allowance for the work he did for his father, so I'd been against it, knowing how tight our budget was. But apparently he'd seen the value in it. Thank goodness.

Margaret, although a wily saleswoman, was the one and only decent member of Donny's family. I trusted her, and so had Donny, so I told him he should get the policy and we could cancel it after she got her commission. Obviously, Donny never informed me that he hadn't canceled it, not that I could begrudge him for it.

Margaret came over the day after the funeral and reminded me of the policy. "It belongs to you. You're the beneficiary," she said as tears formed in her eyes. "At least my parents can't take that away."

We cried on each other's shoulders, which, to be honest, meant more to me than the money. Tears streamed down my face, thinking about the only man I'd ever loved and how the only constant in my life was losing the people I cherished most.

My life in Iowa died with Donny. I was utterly alone and about to return to a place I'd never thought I'd set foot in again—Wilcox, Oregon.

GREYSON MCCOY loves to travel. After years of being tied down to a life of kids, work, running a small farm, and all things domestic, he and his husband have taken full advantage of their empty nest to travel the world.

The joy of writing came to Greyson late in life. While completing his master's degree, he found himself fighting between desperately wanting to write fiction and finishing the homework and papers he'd been assigned.

After his master's was finished, Greyson decided to shirk his life of responsibility and pursue his dream of writing full time. His stories reflect many of the locations he and his husband have visited over the years.

Visit Greyson McCoy on his website at www.GreysonMcCoy.gay (his husband assures him that's a real domain extension) and sign up for his newsletter to stay informed of his journey in the world of romance and all things love.

BRIDGING HEARTS ▪ BOOK ONE

Bridging Hope
Raising kids and finding love is impossible, isn't it?
GREYSON McCOY

When workaholic Pierce Simms's sister passes, he suddenly finds himself unemployed, back in the hometown he fled, and raising his niece and nephew. Despite that, he's confident he has things under control—at least until his sister's high-school sweetheart shows up.

With his teaching grant ended, Dalton O'Dell is at loose ends and tight purse strings. Just as the world crashes down on him, he learns his ex-girlfriend has passed and named him guardian of her two young children. Chaos ensues when he and her brother, Pierce, are forced together to raise the toddlers in Pierce's family farmhouse.

Nestled in the enchanting beauty of the farm, Pierce and Dalton bond over the challenges of co-parenting and their shared grief as unexpected love blossoms. Love might not be enough, however, if they can't learn to bridge the gap between their different worlds and overcome the trauma of their pasts.

Bridging Lives

GREYSON McCOY

Cliff Anderson hopes to build on the legacy of his late parents, but that dream seems lost when his California homestead is lost to a wildfire. Devastated, he travels to Oregon to stay with his aunt and uncle on their dairy operation while he makes plans for his future.

College professor Brandon Forest has always yearned for a family and a home of his own. Maybe that's why, despite being busy with his job and his side gig as a fantasy author, he's stayed on as a seasonal worker at the dairy farm. The farm feels so welcoming, and working on their dairy farm might be the next step in building the life he's dreamed of.

Then he meets Cliff.

As Cliff and Brandon confront their own broken pasts, they build a connection that runs deep. Laughter and shared experiences prove to be strong medicine for the wounds life has inflicted on them.

Cliff hasn't let go of his past or the hopes he had for the farm in California. Will his future burn down as he holds on to lost hopes, or can he blaze a new path with Brandon?

Mending Bridges

Untold stories and unfulfilled dreams. Rhys Healy inherits a house full of both when he leaves the bustling streets of Portland for the serenity of small-town life.

Xander McLeroy is a dynamic force in the world of construction, but life leads him away from that work and back to his roots in Wilcox. Even though he enjoys the comforting world of his past, he expects it to be a lonely place.

True love demands courage and sacrifice. Can Xander and Rhys learn this in time, or will they risk repeating the mistakes of their star-crossed families?

HOMECOMING *for* BEGINNERS

ASHLYN KANE

When Ollie Kent arrives on the front steps of the Morris mansion, he's six months out of the military and the brand-new single parent of an eight-year-old cancer survivor. Now they're starting over back in Ollie's hometown, where he's lined up a job as a live-in caregiver for old man Morris.

So it's kind of a downer when a very hungover, mostly naked man about Ollie's age answers the door and tells him old man Morris kicked the bucket.

Tyler Morris left town at sixteen as a pariah. Since then, he's built a good life for himself as an EMT. But even in death, his father has to get in one final screw-you: Ty can either return to his hometown and act as executor of the family fortune, or let it all go to a hate group.

Between an unexpected job offer and unexpected roommates, coming home doesn't go the way Ty expects. But Ollie and Theo bring the cold, lonely mansion to life, and golden-boy Ollie provides good cover for the town's scorn. The only problem is, Ty's falling head over heels for the world's sweetest and most stubbornly independent single dad, and if he wants to keep Ollie around, he'll have to convince him to let Ty help.

Six Places
TO FALL IN LOVE
LEE PINI

Percy de Villiers has it all: wealth, status, and a famous name—until his father's political scandal brings everything crashing down. Struggling with the fallout, Percy retreats to the South African wilderness to focus on his passion, nature photography. But even in the vast beauty of his homeland, he can't escape the weight of his family's disgrace or the loneliness that shadows him.

Rob Hale, a Hawaiian travel writer by way of Atlanta, has spent years idolizing Percy from afar. When an assignment brings him face-to-face with his photography hero, he doesn't expect their connection to spark more than professional admiration. But a chance encounter leads to an unexpected hookup, and the chemistry between them is undeniable.

As Percy grapples with the emotional wreckage left by his father's arrest, and Rob struggles with his own self-doubts, their fling starts to feel like something more. Navigating cultural differences, class divides, and the looming cloud of Percy's family drama, the two men must decide if they can turn their brief romance into something lasting—or if their relationship will fall apart before it ever truly begins.

FOR **MORE**
OF THE
BEST
GAY
ROMANCE